SHOOTER'S POINT

SHOOTER'S POINT

A Martha Chainey Mystery

GARY PHILLIPS

KENSINGTON PUBLISHING CORP.

http://www.kensingtonbooks.com

DAFINA BOOKS are published by

Kensington Publishing Corp.
850 Third Avenue
New York, NY 10022

All Kensington titles, imprints and distributed lines are available at special quantity discounts for bulk purchases for sales promotion, premiums, fund-raising, educational or institutional use.

Special book excerpts or customized printings can also be created to fit specific needs. For details, write or phone the office of the Kensington Special Sales Manager: Kensington Publishing Corp., 850 Third Avenue, New York, NY 10022, Attn. Special Sales Department. Phone: 1-800-221-2647.

Kensington and the K logo Reg. U.S. Pat. & TM Off.
Dafina and the Dafina Books logo are trademarks of the Kensington Publishing Corp.

Library of Congress Card Catalogue Number: 2001086916
ISBN 1-57566-682-0

First Printing: October 2001
10 9 8 7 6 5 4 3 2 1

Printed in the United States of America

SHOOTER'S
POINT

Why should the Devil have all the fun?
                    —Charles M. "Sweet Daddy" Grace

CHAPTER ONE

"Uh, what we gonna do, champ?"

"We gonna rumble like thunder, strike like lightning."

"Uh, what we gonna do, champ?"

"Tyler Jeffries is gonna get served."

"Uh, when, champ?"

"Tonight, that swole-headed motherfuckah gets served tonight."

Juno Caprice did a little shuffle with his feet, his stocky frame falling easily into a pattern of movement decades old. His right shoulder dipped and his left hand flicked out in an efficient jab. He tagged the exposed gut of the man in front of him. The blow slapped the man's flesh as he rocked his torso from side to side.

"How you feelin', champ?" Caprice said in his rhythmic wail. The cadence of the older black man's voice was reflexively synced to the motions of his body, like a man on a chain gang working the highway.

"I'm feelin' like fire," Joaquin Muhammad responded. He danced backward, his heavily muscled arms working like a race car's pistons, his taped hands creating blurs in the air before him.

"How you feelin', champ?"

"Feel like a stud and look like a million."

Caprice stood flat-footed, his keen eyes scanning his fighter for flaws and hesitation in his tempo. Caprice didn't interpret such deficiencies as a failing of will or desire on the part of his boxer. The veteran trainer foisted those sins upon himself. If his fighter wasn't ready, if he couldn't counter properly in the ring and adjust his strategy accordingly, it was his fault, his shortcoming as the one who should have had his man ready. This total empathy was what made him such a valuable commodity in the fight game, and gave him numerous sleepless nights. It was an obsession that had ruined four marriages.

"Cool down, baby, cool down." Caprice put his large, callused hands on Muhammad's shoulders and kneaded the corded muscle. He was tight, but not too tight. He was hyped, as his granddaughter would say, but not too hyped.

"I'm'a take that fool's head off, Juno."

Caprice smiled knowingly, lowering his hands. How many times had he heard those words or variations of them? How many hopes and dreams had he seen in the eyes of young men who wanted to be the next Ali or De La Hoya, the next Lewis or Mosley? How many had worked like Missouri mules only to find dust in their mouths in the end? But then there was the one, wasn't there? The one who had the right combination of innate talent and hunger, and you were able to impart some of your knowledge to keep him more than just upright in the ring.

The one who made those sleepless nights and broken promises to your family worth it because they shone for a brief and glorious moment in a world where the object was to crush your dreams and toss you aside like a used hamburger wrapper.

Muhammad turned to the pretty woman sitting on a stool. Her miniskirted legs were crossed and her foot bounced to the tune playing on her Walkman. Her eyes were half-closed and she hummed softly.

"Monique." Muhammad stepped toward her.

"Yes?" she said sweetly. Her dark brown eyes nearly matched the color of her smooth, burnished skin. "What does my Latin boy toy want, huh?" She took off the headphones and placed the Walkman on the floor. The young woman reached out and pulled him close, her hands latching onto his hips. The woman kissed the area over his navel.

"Hey," Caprice warned, "I'll get a stroke just thinking about what you want to do to him." He fooled with the bill of his beat canvas cap. The veteran trainer wore the baseball-type hat before every fight of every fighter he'd been training and praying and sweating over since he didn't know when. They didn't always come out on top, but more of them managed to be in the winner's light than not. If that didn't mean it was a good-luck piece, then what the hell was?

"You're so funny, Juno."

"Oh, I'm a goddamn Steve Harvey." He twisted his mouth petulantly. "Beat it."

"I'm helping the contender get ready." Monique got up and stretched. She made a feline sound as she stood on the tips of her toes. It looked like her mini would keep rising, but she stopped and came down flat in her suede boots. "Besides, Juno"—she put an arm around the grinning fighter's waist— "chicks are fighting too these days."

Caprice wasn't going to be baited into a discussion of why women boxers were about as useful to him as nonalcoholic beer. "He needs to get focused."

She twitched a shoulder. "The fight's a couple hours off. King Diamond's set just jumped off." She jerked her head toward the ceiling.

Over the years Caprice had found it unproductive to argue with fighters' girlfriends. She knew he was right, but it was never about that anyway. It was about control, who had it and who could exert it over the object of their desire. He folded his arms and leaned against the wall. "Whatever you think is best for Joaquin."

She put a hand on her hip. "Please."

Muhammad drew the woman close to him so that his forehead touched hers. "Baby," he said quietly, "I gotta listen to Juno. This is the biggest bank I've ever fought for, and you know I can't let my peeps down, yo?"

"I know," she pouted.

"And didn't I promise to take you to New York like you wanted?"

"Uh-huh." She put her arms around his neck and kissed him hard.

Juno wondered if it was something programmed in the male brain. How many times had he seen one of these cats who could take a barroom full of ordinary chumps become so emotionally invested in a broad who couldn't spell an eight-letter word if her life depended on it? Shit, who was he to talk? Monique was fine; he'd tumble too. He had before, Lord knew.

"If you please," Caprice said. "I want him to rest, then we're gonna charge the battery about a half hour before the bell." That was Caprice's way of saying he'd have Muhammad break a light sweat prior to stepping into the ring against the title holder, Jeffries.

"I'll be the one yelling the loudest." She gave her man a peck, laid narrow eyes on Caprice, and left the room.

Muhammad stared at the closed door like a puppy waiting for the return of its owner.

Faintly, over the headphones of the Walkman, the fierce rap of King Diamond's "Ain't No Shame" could be heard.

Bring the pain 'cause I want the gain
Ain't no shame in this strugglin' game
Been like that since Mama worked the line
Gonna find out the capitalist dog done run off wit mine
Then the only thing left is to tear this mother up and seize the time.

The bass guitar kicked in as the rapper stooped over, whipping his dreads around, one hand holding on to the standing mike. Three attractive girls sitting side by side in the front row stood as one and pulled down their tube tops to reveal their bouncing breasts, slick with sweat.

"We love you, King Diamond," the three squealed. One of the young women cupped her ample ta-tas and squeezed the nipples while she puckered her lips at the object of their public affection.

Rapper Galileo "King Diamond" Lawson showed nice teeth and glanced at his homie burning up the ax, Desmond Lee. They'd known each other since junior high and damn near knew what was on the each other's mind before either could say it. Lee too grinned like a leopard sizing up an unsuspecting antelope as the three females snugged their tops back in place and plopped down into their seats. For sure they'd be coming backstage after the set.

As Lee's riff ended, King Diamond heated up the mike again with his blistering lyrics, adroitly attacking everything from corporate greed to environmental polluters. An hour and twenty minutes later, over the speakers in the restroom, two of Diamond's fans were listening to his cut, "Punk the WTO." The two stood shoulder to shoulder, tapping their respective kidneys.

"See? This is what I'm talking about," the first speaker said. He was a stern-looking black man dressed in a conservative dark gray suit, his tieless white shirt buttoned at the collar. "He's got to take his music to the next level."

The second man was Japanese American, dressed in jeans and a flowing shirt of some diaphanous material. His hair was long, and there were silver studs impaled at various points on his face, including his tongue. "Yo, man, King D knows what time it is, and his call is about class."

"But," the first speaker admonished, "this Babylon we live in, my Asiatic brother, is all about the race question. You can't go anywhere without that being paramount when it comes to the law and the ones who run this infidel motherfuckah." He finished and zipped up his pants.

"Economics," the other man responded, as the sensor in his automatic urinal flushed, "is at the heart of the matter, my man. People are victimized by the same ruling class that would subjugate the emerging world in the name of making the cheapest pair of tennis shoes."

The crowd could be heard cheering exuberantly though the crackling speakers set in the corner of the restroom's ceiling.

"The white boy living in a trailer park don't see his interests as tied to the black man cooped up in the housing project." The brother in the suit washed his hands throughly.

"True," his erstwhile debating companion agreed, "yet it's only by organizing them both where they're at that we can achieve a unified front to move on the bosses." He too washed his hands. Each dried their digits under the hot air blower set in the black marble tile of the men's room in the Riverhead Casino.

"That, I'm afraid, my friend, is more of a utopian dream than a reality we're ever gonna see up in this bad boy that motherfuckin' Tommy Jefferson left us."

"Give it up, y'all," the announcer boomed over the PA system. "Give it up, Las Vegas, for King D and the Lowriders."

Whooping and the frenzied stomping of tens of thousands of pairs of feet went up like chants to heaven from the newly finished Ichibhan Arena atop the Riverhead. Actually the stadium, a joint partnership between the Japanese car manufacturer, the Riverhead, and several other players, was not precisely on the roof of the casino. The entrance was reached through a skyway leading from the fourth story of the casino. The bulk of the circular facility was supported by huge Swedish-rolled steel trusses arching up from the streets below. Part of the saucer was built into the Riverhead as if it had crashed into the place. And this being Vegas, the natives decided to make best use of the situation.

The two men continued their conversation as they walked along the circle of a tier while the crowd chanted, "More, more."

"But that's what's so righteous about King D's music," the one with silver studs went on. "Who else has a group like his that brings guys like you and me out to the same cultural venue?" He smiled, stopping to sweep a hand in the air, indicating the gathered.

"Yeah," the other one grudgingly admitted as he took in the panoply of faces and sizes. "But if it ain't about building something from this, a movement, ya feel what I'm sayin'? Then we just havin' a good time and go back to our daily shit of tryin' to get over on one another."

King D and the Lowriders came back on stage, and the applause swallowed up the other man's retort. Each waited, bopping his head to the beat, until the noise subsided to allow for the lyrics.

"I don't agree, homes, I think—" Silver Stud halted and blinked at a woman who was coming toward them along the runner. She was tall, but not that much. Six feet was what he figured. She wasn't like a fashion model, he was sure of that. She didn't exude that fake-ass nonchalance that really was screaming for attention like those kinds did. This one had flesh where it belonged and an upper body that was pumped, but not all veined out like some chicks who worked out.

Suit knew the look on the other man's face and tried to be cool as he glanced over his shoulder. Goddamn, he remarked to himself. They both remained mute as Martha Chainey strolled by them.

"Hi," she said warmly as she moved past in her close-fitting Versace jeans.

The two exchanged shit-eating grins and knocked the flats of their fists together. "We can agree she was fine," Suit commented.

"Uh-huh," the smitten man with silver studs grunted.

Chainey couldn't help but smile, acknowledging her thirty-plus self could still make a man or two fantasize. Not that such was the motivation for her hitting the gym at least three times a week, where she completed sets on the free and machine weights, step aerobics, treadmill and stomach crunches. That didn't include the strenuous brushup training she still maintained in Krav Maga, the Israeli Army fighting art and Gracie jiu-jitsu, and the addition of Capoeria, a Brazilian dance/fight technique wherein the feet were utilized as weapons.

And, she observed, mounting the steps to the entrance to the luxury boxes, there was also the time she was required to put in at the shooting range. Realistically, she concluded, it was her job and not vanity that necessitated keeping her body and mind at the knife's edge.

"Okay," said the burly brother with the orange-tinged flattop that matched his jacket after checking out the gold hologram VIP pass around Chainey's neck.

He stood aside and allowed her through the door into the hall leading to the restricted area. It was reserved for those glitterati who could pay or finagle, or who knew somebody who'd paid the $220,000 a year it cost to rent one of the suites. Chainey knew the owner of the Riverhead, Victoria Degault. The two women, though of different economic and racial backgrounds, shared a secret that bound them in ways few other people were.

The boxes had taken their style cues from several sources, including Beaux Arts and '60s steak house, remixed with the usual Strip flair. Apparently the idea had been to design each suite in a different style—one would be quasi-Aztec, another Louis XIV—and so on. But that had been abandoned when it was concluded that the rooms would be assigned a pecking order depending on taste, and some would not want, say, to rent the Wild West Room if it was perceived to be too tacky even by Vegas standards. So it was one-style-fit-all. And the waiting list was many names long.

"What's that look?" Rena Solomon clapped as the platinum-selling rapper and his posse tore up their encore number down below.

"Distraction," her friend said cryptically as she poured some more Merlot into her glass. Bose speakers were hidden strategically around the suite, providing a rich, modulated surround sound in the comfortably appointed box. This in addition to the arena's array of gigantic Aiwas intended for the hoi polloi below.

The room also contained two leather couches—one black and the other off-white—a wet bar, a mini-fridge, a big screen that piped in the image from the stage, and three pretty good prints on the wall. One of the pieces was a Roy Lichtenstein swipe of a fighter airplane comic book panel. There was also a glass-and-chrome coffee table covered with hors d'oeuvres such as spinach dip and hummus, leather chairs, and several authentic Cuban Cohiba cigars lay next to a silver ashtray.

Solomon raised an eyebrow but let it ride. There were several holes in her knowledge of what this former showgirl knew about the other one. But there were a few things Solomon knew that Chainey was not hip to either.

"Isn't that the high holy one? She must have just arrived." Solomon tilted her head to the right as Chainey sat down beside her friend. Two boxes over, as the structure made a curve, they could see the people in the other suite. The woman she meant was a seemingly plain-looking individual with ironing-board-straight mousy brown hair. She sat impassively in her chair, her hands folded in her lap.

"The one-and-only postmodern guru of the bullshit, Naomi," Anson Hiss groused. He was the owner/publisher of the twice-weekly alternative paper called the *Las Vegas Express,* for which Solomon was one of three investigative reporters. He tossed a handful of cashews into his mouth and smacked on them, chasing the nuts with a cold Pilsner.

"You know the contradiction of the city's number-one muckraker indulging in bourgeois largesse while passing judgment on the patricians will make your head explode," Solomon chided.

"I'm just here to give props to my man, see that he serves that fool Muhammad, am I right?" Hiss held out a hand to the casually dressed man dangling a tasseled Lorenzo Banfi sitting next to him. "Oh, you gonna leave me hangin'?"

"Sorry, but you get no dap from me on that score." Simon Kuwada shifted his gaze from the joking beer-gutted publisher to a more pleasing sight. It wasn't the first time this evening he'd checked out the woman. "Who do you like in the fight, Chainey?"

" 'Fraid I have to agree with Anson. I think Jeffries is gonna show Muhammad what time it is."

"You willing to put money where your hype is?"

"I can't stand the same table stakes you do," she answered, returning his look as she sipped her wine.

He spread his manicured hands. "A friendly wager."

"Dinner and a show," Solomon contributed, playing an unsubtle matchmaker.

"Sounds good to me," Kuwada managed in a neutral tone.

Chainey made a quick face at her friend, then got up and reached across Hiss to shake Kuwada's hand. "Bet."

"Very good," the son of the founder and executive vice-president of Ichibhan Motors replied. Their eyes held on each other for a few beats, then he withdrew his hand. "Seems I win either way." Idly, he fingered a Asanti bracelet of thick gold links.

Her lips compressed, Solomon murmured, "Um," quietly.

"Back to the Nymnatists," Chainey said, wishing to take the conversation in another direction. "Looks like a couple of them are bopping their head to King D." She placed her glass on the end table set between her chair and Solomon's.

The rapper had just finished his last encore, and he and the band left the stage to a standing ovation that literally rang to the rafters.

"That one with the slicked-back hair is a fellow traveler," Hiss noted, tipping the bottle to his lips. "Jeff Zanko, he of the www.CheapAss who made his money before dot-comers went bust. I've been collecting some material on him and a few of the other Gen Y multimillionaires. I want to do a piece on what they give to and how they use their money to meld technology and society."

"But he's not a Nymnatist?" Chainey asked.

"Anybody want anything?" Kuwada was heading for the wet bar. Everybody indicated they were fine.

"Oh, he's given them money," Hiss continued, "but no more than he's donated to some political candidates, and much less than he's seeded into his foundation on K through Twelve education."

"But he likes their company," Solomon added.

"Maybe he just wanted a good seat for the fight," Chainey half-seriously expressed.

"He could buy out a row of luxury boxes if that was the case."

Kuwada stood in the rear of the suite, enjoying a bottle of carbonated water.

"*Time* and *People* have anointed Naomi a bona fide celeb," Hiss pointed out. "And bright stars enjoy, indeed, feed on each other's celebrity."

"Careful, Anson, them suds is making you poetic." Solomon playfully tapped the back of her hand against her boss's knee. "Hey, isn't that Ione Whatshername in their box?" She resisted the impulse to jab her index finger at the booth.

"Yeah." Chainey stared. "I didn't know she was a follower."

Hiss nodded his head in the affirmative. "I understand she's putting together a big-budget movie based on one of Naomi's self-help tomes, *The Shackle of Dreams*. It was a best-seller."

"What exactly do the Nymnatists espouse?" Kuwada sat down again. "You know, I hear what people say and have read a couple of pieces on them, but as far as I can tell, it's just positive thinking wrapped up in a bunch of gobbledygook."

"My fuckin' point exactly." Hiss triumphantly thumped a fist on an end table. "But once you dress up warmed-over Dale Carnegie with twenty-first century buzz words and clever turns-of-phrase and get a few high-profile suckers to swallow the pablum, then you're over like a fat rat."

"You sound kinda jealous there, ya know?" Solomon kidded.

"Well," Hiss admitted, finishing his beer, "it is a good hustle."

The door opened and their hostess, Victoria Degault, entered. She was a handsome woman dressed fashionably casual in a D & G silk jacket, Hilfiger jeans, and a Donna Karan sweater. Behind her stood a man in his late fifties wearing a suit and loafers.

The owner of the Riverhead Casino moved farther into the room. "I don't know if everybody knows Dean Tosches, owner of the High Chaparral."

"Hello," Tosches said, raising his hand in a brief wave. He was an individual with a solid build and tanned skin. His hair was too black given the lines in his face, indicating frequent visits to the salon. His eyes moved constantly about the room, like a thief casing the joint.

Chainey made introductions as the stage crew down below set up the ring for the matches. The intermission entertainment consisted of three cages that looked as if they'd been props in a science fiction gladiator film. These were lowered over the stage. In each cage a pretty woman in lingerie danced to recorded music, their gyrating figures televised on the gigantic monitors that arched up to the domed roof on three sides of the arena.

"Quite a coup getting Muhammad and Jeffries to have their title match here, Victoria," Hiss complimented. He was already working on another beer.

"It's good for the gate but hell on the nerves," Degault said. "Putting up with the demands of Naomi and her bunch would try Jesus's patience."

"But he wasn't in it for the money," Hiss the atheist reminded the flock.

"Be that as it may," Degault countered, "we had to go in on some co-op advertising with the Nymnatists, reserve two other suites for her friends and goddamn Fruit of Nymnatists guards, and then Naomi of the one name got the gaming commission to allow her to pipe in her suggestion in Jeffries's corner—" Degault stopped herself from further ranting and merely made motions with her hands.

"What do you mean, pipe in?" Solomon asked.

"At first," Degault answered, "she wanted to be physically sitting in the champ's corner, but the commission nixed that in a hurry. Only essential personnel are allowed. But she knew the right calls to make and got the commission to allow Jeffries's cut man to wear a headset so she could communicate with him while she stood below the ring."

"Which is a riot, considering," Tosches added but didn't go on.

Degault shot him a look and quickly added, "That group have their hooks in deep into Jeffries."

"He's awfully valuable to them." Hiss burped quietly. "In his last fight, Jeffries made between sixty-five and eighty million, give or take a few either way. Beside the IRS, no one knows how much he 'tithes' to the cause, but that's not even the biggest benefit. His face is known all over the world, and who could ask for a better model of sportsmanship and clean living?"

"That pulls in more suckers, that's for sure," Solomon added.

"But all isn't home on the range in his camp either," Chainey contributed. "Yank Turner isn't burning any incense to Naomi's statue, and he's been pretty vocal about it."

"True," Degault concurred, sitting on the arm of a couch. Tosches busied himself at the bar. "But the way I understand the pecking order, all things involving ring strategy is Turner's job. When it comes to the money and the public face, that's the champ's and the Nymnatists' purview. You know that Jeffries has a house in town here, and a four-star training facility he maintains over in Echo Bay, near the lake. He's been ensconced there for the last month. Not Naomi or Haulsey, the guy who heads up her security force the Fruit of Nymnatist, not one of the Numb-nutters are allowed to mess with him. That time is all Turner's."

"That's what I'm talking about," Hiss gurgled. The beers were starting to effect him. "Yank Turner's gym is the home of champions." He shook his beer bottle above him in a salute. "That would-be pretender to the crown is gonna be carrying his head home in a basket after tonight."

"We'll see who gets what handed to them tonight," Simon Kuwada said quietly. He and Tosches exchanged knowing looks.

"Prelim with Prince Nahim and Conrad Jones is about to come up." Solomon was standing, staring down into the arena. "I'm going to go out and mix with the masses, get the pulse of the crowd. Always good for a sidebar or two, huh, Anson?"

"Yep," the publisher replied, while he rummaged in the fridge for another brew.

"I'll go with you," Chainey said. "I want to say hi to Moya Reese."

"The woman boxer also on the under card?" Tosches asked with interest. "How do you know her?"

"She was a dancer for a hot minute," Chainey responded. "We did a show called the 'Shogun' at the MGM for a few months. She'd always worked out too, and this promoter gets to chatting her up, and she figured there was better money to be made in knocking heads than knocking your boobs together."

"My, my," Kuwada remarked.

"We'll be back in a bit." Solomon and Chainey made to leave.

"I'll watch Anson drink in the meantime," Kuwada cracked.

"And count your receipts." Chainey put a showgirl's smile on her face and exited with her friend.

"He does have his own Gulf Stream." Solomon made big eyes at Chainey.

"I don't care how big Mr. Kuwada's jet is, girl."

They both laughed. A tall, muscular, dark chocolate of a man in a golden suit, an electric blue shirt, and a tie crossed in front of them as they walked along the tier. He touched the brim of his Homburg. "Ladies." His teeth were shimmering, as if they'd been coated with an incandescent material. The elegantly proportioned man went down a set of stairs. Coming along the tier from the opposite direction were two women in pale pant suits, chatting. Each was armored in Tiffany-league jewelry. They looked as if they'd taken a wrong turn on their way to a Republican rally.

Solomon made notes on her steno pad. "Even the blasé have to give it up on this one." She smirked to herself as she scribbled her impressions. "From eight ballers to soccer moms, and all sorts between and beyond," she murmured.

Chainey nodded in assent. Two rows below her, a young woman with green dreads and a tattoo of a stylized cheetah's head on her exposed back stood up to let a gray-haired older gent in a linen suit and bow tie get by. The two sat side by side. "You ain't never lied, Rena." The women went down the stairs toward the bottom tier.

"You got these Nymnatists who cut across all kinds of social and racial lines," Chainey continued. A brawny Chicano in khakis and an athletic T stepped into the aisle, holding on to a cup of beer. His corded arms were adorned with intricate tattoos of vines, cars, and comic-book-proportioned women. He went up the stairs past the two women.

"And some who wouldn't know a boxing match from a game of checkers," Solomon observed. "But because the great and wonderful Naomi has decreed that boxing is cool, is pure"— Solomon closed her eyes and fanned out her hands in an imitation of the Nymnatists' leader—"it is so."

Above them there was a sudden squeal, and heads turned toward the source. The tough-looking tattooed man was standing in front of one of the Eagle Forum babes, and it was she who had made the noise. A couple of the security personnel, in bright orange nylon windbreakers with the words STADIUM PEACE stenciled on their backs, moved toward the threatened matron.

The woman giggled and threw her arms around the illustrated *vato*. They bear hugged each other, some of the beverage in the man's cup splashing onto the back of the women's coats.

"You know, the weird part is, they're just as likely to be here to see King Diamond as to be here for the fight," Chainey said as the two women went on.

"Yeah, he pulls in a cross section too, doesn't he?" Solomon sidestepped a couple kissing passionately. On the back of the woman's sweat top was the old communist hammer and sickle symbol. A very recognizable anthropomorphic corporate mouse was skewered on the sharp point of the blade. The duo moved on.

Las Vegas was the home of spectacle, which always presented the problem of how the players on the Strip managed to outdo each succeeding pageant of the senses. When Degault, Kuwada senior and son, and their partners erected the stadium, they knew they needed an inaugural event that would get the attention of even those whose mantra was "Been there, done that."

Blood, sweat, and sex were always a sure way to capture the public's imagination and get it to willingly part with its moola. Some would argue that the desire to be desirable was at the root of the gambling urge. A Shriner with an aching prostate and cigar breath certainly had a sudden panache when he was making his point at the craps table. And so the partners in the new stadium put together a package that would appeal to the conventioneers, the sharks, the whales, and the minnows—the moms and pops of however America was seeing itself in this bold new century.

The first segment was the just-concluded rap concert of King Diamond. He was a multimillion CD selling, multimillionaire twenty-six-year old from Carson, California, a small city lodged between Los Angeles and the more infamous Compton. Hardscrabble Compton was the birthplace of gangsta rap, giving rise to such superstars of the genre as Dr. Dre and Ice Cube, among the founding members of the less-than-PC Niggaz Wit Attitude. One of the other original members, Eric Wright, Eazy E, had died of AIDS, a victim of the persona he had crafted only too well. By contrast, Carson was more of a middle-class enclave of newer tract houses and a university where the '84 Olympics had their bike races. This was a town where whites, blacks, Latinos, and Samoans sought refuge from their jobs, working miles away in downtown L.A. in some anonymous county office, or maybe a start-up software firm in one of the tonier South Bay cities of Redondo and Manhattan Beach.

Small wonder, then, that the half-black, half-Samoan Galileo Lawson would emerge with a different outlook than his contemporaries in less-than-burgeoning Compton. Lawson was a straight-up product of the middle class who not only understood his class origins, but flipped it and spun it in his music. The King Diamond alter ego was not so much a roughneck act as it was an interpretation of his life and times. His was an era in which the gap between the haves and the have-nots was growing, at the same time the dotcom-ers were raking in millions not for what they produced but for what others projected they *might* produce.

"You're cool," the dour-faced security woman pronounced after studying the women's gold passes. She stood aside, and Chainey and Solomon entered the secured area that led to the dressing rooms beneath the stage and the ring.

"Dah—mnn, I know y'all are here to give me my rubdown." The Welterweight Belt holder, Prince Nahim, nee Curtis Parsons, was laying stomach down on a padded table, a towel loosely draped over his lower body. He could see the two pass by as his door was ajar. Sammy Davis sang "What Kind of Fool Am I" on a CD player in the room.

"Maybe." Solomon peered inside, an eyebrow arched.

"You better come on." Chainey nudged her along.

"Don't be in a hurry on your way back, a'write?" the boxer yelled as they moved along.

Though open at the end, the hallway was constructed to absorb sound. Even their footfalls seemed to be faint echoes of another time.

"Here." They halted before a door with Reese's name written in marker on a piece of cardboard slotted into a frame. Chainey knocked rapidly.

"Yo," a male voice rumbled from the other side.

Chainey announced her name and why she was there.

"So?" the gruff voice said.

"Fletcher," a female voice said scoldingly. The door was opened by a woman five inches shorter than Chainey. She was a shade darker than the taller woman and had short, pressed hair on top of an oval head. A thin scar ran along one side of her nose and she was dressed in a matching sports bra, athletic T, and loose shorts in a faux cheetah pattern.

"Hey," Moya Reese said joyfully, opening the door wider and wrapping her arms around Chainey.

"Good to see you too." Chainey returned the hug. They parted and she introduced Solomon.

"You gonna quote me in something?" Absently, Reese rubbed the fresh wrappings around her right hand.

"We ain't got time for this reunion shit," the man bellowed from inside the room. "We got fightin' and feudin' to handle, Moya." He was an older black man of indeterminate age, slightly stooped, with a face full of crags like the side of a mountain. His arms seemed much too long for his body, as if they had been grafted on, taken from some other man who no longer needed them.

"I'm just sayin' hi, Fletch." Reese turned her head sideways to speak to him. Around her neck was a thin silver chain that had a circular object attached to it.

"First got them goddamn Numismatists, or whatever the fuck they call themselves showin' up, and now this," he mumbled. "This ain't the goddamn 'Oprah' hour, ladies." On the floor was an open satchel from which scissors, a nail file, and other boxing paraphernalia poked out.

"Look, I know you have to get your head in the game," Chainey said. "I just wanted to say hello. And after your fight, which I know you'll win, come on up to the skybox we're using."

"You all that, huh?"

"I'm just one of the field hands." Chainey told her which aisle to take to the box and said she'd leave her name with security. "Rock 'em, baby."

"I will. I'll see you after the bout."

"Can we take care of our shit now?" the grumpy trainer asked sarcastically.

"Of course, your majesty." Moya winked at Chainey and quietly closed the door.

There was a commotion in the seats just below them as the duo went back into the arena. Several orange jackets were swarming into a knot of people.

"Bullshit," an unseen combatant hollered from the tangle. "You motherfuckahs sold out the working class."

"You wouldn't know the working class if they came up and slapped you upside the head with a pipe wrench," came the answer.

The two went on, bemused looks on their faces. "It's gonna be a hell of a night," Chainey prophesied as they ascended to their swank aerie.

He got ready in a cramped section of the stadium to which bunched conduit wiring led, and from there outside to juncture boxes, several feet above where the seats ended. He'd been given the right pass to get by security and shown on a plan the correct ladder inside a hidden access closet to take him to his perch. From here he had an excellent view of the ring, looking down between a battery of lights. The man took deep, regular breaths to keep himself steady. He didn't like wearing gloves, but it was a necessity. He dabbed at the sweat beading his forehead, then wiped his sheathed hand against his pant leg. Could they tell his DNA if he left the most minute trace of perspiration on any of the surfaces around him? Probably. So much to consider to pull this off. This was a different kind of stealth than what he'd practiced in the bush.

Then there was the strain of having to lay still after doing the deed. That was going to be absolute hell. But there was no getting around it. Afterward if he ran out of here, as would be the natural inclination, he might be spotted, something might happen. All those people running around, screaming, looking for cover, maybe lashing out at one another—frightened that the person next to them was the one. Get him before he gets you. People sure were something. He was glad he hadn't spent much time among them in the last thirteen years. Absently, he rubbed a gloved index finger over and over the emerald-tinged eyepiece of the rifle's scope.

CHAPTER TWO

Reese followed her wild swing with a hard, compact right that was timed a bit off. But it did its job and landed flush with a smack against the cheek of her opponent. Spittle erupted from Raven Kim's mouth, and her lips curled in a sneer.

"That all you got, bitch?" Kim uttered around her blue mouthpiece. She shot an underhand left into Reese's ribs, eliciting a wince from the other fighter.

"Break," the referee commanded. He used his arm like a scythe to separate the two women.

Resuming, Reese didn't do as expected and lower her elbow to protect the bruised area. Instead she got up on the pads of her feet and tagged Kim with a stiff overhand left off center in her torso. She immediately followed with the right to the stomach that caused a look of concern from the other fighter.

Kim went to some footwork and moved back and to the side, hoping to clear enough space to level her own blows. But Reese wasn't going to lose the momentum and kept on the woman, taking defensive shots from Kim to her forearms, guarding her upper body.

"Back the fuck off me," Kim wheezed. The braggadocio was in her words but not on her face. She was worried.

Again the ref issued a warning. When he put a hand on

Reese's shoulder, she used the few seconds of instruction to lean on Kim and get some rest. As soon as they broke, Reese ducked, while Kim let loose with a stiff, hacking chop that grazed the back of the woman's shoulder blades. Kim tried an uppercut, but Reese had anticipated such a tactic and moved her head to the side. She backed the other fighter off with some hard ones into her body, and the two were now along one side of the ring. Kim's back was to the ropes.

The bell signaling the end of the round sounded, and they went to their respective corners. Reese sat heavily on the stool. Drake, the corner man, squeezed water over her head and wiped at it with a coarse sponge.

"Don't let her bullshit rattle you," Fletcher Rhone admonished her. "I want you to stick to the game plan. It's working; she's not rocking you and you got her looking twice." His stale cigar breath revived Reese better than any smelling salts could.

Drake rubbed her arm and said, "Get her in the body, she hates that." He worked in ointment beneath her eyes with his thumb to reduce the swelling.

Reese let her mind create the image of her downing Kim with a fantastic feat of fisticuffs as her trainer/manager droned on. She was on her feet with anticipation and anxiety before the bell rang and the card girl pranced around the ring in a thong bikini, announcing the next round.

The two marched into the center flat-footed. Kim, a Korean-American fighter, shook her head, her ponytailed brown dreads wiggling like Martian tentacles. "That's your ass, girlfriend," she promised. She went low, then up top, catching Reese along the side of her nose. Blood reddened the black woman's nostrils. A gleeful light shone in Kim's dark eyes. She stepped up her pace, and that was when Reese sandbagged her.

Kim had turned the left side of her body to provide more leverage in delivering a strong right. As she did so, Reese countered with a combination that made her opponent wheeze gusts of air. Then Reese got her attention with a punch to the midsection that dropped Kim to one knee. Some in the audience clapped; others booed. A plastic cup was tossed through the air. The orange jackets quickly descended on the assailant.

"Step back," the ref ordered, inserting himself between the two contestants. He began his count. On seven, Kim got up, bouncing to her feet and moving her head as if it were attached to her body by a gimbal.

"You all right?" The ref stared intently into the boxer's face, searching for traces of disorientation or injury.

"Yeah, yeah," Kim growled. "Bring it on."

"It's your world." The ref stepped out of the way. "Fight," he shouted.

The two came together and mixed it up in a flurry of blows. Little damage was done but each woman licked wet lips as they parted. Kim slapped a foot onto the canvas and twisted a fist aimed at Reese's head, using her hip for torque. The blow got a piece of the other woman, who took the brunt on her tricep.

Reese pressed in, not willing to back up and give Kim any play. She took two to the face that got parts of the crowd cheering. But the second hit wasn't as hard as the first. Kim was running out of gas, and she knew she had to get busy in a hurry.

The Asian American woman went right at the African American with another uppercut intended for the latter's jaw. Reese took it, and some incorrectly assumed she was going to drop at any second. True, she was feeling woozy, but she knew just what she had left in her arms.

Reese clipped Kim in the solar plexus and got her blinking on a jab that ended at the cheek. Kim tried to get her offense in gear again, but Reese had enough saved up to be nanoseconds faster—the margin that decided victors and could-have-beens that Rhone had ingrained in her. Reese's glove found its sweet spot on Kim's chin, and the woman's eyes did a roll in her head. Reese showed no mercy, sending Kim back against the ropes with a pop to the eye socket. She crowded in and worked on Kim, who slipped some knocks but took some more too. Her head lolled, and then the ref intervened.

"Step back," he said, his spread fingers pushing against Reese's breastbone. He counted again, and Kim shook him off just as he started to say "Nine." Reese glanced back at Rhone, who could sense the end too. He gave a slight nod, but Reese had already turned back and pounced on Kim.

There wasn't much to do, and her fourth rap sent the ref between them again. Kim's arms were down and a cut had been opened over the eye socket that had been attacked several times. She still had a defiant stance, but that was only willpower. The crowd chanted "Fight, fight," but the ref knew better.

He made a motion to the judges and called the fight. A round of catcalls was overcome by the stamping of feet and secreams of approval. The technical knockout occurred two minutes and three seconds into the fourth round.

The announcer cried, "The winner of the WCB-sanctioned bout, Moya Reese." The ref held her arm aloft as her crew piled into the ring, everyone hugging each other. Reese smiled. Later, the camera that zoomed in on her would record that momentarily her eyes scanned the gloom above and behind the lights and the audience. And just as suddenly the nervous knotting of her brow disappeared when she refocused on the cable announcer thrusting a mike at her swelling face.

"What I tell you?" Tyler Jeffries grinned magnificently at the monitor that displayed Reese enjoying her win. "I told you Moya would clean her plow. You think just because Raven acts black she's tough." He snickered at his own joke.

Yank Turner scratched his trim belly. "Let's just concentrate on what you gotta be doing. Get your rubdown going." He resumed cleaning the briar of his pipe with a pocketknife, knocking out the tobacco remains against the side of a table.

On the monitor suspended from the corner of the ceiling, the ring announcer introduced the third and final undercard. This bout featured two welterweights, Esteban Vargas, the current number-three ranked, and the younger, greener Floyd Reynolds.

Jeffries picked up a copy of that morning's *New York Times* front section. He removed a large towel from around his lower body and lay on the padded table nude. The world heavyweight champion, at least as far as two of the three entities that bestowed a belt were concerned, was six feet, four inches of proportioned manhood with a fifty-six-inch chest and a forty-inch waist. He was better read than most professional boxers, and his brother-in-law, a lawyer, handled his contracts and legal affairs.

In '96, Jeffries had failed to qualify for the Olympic boxing team. Oddly, he attributed that slight to his not doing his rubdown in the buff, though previously he'd never had it done unclothed. Since then, since turning pro and generating a combined purse—what with satellite rights and endorsements, from video games to signature boxing gloves—of more than $150 million, no one could tell him different.

Yank Turner smiled inwardly—goddamn fighters were a superstitious lot. They had to have their mother or their squeeze or both sitting in row four. Or take Sugar Ray Robinson, insisting on drinking fresh cattle blood from the slaughterhouse before a match. He believed in the old folk tale that the blood of an animal or slain opponent imparted to you some of its strength. It couldn't be its luck, since the creature whose fluids the fighter was gulping was the one who'd been killed, Turner surmised.

"I'll say this again so it's on the record," Turner said in his quiet but forceful way. "I don't much like that guru of yours roostin' in my henhouse."

Jeffries raised his eyes above the folded newspaper he was reading. "Very colorful there, Yank."

Will Masters continued his rubdown of the champ. "Is that sore?" He kneaded an area above Jeffries's kidneys. Two days earlier he'd been unexpectedly blistered there by his sparring partner, Ray "Busta" Brown, an ex-heavyweight contender who never held a belt but came close twice. They'd picked him because Brown still had something to prove, and was known to pour it on when the main attraction lagged.

"I'm not pissin' blood." Jeffries yawned, displaying wide, strong teeth.

"I ain't foolin'." Turner's voice went lower, indicating how serious he was.

"Naomi is only there to boost my Q, Yank, that's all. How I fight is your business." He continued reading an article about an experimental procedure dealing with Alzheimer's. He'd have his broker look into the company advancing the work.

"You people got too many code words goin' on, you know that?"

"It's jargon, just like in our profession or the medical field"—he waved a hand listlessly—"or whatever. They've been good for me in a certain period in my life."

"Turn over," Masters said.

Jeffries rolled fluidly onto his back, holding the folded newspaper over his face. "And anyway, Yank, I've been—"

There was a knock at the door, and before anyone could answer it was opened. In stepped Wilfred Haulsey, head of security of the Nymnatists. He was tall, white, blue-eyed, in his mid-fifties and in great shape. He was a ramrod, sharp in his steel blue suit and polished burgundy wingtips. The security chief was a casting director's idea of what an ex-military man should look like—because he was.

"What?" Turner barked.

"Everything okay, Tyler?"

"Of course." Jeffries stretched like a lion deciding whether to chase its food or get more sleep. "I don't have a care in the world."

"She just wanted me to check." Haulsey had been in the army Rangers for some twenty years and could take in a room and assess potential danger in a fraction of a second. He purposefully avoided locking eyes with the glaring Turner.

"You checked," the irritated trainer-manager snarled.

A twitch came and went at one corner of Haulsey's line of a mouth. "Very good, then." He narrowed his eyes and left quietly.

"How does that punk sit down with that big a stick up his ass?" Turner railed.

"He just does that because he knows it gets to you. Relax, Yank."

"You do the relaxing and let me handle the worryin.'

On the screen the challenger got a good one in on Vargas. The latter reeled back and had to get his arms up as the kid pressed him. Masters finished the rubdown, setting aside a liniment of his own making.

"Get twenty, okay?" Turner shut the monitor off just as Vargas was getting his rhythm back and was backing the kid up.

"I'm already there, baby." Jeffries let his eyes close as Masters turned off the lights and he and Turner stepped out of the room. The champ began to doze, collecting his energy and reviewing how he was going to school that clown Muhammad. Joaquin Muhammad; what kind of name was that for a dude from El Salvador? Ragosa, that was his real name. Man has a name, he ought to use that name, not be something he ain't.

But then, what did they say in the Nymnatists, "Re-creating oneself is part of the process of removing all shackles. By adopting the persona, we unlock the inner truths whispering to us." *Yeah, Tyler, get your Q together, brother.*

Jeffries daydreamed that he was driving a bulldozer and had picked up a bunch of dolls in the scoop. He was delivering these dolls over a craggy landscape where bombs exploded in the far distance. His destination was a large house on a hill. As he got closer to the house, he could see the front door opening. In the doorway stood his wife, the woman he'd recently separated from. He'd told no one about it, not even Yank. But the old pro probably suspected something, since she had yet to appear at the stadium.

His wife, Charisse, had a quizzical look on her face. It occurred to him that she was looking past him and the bulldozer he rode on. What the hell was she looking at, and why did she seem so agitated?

"What I tell you?" a sloshed Anson Hiss slurred. He leaned onto the ledge of the sky box, his hot breath frosting the glass in front of him. "Didn't I tell you Jeffries is the man?"

"There's plenty rounds left," Kuwada observed. He tried to

look composed, but worry had tightened his lithe form. In this fifth round, Muhammad had been on the receiving end of an aggressive attack by Jeffries. He turned from the monitor to the ring, as if one version would be better than the other.

"Not enough for your boy to get good," Hiss gleefully replied.

In the ring, Jeffries had backed up the boisterous Muhammad on the ropes and was methodically hammering at his midsection. Muhammad's tongue slapped against his mouth guard, and a welt was reddening on his cheek. But as Jeffries came up with a cross to the other man's nose, Muhammad slipped in a blow that caught Jeffries full on the jaw.

Vociferous crowing went up from the crowd.

"That's what I'm talking about, Larry," former Heavyweight champ George Foreman said excitedly as he provided color commentary at ringside.

Muhammad had stunned the champ and now was boxing his way out of immediate peril.

"That remind you of Kinshasa, George? When the other Muhammad, Ali, worked his rope-a-dope on you?" Larry Merchant waxed euphorically next to his partner.

"Right, exactly, Foreman answered. "Jeffries better figure out who should be whispering instructions in his ear, if you understand my meaning."

"Oh, I do, I do," Merchant agreed.

Back in the skybox, Moya Reese was wide-eyed as she too stood to view the combatants. "Come on, Tyler, come on." After her match Chainey had phoned downstairs for her and reinvited the new champ upstairs.

Chainey raised an eyebrow. "Tyler, huh?"

Reese ignored the comment. "Left, get your left up and your shoulders squared, come on," she muttered. "That's it, that's it," the woman boxer said, louder. "Move to his right and work that side." Reese began to go through some motions, seeking to telekinetically transmit what she wanted Jeffries to do directly to the muscles of his body.

Solomon and Chainey exchanged glances. Tosches watched Reese go through the motions. Victoria Degault studied the monitor, enraptured at the savage grace of the contenders going about their job.

"Didn't know you were such a fan, Victoria," Hiss commented. He twisted the top on his umpteenth beer.

"Neither did I."

On screen, Muhammad solidly hit Jeffries along the temple as the bell rang, ending the round. The camera followed Jeffries to his corner. He sat, sucking in air, as his corner man squeezed water from a sponge over him. Yank Turner was talking to him and Jeffries was nodding, his eyes locked across the ring.

Turner's mike broadcast his short, clipped admonishments. "Goddammit, go to his left more, use that speed to get him weary, ya hear me? Stop trying to show everybody how tough you are and stand there taking his punches. This ain't no fuckin' show like wrasslin'. This is a goddamn for-real boxing match, and you use everything at your command to outsmart the other man, ya hear me?"

"Yeah, yeah, I'm on it, Yank," came Jeffries's muffled reply as his face was wiped with a towel.

A female hand came from between the ropes, and for a second Degault assumed it belonged to the champ's wife. But she realized the hand was white, and could then see it was Naomi touching Jeffries's arm.

Turner looked down at the leader of the Nymnatists, who was standing outside the ring and also talking to the fighter. So much for radioing in her bullshit, he reflected.

Naomi wasn't miked, so her words weren't being picked up. But Turner's grumblings were very audible.

Picking up on the vibe, Foreman piped in, "This is what I'm talking about, Larry. I'm not one to tell anyone what religion or way or whatever you want to call these Pneumatics—"

"Nymnatists," Jim Lampley corrected.

"As I said, whatever," Foreman went on. "I believe in the Lord Jesus Christ, but you don't see me having my pastor in the corner with me, do you?"

"Well, George," Lampley demurred, "strictly speaking the Nymnatists by their own reckoning are not a religion."

The sixth round bell rang. "My point is, there ain't but one person you need to be listening to at a time like this, and it ain't somebody with nice nails."

Muhammad was dancing, his arms relaxed in an effort to sucker Jeffries into taking a punch. The champ knew that game and bided his time, racking up the punches-thrown stats as he leveled a series of one-twos at the darting and ducking Joaquin Muhammad.

"Still confident in the outcome, Anson?" Kuwada smiled sideways.

"I got a hundred says I am, Mister Car Manufacturer." The alternative news publisher produced a crisp note and gently laid it on the coffee table. "I realize this is just lint to you, but how 'bout it?"

"Anson," Solomon warned.

Kuwada placed his tumbler of Glen Fiddich next to the bill. "You're on, my friend."

The two shook hands.

Under the lights, Muhammad smacked a fist into the champ's hard gut, and a collective "ah" erupted from the crowd gathered in the skybox. Lampley was spitting into his mike and Jeffries countered with a stiff left that clearly stunned the challenger.

"Hmmm," Hiss bobbed his head appreciatively. "Now who's the man?"

"I wouldn't get all giddy just yet, Mr. Hiss." Victoria Degault sat forward expectantly, her forearms across her spread legs.

Tosches took this in. "Not worried, are you?"

"There's no sure bets are there, Dean?" She held out a hand and he took it. He stood next to where she sat, their fingers gripping the other's with force.

Muhammad pounded several into Jeffries's ribs while the other man got some raps into the challenger's upper body. The crowd was ecstatic, and the noise they generated vibrated on the windows of the skyboxes. The chants of each man's name were like two competing cults having a showdown, each seeking to demonstrate that its magic was more potent that the other's.

"Use your arm length, Tyler, use it to get breathing room."

Reese was still at the window, transfixed by the scene below. Her words were chants to empower her Templar of the squared circle. "That's it, Tyler, work it, work it." She was throwing shadow punches and accidentally knocked over the small backpack/purse she'd brought into the room. Some of its contents spilled across the floor.

Solomon winked at Chainey. "Yo," she said quietly into her friend's ear, "what up with that?"

"Maybe she's got a wad on him," Chainey hazarded. She bent and helped Reese retrieve her items. She picked up a slip of yellow carbonless paper. "The boxing game is picking up, huh," she quipped, handing the woman back the receipt. It was from the Terrace, one of the themed restaurants inside the Treasure Island Casino, and signed to her room.

"I'm doing all right," Reese allowed, straightening up to see more of the fight.

"Is that previous remark of yours supposed to be a double entendre, Ms. Chainey?" Kuwada had his eyes locked on the screen.

"However you like it."

That got his attention, and the two momentarily forgot about the fight. Then George Foreman bellowed.

"Like his namesake, Muhammad can take a punch," the ex-champ and greaseless-burger-grill pitchman blared into his mike. "Jeffries is pouring it on, but Muhammad is still on his pins, slipping some blows and getting some in too."

Jeffries's head was snapped back from a crisp right and Muhammad got overconfident and tried to finish him off, crowding in close. For his effort he received a sharp blow that got him blinking.

"Well, well," Hiss kidded, slapping Kuwada on the back. "Care to go double or nothing?"

"My pleasure," Kuwada said, a flinty edge to his voice.

The bell separated the two, and Muhammad trudged back to his chair, his big arms lank at his sides.

"I don't know, Jim, looks like the Salvadoran Scrapper is about out of tricks," Larry Merchant appraised.

"That's a possibility, Larry, but don't forget there were those counting him out seven months ago against Ringo Threadgill, and he came back and won in the tenth round."

Merchant chortled. "Jeffries is a different matter altogether than Threadgill, *mi amigo.*"

"On that we do agree."

Over this commentary, viewers saw Juno Caprice's butt. He was bent over his fighter, his hands kneading Muhammad's shoulders as he gave him instructions. His mike picked up his words: "Look, Joaquin, don't go right at him, you know that's not what we trained to do. I want you back on your bicycle, make him come after you. He hates that, especially when he figures he's about to put someone down."

Muhammad's reply was drowned out as the view was switched from the corner to another camera focused on the audience. There was a flurry of arms and shouting, and the lens zoomed in on a throng of people in the upper decks.

"What the hell?" George Foreman breathed into his mike.

"Indeed," Lampley concurred once more.

Several men in iridescent, retro Super Fly suits topped with hats that had bright feathers sticking out of them were involved in some pushing and shoving with middle-aged women in full nun regalia.

"Only in Vegas," Larry Merchant noted.

A camera went to Jeffries, who wasn't watching the ruckus. He was sizing up his opponent. Conversely, when the camera swung to Muhammad, he had a bemused grin on his face as he watched the goings-on. The disruption was dealt with, causing a delay of some four minutes before the fight could resume.

Several seconds elapsed as each man sought to get his rhythm back, before they both stormed around the center of the ring. Jeffries banged Muhammad under the heart, and he woofed out a ball of air. He counterpunched, then got clear. Following his trainer's advice, Muhammad got moving, earning an exasperated look from the title holder.

"Uh-oh," Foreman warned, "be careful, Tyler. Don't get too anxious."

Jeffries was swearing over his mouthpiece. "Stand still, you fuckin' rabbit." He stalked Muhammad, trying to cut off the ring on the other man.

"Your mama." Muhammad got him with light taps of the back of his hand. "I'm gonna give you a boxin' lesson, homeboy."

"I got your homeboy," Jeffries grunted. He pounded forward and let loose with a strong right, but Muhammad managed to duck most of its force. Muhammad moved backwards out of range again.

"Shit." Jeffries charged and threw another right. As he did so, Muhammad delivered his own right and grazed the champ's jaw. Jeffries's upper body suddenly stiffened.

"Is this like Ali's invisible knockout punch of Liston?" Merchant asked.

Joaquin Muhammad was openmouthed as Jeffries toppled over flat on his face. The referee stepped forward and pushed the challenger back. The ref started to count, then stopped before he finished. He bent down.

Everyone in the skybox stared at the screen. Reese had a hand over her mouth. The camera dollied in, the image went out of focus, and it was several moments before the lens was rotated to provide clarity. The referee was looking all around, unsure of what to do next.

"He's dead. He's been shot," he said in a strained voice.

CHAPTER THREE

"What?" Merchant and Foreman roared in unison at the referee's pronouncement. The crowd also heard the somber words, and stunned disbelief settled over them. This lasted about half a minute; then disorder and confusion overtook patience and common sense as people began scrambling for exits, the ring, the locker room, anywhere but where they were.

Somehow one of the chairs had been uprooted from its moorings in the row below the skyboxes, and it was tossed into the sea of swarming bodies.

"Shit," Kuwada swore as the seat sailed like a groupie into the mosh pit. "Those fucking things cost us three-hundred-forty-five-dollars per." He made for the door.

Reese was moving past Chainey, muttering, "They were serious."

Chainey was paying more attention to Victoria Degault. The casino owner was swearing into her cell phone, which had rung right before the chair had been launched into space. Outside the skybox window, teams of orange jackets and uniformed Las Vegas Metropolitan Police Department officers in their tan uniforms were scurrying about like worker bees bereft of their queen.

"Goddammit." Degault hurled the cell phone, and it broke against the edge of the coffee table.

The door to the skybox was open, and people could be seen running back and forth along the hallway. Reese and Kuwada had joined the action for their own reasons.

"What is it, Victoria?" Tosches put a hand on the woman's arm.

Degault said something to him that wasn't audible across the room where Solomon and Chainey were standing. Hiss had fallen asleep. His feet were spread out, his arms flopped over the chair's arms, and his head was back, his mouth open. He was blissfully *zzzing* as Rome lit up.

Solomon suddenly came to life. "I better make like a good reporter." She dashed for the door and bumped into one of the security crew. "Come on, I'm deputizing you."

The confused man looked at Degault, who gave him the high sign. They went off. Degault closed and locked the door. She and Tosches exchanged more words, while the owner of the High Chaparral was not too subtly peeking at Chainey. He turned back and said something else to Degault, then solemnly nodded his head.

"Could we have a minute, Chainey?"

"Like I have a reason to be out there?" Chainey jerked her thumb at the window. A cup of beer went splat against the pane.

"True," Degault said. She sat on the couch and crossed her legs. Her forced composure was a studied contrast to the general bedlam out in the stadium proper. A voice hollered for calm over the PA system, and Tosches turned the speaker down. His cell phone rang and he extracted it from an inside pocket. He went to another part of the room to talk on it.

Degault addressed Chainey. "I need you for a job."

"Find out what happened to Jeffries?"

Degault luxuriously waved a hand. "Oh, I'm sure the police will be sufficient for that."

"Then it must involve money." Chainey wisely didn't add that she concluded that because she knew green might be more important to Degault than life. Considering how her brother had met his end, that would have been an unnecessarily cruel quip.

"Five mil and some change, five million seven hundred thousand to be exact," Tosches added. He tucked his phone away.

"The phone call." Chainey pointed at the now useless cell phone.

"The robbery went off right before Jeffries went down." Degault stared at the broken phone. "They murdered a decent man as a diversion so they could get away." She was about to go on but didn't.

"But if the casino's been hit, why not get the cops or your own security on it?" Chainey asked.

Degault looked at Tosches, who was bending down, peering at Hiss's face. He straightened up, convinced the man was actually out. "Because it's not table money," Tosches clarified. "This was off-the-books stuff, the fade-line action, dig?"

Chainey had to smile at the antiquated hepster term. "Then what? You guys bet on the fight," she said declaratively.

"Right," Degault confirmed. "The money was tucked away in a safe hidden in a room known only to a few."

"What's my end?" Business was business, and Chainey knew these two wouldn't respect her unless she showed them she could be as single-minded as they were.

"Let's say three percent," Degault proposed. "That should come close to two hundred K, tax free."

Chainey shook her head. "Five percent."

Tosches got a sour look, but Degault acquiesced. "You cover your own expenses."

"Deal."

A knock sounded on the door and the lock jiggled.

"Ms. Degault, Ms. Degault, you all right in there?"

"That you, Barry?" Degault took several steps toward the locked door.

"Yeah, you okay in there?"

"We're fine. How's it going out there?"

"Crazy as shit, like when the Lakers won but worse. You better stay put."

"Okay, thanks." The man's feet pounded away across the carpeted hall.

"All this still doesn't explain why you don't have your own security people sniffing out the ducats. Not that I'm eager to turn down the job." Chainey looked over her shoulder and saw that there were more cops in the arena, some of them shouting instructions over bullhorns.

"That guy just at the door," Degault responded, "he's been with the casino's security since the day it opened. He's one of not many I'd trust internally to handle this, if he was capable of doing it." She halted, a visible change overtaking her aging model's features. "Since Frankie's death," she began haltingly, "since then I know for a fact that the Nevada Gaming Control Board has been on me—"

"Like a goddamn tick," Tosches interjected. "The skinny is, they've got somebody undercover here, or turned someone to rat out Victoria."

"We've added a lot of people with the stadium opening and so forth. Therefore there's a need for this to be handled fast and discreetly." Degault uncrossed her legs. "Well, what do you think, Chainey?" She held her arms open in an inviting manner, a sleek tigress who could make it unpleasant for Chainey should she turn down the request. It wasn't the same as last time, when her brother had a gun literally to her head to find the dough she'd been transporting that had been ripped off. Then it was clear, either get the money back and quick or she'd be whacked.

But this—she could walk away, and what could Degault really do to her? She'd be disappointed, she'd be pissed, she'd talk bad about her, but to whom? The money wasn't supposed to exist, and with big ears in her organization she had to be mum anyway. On the other hand, Chainey's job as a courier of Truxon, Ltd., depended on the goodwill her boss, Ira "Mooch" Maltizar, had built up over decades doing this kind of under-the-table work for the shot callers in town.

"Well?" Degault repeated, her pointed politeness slipping.

"I'm in," Chainey said. "But you cover my expenses if it gets to that."

"It's the principle that matters to me," Degault emphasized.

"I can't have the others on the Strip seeing me as weak, you understand, Chainey?"

"Not being able to handle your business, as the kids say."

"Exactly. I'll cover whatever expenses you run up."

Tosches pointed at Degault. "Within reason, right?"

"I'm not worried about her running up the bill." Degault stood up and offered her hand. "It's a deal."

"Good." Chainey shook the woman's hand.

Tosches smiled, giving his benediction. "Looks like things are getting under control out there." He tapped the window with an index finger. "I better go see what's happening over at the Chaparral." He walked over and kissed Degault briskly on the lips. "I'll call you later."

"Okay," she said, patting his arm. She kissed him again and Tosches exited.

"Who bet in this pool?" Chainey was beside her, and the two women also headed for the hallway.

"Do you really need to know that?" Degault bristled.

A man with flowing hair and pink jeans, and wearing a fluffy angora pullover sweater, came skipping and laughing along from the entrance. He was easy to make as a man because of the stubble on his face. The happy fellow had a rucksack draped around his torso and was throwing objects from it.

"Aw, shit," Chainey bellowed, ducking instinctively. Several pinpricks hit her arms and face but nothing exploded.

"Come here, Johnny Appleseed." A member of the LVMPD grabbed the overgrown sprite from behind. "You ladies okay?"

"Yeah." Victoria Degault rubbed the side of her head.

"I've never been assaulted by an acorn before," Chainey remarked. She'd plucked one of the mini grenades off the floor.

"That's how mighty oaks grow and the capitalist sycophants will be toppled," the man under arrest said joyfully as he was handcuffed and escorted away.

"You think he was a Jeffries or a Muhammad fan?" Both women laughed nervously at Degault's joke. Instead of heading out into the arena, the casino boss led them deeper into the hallway. They passed several people standing in the doorways of their luxury boxes.

"Is everything okay, Victoria?" someone asked.

"I heard the gunshot right above me," another stammered.

Degault mouthed platitudes about order being restored, the situation soon being stabilized, and so on. It reminded Chainey of a History Channel doc she saw that had then-President Nixon in front of the cameras, going on about how American victory was assured in Vietnam. She hoped that particular ignominious outcome wasn't going to be the reality of this predicament. Whatever the hell it was, exactly.

They got to a door marked REPAIRS set along one wall in the crook at the end of the hallway. Degault swiped a card with a magnetic stripe through the electronic lock and they stepped through.

"This will take us down and across to the Riverhead." Degault went down steel steps to a landing.

"You still haven't answered my question, Victoria."

"You noticed that, huh?" The landing was lit by wall sconces. Beyond it was a dark maw Degault illuminated by touching a panel.

"Very Indiana Jones of you."

"No sense building a place if you can't include a private entrance and exit for some of your best clients." She started along the metal tunnel. The walls had colorful photos and prints at intervals along the passageway. The subject matter ranged from city scenes to a couple of '30s-era Soviet realism shots.

They walked along. "I put some money down, of course," Degault said without introduction.

"Even I figured that one out." Chainey paused at a handsomely rendered depiction of the Rye Breaker, a nightclub in West Vegas, black Vegas. Standing before the club was the original owner, a man named Wilson McAndrews. He was dressed in a stylish late-'80s Pierre Cardin sport coat, one hand in his pocket. He'd been a big, muscular man with rugged features. The kind of man who wasn't pretty, but who got a woman's attention. McAndrews had been the man you went to see if you had trouble and the normal channels wouldn't or couldn't do anything for you. He'd also been Chainey's lover at one point. He was dead now, having died violently after pulling off one of the biggest heists in town.

"I didn't know you knew him." Chainey tilted her head at the print.

"Dean knew him. He had this photo among some old things and asked if I wanted it to blow up. We both thought a guy like McAndrews would appreciate being hidden away, only seen by the movers of the city."

"Yeah, he would." Chainey choked back further comment.

The two reached an access door that opened onto another hallway, this one inside the Riverhead Casino. "This way." Degault walked briskly to a private elevator that took them to a long, rectangular room Chainey hadn't been in until now—though she had known it existed.

"Well, well," she said appreciatively as the doors slid back to reveal the monitor operation. There was a wall of TV screens relaying myriad images from fiberoptic cameras hidden all over the Riverhead's main gambling floor and elsewhere. The patrons went about their delusional pursuit of easy money, apparently oblivious to the commotion happening less than four hundred yards away.

At intervals before the monitors were control panels and a small squad of security people whose eyes roved over their own set of screens. Each person wore a stylish headphone set, and there were several supervisory men and women in tailored suits who marched back and forth behind the seated sentinels.

Flung on one of the keyboards was a printout update from G.O.L.D., the Griffin's OnLine Database service. This cyber-age firm supplied insider information on suspected cheaters and rings operating from Vegas to Monte Carlo. This one and a few others had replaced each casino's legendary black book, the book in which card counters and their ilk were listed in the old days.

"Ms. Degault," one of the personnel said.

"Bill." Degault walked through the room, Chainey beside her.

Bill fell into step.

"I think I got someone past-posting," one of the people at a monitor announced. That was a method employed at the roulette table; a decoy distracted the dealer and an accomplice put a bet, usually cash, down on the right color and number combination after the roulette marble had come to rest on that particular slot on the wheel.

"Give me a print from the tape, will you?" one of the supervisors asked.

The one who'd spotted the cheater hit a button, and some internal gears could be heard turning.

"What's the mucker doing?" the supervisor asked. The mucker helped the dealer clean up losing bets from the roulette table and was supposed to help look out for those attempting to beat the house.

The trio were already at the other end of the room as the printout was examined. Later, Chainey knew, there'd be a meeting where the least the dealer and the mucker could expect was a reprimand. If it was determined they'd been partners in the effort, their names and faces, along with their accomplices, would go out to all the casinos on and off the Strip. Like horse thieves in the Old West, they'd be persona non grata all over town.

Bill swiped an electronic card key, there was a buzz, and Degault swiped her card to complete the process.

"I guess they didn't come in this way," Chainey remarked.

"Hardly." Bill held the door open and the two women entered another passageway. Bill let the outer door click shut, then the three walked along, took a turn at a T, and came to a blank wall.

Chainey looked at Degault, who waited patiently. Bill punched in a sequence of numbers on his cell phone and a panel slid open in the wall. Degault pressed her hand to a plate inside the panel that scanned her palm. A seamless door swung inward on hydraulic hinges in the wall. This, in turn, led to a box of a room sheathed completely in stainless steel.

"Damn," Chainey exclaimed.

"Frankie saw one-too-many episodes of the old 'Mission:

Impossible' show on cable," Degault said apologetically. "He got carried away with the concept of the secret room." The three stepped inside and the outer door closed.

Part of the floor of the steel cube slid back to reveal a recessed safe. Chainey stood over it, estimating it was at least four or five feet deep and three across. She looked around the room and up at the overhead floods. There were three-inch-square grills letting in forced cool air. "Okay, how'd they do it?"

"We're still working on that," Bill said.

"We?" Degault questioned anxiously.

Bill held up his hands in a defensive posture. "I meant me, Victoria."

"So, if the only way in is the way we came"—Chainey pointed at the door—"and you were back in the monitor area, with all those other people, how'd you know the safe had been hit?"

"This." He took a pager off his belt. "It beeped me that the safe had been broached. It took me less than a minute to get in here, and this is how I found it."

Chainey had never read an Agatha Christie novel, but from what she understood, this kind of locked-room puzzle was at the heart of some of her stories. She sure as hell hoped she wasn't going to have to bone up on the woman's mysteries to find the missing cash.

"Besides, Victoria," Bill continued, "I'm the only one who specifically knows what's in this room and what it's used for."

"You're the one responsible for tucking the bills away?" Chainey was back looking at the opened safe. There were scorched smudges around its hefty edge.

"That's right."

"How?" Chainey fixed him with an even look. "How do you get the cash past the other employees?"

"The other hallway off the T leads to the rear of my office," Degault provided.

"So, who was in your office laying bets, Vikki?" Chainey allowed a hollow smile to curve her lips. Degault hated not being called by her full name.

"Thank you, Bill." She gave the supervisor a pat on the shoulder, dismissing him.

"I'll be in the monitor room if you need me." He started to walk out. "Oh," he added, standing at the door, "we heard from the floor that Sheriff Lambert is closing off the area around the Strip because of the shooting. So there's a good chance the crew is still in the vicinity."

"There's not enough personnel on the Vegas PD to do that," Chainey stated. In 1973 the Clark County Sheriff's Department and the Las Vegas Police Department had been merged into one. But given the number of people who were always in town and the exploding population, the force was completely out-stripped.

"He was already prepared for something to break out. The National Guard has already rolled into town." Bill departed.

Degault folded her arms. "I bet in favor of Jeffries."

"So did I, but not with the weight you can put on the table."

"Dean put some money down too, on Muhammad."

"Did Simon?" Chainey asked.

"Yes, also on Muhammad, as I'm sure you guessed from his and Hiss's conversation. And Mr. Lawson, a.k.a King Diamond. As he put it, 'I got to put up the cheddah for my boy Jeffries, even though he's hooked up with that nonsense.' "

"Okay." Chainey nodded. "Anybody else?"

Degault looked at the empty safe. "The one that's got me thinking is the Nymnatist bet."

"You mean Naomi likes a little action?"

"It was Haulsey who came to my office to lay it down, but I'm sure it was her money. Or the church's, or however they refer to themselves."

"So she bet on a sure thing, just furthering their interests."

"That's just it," Degault said. "He put money on Muhammad."

Chainey speculated on what that might or might not mean. "Well, if they capped Jeffries to make sure they could collect, why steal the dough too?"

Degault lifted a shoulder. "All bets are off with Jeffries dying violently. Technically the fight's voided, so everybody picks up their marbles and goes home."

Chainey looked around the room again. "I haven't got the brain power to figure out how they did it, but if I find out who, then we can ask them."

"It's not about the money, Chainey—"

"It's about the rep, I know," she said, interrupting. "I'll see what I can shake loose."

"That's all I can ask."

The two went back the other way to Degault's office, and Chainey went out that way. She crossed the marble-and-gold-leaf foyer with its twin massive doors inlaid with the four card suits leading to Victoria Degault's plush office. Chainey also passed the door that used to lead to Baker's office. He'd been Frankie Degault's personal enforcer, and had kidnapped the ex-showgirl to live out an S&M rape fantasy he'd been carrying around in his demented mind for some time. This as Chainey was chasing down seven large that had been ripped off from her as she made a delivery of the cash on Frankie boy's behalf. She'd managed to overcome Baker, leaving him wounded and out of favor with his boss. Now Frankie Degault was dead and Baker . . . who knew where he was?

She descended in the private elevator that let out near one of the kitchens. Chainey was surprised she could review distasteful events so dispassionately. Vegas taught you that only the survivors had the luxury of hindsight, and they could call it any way they wanted.

Walking toward the front of the casino, Chainey encountered three Las Vegas cops in riot helmets, T-handled batons at the ready, jogging past. Her eyes followed the figures as one of the public elevator cars came to rest on the ground floor. Out poured green fumes, and someone inside of the elevator shouted, "Viva, Sub-Commandante Kahli. *Qué viva la revolucion.*"

"Wow, we don't get that back home, Ma," a man said in a flat monotone to his wife. Both were dressed in shorts and tennis shoes.

"No, no, we don't, Pa," the woman said in an equally spiritless voice.

The Jacobins from the elevator—young people in jeans and T-shirts, some with handkerchiefs tied around their mouths or Kafirs on their heads—darted off in various directions, moss-colored smoke trailing after their darting bodies. The Vegas police did a Keystone Cops bit, looking everywhere, starting in one direction, then turning to go in another.

Chainey continued toward the main entrance. Purposely, she segued to one of the bars off the casino. Sure enough, the TV was on and, unusually, several people were actually watching it. Normally the denizens of the bar were too busy drinking and plotting their next strategic approach to cards or the craps table to pay attention to anything else.

"Let me make this explicitly clear," Sheriff Gil Lambert was saying into several microphones thrust up at his jowls. "A four-mile area in all directions will be put in place by this state's National Guard, with an assist from our fellow sunshine soldiers in California." Chainey recalled that he liked to be called chief and used the term interchangeably with sheriff.

A chorus of questions were hurled at him like hail. Lambert maintained a stolid appearance, his eyes cast toward the ground. Eventually he held up his hand for the electronic rabble to hush. They didn't quiet down, and he merely smirked as the Cheshire cat had done in the *Alice in Wonderland* cartoon Chainey had seen as a kid.

Lambert dug a finger in his ear, adjusted his crisp straw cowboy hat, and looked over at one of the cops standing near him and waited. The minions of the once-esteemed Fourth Estate finally figured out he wasn't going to try and answer their repeated rapid queries.

"As I was saying," Lambert began again, his hand held aloft, "the area proscribed will be controlled access and egress for the next twelve to fifteen hours at least."

More clamoring started up, and this time the hand gesture got the proper Pavlovian response. "The assassination of a beloved public figure such as Tyler Jeffries cannot be taken lightly. I have assured the governor that my office will exhaust all mea-

sures to identify and bring to justice the instigators and perpe-
trators of this heinous act."

He paused, and only the snapping of cameras could be
heard. "We have been compelled to take these strong steps due
in no small part to the presence of self-styled anarchists like
black bloc and ultra-leftists such as the revolutionary Communist Party, some of whom disrupted the WTO in Seattle and the
Democratic Convention in L.A. This on top of the myriad other
folks we have in town for the event means we must, again I say,
take extraordinary measures to ensure that order and sanity are
preserved."

Chainey began to leave the bar, but she picked up on Lambert's last words. "Any further questions can be routed through
Ms. Harris, who some of you know, in my office. Thank you, and
we will keep you abreast of our progress."

"Gawd," an old-timer teetering on a stool at the end of the
bar exclaimed. "Goddamn Douglas MacArthur had nothing on
the chief, huh?"

"I shall return," his companion, a woman in white stretch
pants and a white-streaked black beehive added. She jiggled the
ice in her glass over her hair, her forehead against the edge of
the bar, saluting the madness of it all.

CHAPTER FOUR

As Chainey began her hunt, Rena Solomon was next door at the Ichibhan Stadium, getting some good dirt for her story. All about her the cops had German shepherds and blood-hounds sticking their wet noses into every conceivable hiding place.

"You better back the fuck up." The cop's meaty hand was pressed forcibly into the wide expanse of the Fruit of Nym-natism's protruding chest.

"You better withdraw that paw or they might start callin' your impudent ass lefty." The security squad member was at least six-five and 310 solid pounds, and it looked as if he was quite used to getting his way.

The cop's hand made a squeaky leather sound as he tightened his grip on his T-handled baton. And he wasn't alone either. "Is that right?"

Solomon had her recorder going and was taking notes as fast as she could. Abstractly, she imagined what would happen if she were getting beaten down; would she be coherent enough to re-call each excruciating blow when she wrote the story later?

"Sergeant Carter," Haulsey and more of his security detail re-proached the beefy man as he strode onto the pathway between the ring and the seats. The police had made an effort to cordon off the area where Jeffries had gone down. His powerful body was on its side in a partial fetal position. One of his arms was cocked over his head, and it looked as if he were in deep slumber. The lack of motion of his abdomen was the only indication of his true condition.

"Great, another one of these numbnutters," one of the cops muttered.

Haulsey stood at parade rest, hands clasped one over the other behind his back. "That disparagement is not necessary."

"What is necessary is for you people to stop trooping all over this crime scene." Chief Lambert came in from the opposite direction along the pathway. Several National Guardsmen cradling rifles accompanied him. "You have ten seconds or you will be arrested for obstruction of a police officer as he performs his duties."

"But—" Haulsey began, clearly perturbed by the numbers and authority Lambert commanded.

"Nine," Lambert announced. He stood directly in front of the taller Haulsey.

The seconds crawled by and Solomon took it all down. She was the only media person able to finagle her way this close. The combination gold pass and having been seen by the stadium security with Degault had bought her passage.

"Very well," the ex-Ranger relented. His head spasmed quickly and the FON came off the ring and lined up around Haulsey. To the man and woman they remained at the ready, not deigning to lose any more ground or face.

And Lambert was wise not to push it further, since he knew he might need the Nymnatists' cooperation along the way to resolving this business. He tilted his head up and said, "Doc?"

Hidden until now were three members of the medical examiner's office. Two were younger assistants, a man and a woman, accompanying the older man Lambert had addressed. He was stoop-shouldered, and the suit he wore hung on his lanky frame like sewn-together sackcloth.

The doctor crooked a finger, beckoning the sheriff, who clambered into the ring. The two men put their heads together.

Several minutes elapsed as people shifted on their feet. Solomon tried to angle closer to catch a phrase or two.

"Not today," a cop said, blocking her path.

Then Naomi showed up with another woman in a severely cut designer suit. Solomon remembered seeing her in the Nymnatist's skybox earlier. "I'd like to know how Tyler died, Chief Lambert." The leader of the Nymnatists' voice had the quality of a newscaster's, forceful yet pleasant.

Rather than be brusque, he asked, "By what authority, ah, Ms. Naomi?"

"This," the woman next to the leader of the sect said. Her manner was as sharp as her attire. She produced some folded sheets and handed them up to Lambert.

"The wife's rights supersede this power of attorney," Lambert said casually, refolding the papers. "And as far as I can tell"—he shook the paperwork—"this has to do with Mr. Tyler's financial affairs."

"And to matters of his welfare," the woman said. "That is what we're concerned about, as much if not more than you, Chief."

"I know you're licensed to practice in Nevada, Ms. Willoughby," Lambert began, "but that doesn't mean you'll run roughshod over this situation. The governor has declared a state of emergency in Las Vegas, and for the time being that gives me carte blanche."

That was it, Solomon told herself as she completed her notes. Davis Willoughby had been on the cover of several national magazines and all over the tube two or three years earlier. She had been the lead attorney in a legal appeal the Nymnatists had mounted when the nonprofit status of their MindFood organization had been revoked by the IRS.

MindFood was a series of storefronts the parent organization had seeded throughout various inner cities and rural areas. It was an after-school, free-of-charge program that provided tutoring in reading, math, and science. Given the dire state of many public school districts, desperate parents were willing to overcome their distrust of the Nymnatistic way to at least be able to provide their children with some academic help.

But the program had come under scrutiny after several regional MindFoods had done direct mailings wherein scorecards were presented, ranking local candidates for school board races. Willoughby's team had successfully argued on appeal that the report cards were in keeping with nonpartisanism and grassroots outreach.

"Really?" she declared dubiously.

"Exactly," Lambert answered and resumed talking with the medical examiner.

Willoughby said something to Naomi, who maintained a placid appearance. The lawyer whipped out a sleek post-Matrix II-style cell phone and turned her head as she made a call to confirm what Lambert had said. Solomon had an opening.

"If I could ask a few questions, Naomi?" She flipped her gold pass over to display her press credentials. Haulsey and two of his dragoons were already in motion.

"I've never read your paper," the quasi-religious leader began. Without looking in their direction, she held up an index finger, and the three FONers halted in midstride. "But we have members here in Vegas who have spoken well of the publication. The last town crier in the desert." Her eyes sparkled at her wit, but her face retained its masklike composure.

"Will the murder of Tyler Jeffries hurt the Nymnatists?"

Willoughby arched a neatly plucked eyebrow as she continued talking on the phone.

"The senseless slaughter of any one of us hurts more than just the immediate family, Ms. . . . ."

"Solomon; Rena is fine."

"Rena," Naomi said her name as if it were coveted aged cognac. "But of course I know what you mean. I'm simply not being coy when I say that the child who dies hungry, alone, and afraid in Sierra Leone is as significant a loss to the universe as is the heavyweight champ beloved by millions."

"But the child in Sierra Leone doesn't bring in converts and resources."

Willoughby thumbed her cell phone off, and it disappeared into her pocket as she said, "We're done here."

Solomon made a note of that. Naomi smiled like a patient mother who must endure the caprice of her headstrong children. "We can spare a few moments, Davis. This is, after all, the calm in the epicenter of the chaos sure to descend."

Willoughby was practiced at keeping contrary emotions from showing and did so now. She merely looked at the reporter with smoldering indifference.

"What you say is accurate, Rena," Naomi said. "Naturally when we are fortunate enough to have someone of Tyler's caliber, we take advantage." She halted and looked past Solomon's shoulder into the ring. The techs had loaded the champ's body on a stretcher and were taking it out under police guard. Jeffries's heavily muscled body had a sheen of sweat covering its magnificent proportions, and it seemed as if any moment he might, like a bronze Lazarus, rise and finish the fight.

National Guardsmen came into the arena and were now helping the police search each person who was trying to get out. Simultaneously, the cops were using dogs to scour the premises. This must be what a coup was like in Eastern Europe or South America, Solomon reflected, as Naomi cleared her throat. You show up with enough guns and you're bound to get people's attention. As a sidebar, she'd have to get out of town and talk with some of the NRA enthusiasts to get their reaction to the controlled—or was that confined?—madness.

"I know there is a better peace than this," Naomi muttered as Jeffries, the media-adored gladiator, was taken away.

"I should get over there to the morgue," Willoughby said, more to herself than to anyone in particular. "Charisse will probably be there."

Naomi quietly communicated something to her lawyer by turning to look at her, blocking her face from Solomon's view. "I think that's a good idea, Davis," she eventually uttered in a normal tone of voice.

"I want a copy of the transcript of this." The lawyer pointed at Solomon. She and everyone standing within earshot knew the tough woman said the words more for effect than anything else.

Naomi went on. "As I was saying, it's only good business to exploit one's talents. Nymnatism is about exploiting the best in all of us. We use"—she touched a hand to her bosom—"the term *exploit* in its best sense, that of achievement, of course." On Naomi's left-hand ring finger was a rock of seven karats, at Solomon's guesstimate. Achieving was an understatement.

"Let's get to the big questions, Naomi." Both women had moved away from the ring and were standing in an aisle leading to the dressing rooms. A German shepherd with off-colored eyes sniffed at Solomon's pant leg as its owner moved the dog forward. "Who killed Tyler? Had he been getting death threats? There is a breakaway faction out to expose you, they say. Do you think that is related to this?" Solomon didn't believe so, but she wanted a way to talk with the ex-Nymnatists and not make it seem she was courting the opposition.

"All movements suffer those who for petty or insecure reasons seek to undermine the good works of others. Particularly when they can't put their names on it or take sole credit." Naomi touched a finger to her lips, considering her next phrasing. "But I don't for a second believe that the detractors who were at one time supposed members are responsible for this sick crime."

Solomon had been listening carefully. "But other detractors could have a hand in this?"

"You'd be surprised at the amount of heinous"—she shook her head in disgust—"simply heinous material directed at us each week. I don't maintain the FON for affect, Rena."

Solomon had previously done some research on the organization's principal players. Haulsey, the ex-Army Ranger, had been in charge of a seek-and-retrieve mission when the U.S. had invaded Panama, tracking down their uppity bad boy, Noriega. Pineapple Face, as he was nicknamed, had before then been useful to the State Department but became a liability when he started believing he and the U.S. were equal partners. The former military man was sure to have brought a few buddies with him to this civilian gig.

Looking askance, Solomon could see Lambert getting antsy. *Get going, girl.* "Given that the Fruit are not window dressing, that must mean you're going to put Haulsey and his crew in motion. What direction in the deep, dark woods would that be, Naomi?"

The leader of the Nymnatists snorted a short burst of laughter, then got serious. "I want to see the bastards who killed Tyler Jeffries get what they deserve."

Lambert was climbing down from the ring.

"Would Sub-Commandante Kahli be on that list, Naomi?"

The other woman folded her arms.

"I understand her crew has had physical confrontations with some of your members at spiritual fairs and that sort of thing."

"They even tried to crash into our retreat facility in Reno," Naomi added.

"A bunch of tofu-eatin', Che Guevera–pretending buffoons could hardly be smart or organized enough to pull this off." Haulsey had also stepped over and now stood slightly behind and to the side of Naomi. Her body language briefly, and genuinely, relaxed, then resumed its public posture.

"We'll see," Lambert countered. "I'd like a few words with you, Ms. Naomi."

"Convenient, now that my lawyer has stepped away."

"I don't mind waiting; this is not a police state, just a police emergency."

"You must read more than *USA Today*, Chief," she complimented.

He laughed, shifting his long frame on his big, flat feet. "My wife tells me what's been in the *New York Times* the previous day."

Solomon left them to their cocktail-hour banter. She could head to the morgue; she had a contact there, and she was curious to see how the new widow would interact with Naomi's hatchet woman. But the ex–chorus girl, now reporter looked through the gauntlet of humanity and settled on Victoria Degault. The boss of the casino was huddled with someone it took her several blinks to realize was Juno Caprice.

Now that, she acknowledged to herself as she tried to get closer to them, was very interesting. The two of them were standing at an angle to her, up several tiers, near one of the exits. Solomon was simultaneously attempting to move briskly and at the same time not have Degault's attention suddenly swing toward her. But quick movement was difficult. People either stood around offering competing theories on who had killed Jeffries to each other or were jostling to try to get out. By the time Solomon got to where Degault and Caprice had been, the pair had gone their separate ways. Degault was walking around the middle circular tier of the arena. Muhammad's trainer was lining up to exit through one of the tunnels running under the upper-tier seats.

"Mr. Caprice," Solomon said, cutting around a set of bodies who seemed to be circus acrobats, dressed as they were in tight striped pants and loose silk shirts. Maybe they worked for the Siegfried and Roy–trained white tiger act and had taken a wrong turn on their way to rehearsal.

"Yeah," he groused without turning around, his hands jammed deep in the pockets of his baggy pants.

Solomon introduced herself. By that time the older man had half turned his head and brightened at the fact that it was a youngish woman asking him a question. "You write for what, *Boxing News,* you said, honey?"

He'd heard right, just wanted an excuse to call her honey. But she played it off. She explained again and touched the man's arm. "If I could just have a few moments of your time, sir . . ."

"Well, I guess." He followed her to the end of the line and out the passageway. The two stood near the corner of the tunnel. Solomon calculated that she could get to Degault later if need be—at least she hoped so.

"Now what can I do for a pretty something like you?" Caprice leaned the upper part of his body toward her as he left his backside pressed to the wall.

"How has Joaquin Muhammad taken this?"

"Bad; shit, he was about to open up on Jeffries. Goddamn shame is what it is, okay?" He took one of his hands out of his pocket and pointed at her pad as she scribbled. "Please make sure you get that down, okay? I don't want nobody thinking I ain't got no heart."

"Can I talk with Muhammad?"

"I'd rather you not, young lady. He's awfully shook up about this craziness." Caprice massaged the lower part of his face with one of his large callused hands. The hands were like pieces carved from ancient wood, all cabled veins and gristle. The hands of a man who'd been involved in some manner of physical activity since before Solomon was born, she realized.

"Does he think the shot was intended for him?" she suddenly stammered, picking up on the subtext in the man's voice. "Had something happaned to Muhammad recently?"

"I should have known you wasn't gonna ask no fluff questions." The older man adjusted his worn cotton cap. He needed its luck now. "Let's just say, in this great land of ours, there are some who don't cotton to a brown man who likes black culture so much he goes around with its women. Me, I like all kinds." He touched the bill of the cap. "And I got the canceled alimony checks to prove it."

"So the brothers jam him up?"

"Yeah, but it ain't like we ain't been used to it. And you gotta balance that with the fact that Muhammad gets a lot of respect in the black community too. He gets invited to all kinds of events."

"No doubt," Solomon said as she made her notations. "But what particularly has happened recently?"

Caprice regarded her for several moments. Not too far away, one of the police dogs was barking fiercely. "It happened to his old lady, Monique."

"She's African American?"

"Yeah. He met her on the set of a music video. She was one of the backup thong wigglers, or whatever the hell her job was."

"I see," Solomon said, suppressing a smile. "And somebody did something to her?"

"A note was left on the window of her car. Now you realize," he said forcefully, "I didn't tell them Vegas cops this. They only wanted to know if I'd seen something when Jeffries got shot."

"You won't get in trouble by telling me this," she hedged.

"Not that I care for my sake," he resumed. "I just don't want to do anything that will hurt Muhammad. I never do that to any of my fighters," he said proudly. "Anyway, this note stuck out, one, 'cause it was on Monique's car, so that meant someone had been following her."

"And two?"

"Two, it had a name signed on it."

"Whose?"

"The Black Jihad." Caprice briefly rubbed the top of his cap. "Somebody had to explain to me what *jihad* meant."

Solomon had never heard of the group, but the name suggested some sort of Muslim affectations. Or it could easily be a white militia group looking to blame the Muslims, playing into common stereotypes. "What did the note say?"

"Like a left hook, direct and to the point, see?"

She didn't.

The old trainer illuminated. "It only said, 'Be with your own. This is his only warning.' "

" 'His'?"

"Right. Like the note was really for Joaquin. So naturally, being not the most collected sort, she goes and tells my fighter this, rather than come to me with it. This is three weeks ago," he declared, dumbfounded. "What in the hell was this chick thinking?"

"Of course he was rattled."

"Really, not too much," the trainer said with admiration in his voice.

Suddenly there were shouts and cursing, and they looked over in the near sets to see a group of men and women in business attire being manhandled by some Guardsmen. One of the men, in a diMarco suit, Solomon noted, threw his cell phone, and it bounced off a helmet. The two watched until the rowdies were removed. Life during wartime, Solomon wrote, recording the incident.

"Juno, you mentioned Joaquin wasn't particularly bothered?"

"Naw, like I related, he's grown kinda used to this stuff. He played it off; we didn't even talk about it, though I made sure we added a couple more guards to the entourage. Even had me a retired cop from Philly on the payroll. And there was nothing else, so we figured everything was cool."

"Had you told the cops about the threat?"

"Of course, but it ain't like they've turned up anything," he spat out derisively. Caprice stopped talking and bit one corner of his bottom lip before he spoke again. "When Jeffries went down, the first thing Joaquin hollered when he looked at me rushing over to him was about this goddamn jihad out to get him."

"So he's convinced the bullet was meant for him?"

The older man merely fidgeted with his cap for the umpteenth time.

"And now he's in hiding," Solomon finished. She wasn't going to corner the trainer for access to Muhammad because it wasn't going to be granted. At least not if she insisted on getting the interview, she sensed. "Here, take this, please." She stuck out her card, but Caprice glared at the item as if it were used Kleenex.

"Juno," she went on, unfazed, "this is one big mother of a story. This is the first time in the history of boxing, I can say without fear of contradiction, that a heavyweight champ has been literally assassinated during a fight."

As she finished speaking, what Solomon had feared happened.

The international sporting press, present to cover the fight, had shut down temporarily following the crack of the rifle. The swarming-about of the cops and the National Guard had contributed to a rolling shock among them. Some, Solomon saw, had scrambled to get photos of Jeffries's body and interview his trainer, Yank Turner. And a few had sought out Caprice. But as the cops were attempting to secure the scene, the media hounds had been driven back.

So Solomon had waited in the cut and had made her move after her colleagues had been forced from the stadium or gone off to develop other angles of the story. She was the only one with a gold pass, and thus had avoided being ID'd with her brethren. But now a few, hoisting minicams and portable mikes, were back, and heading for Caprice. Fortunately, they were on the opposite side of the rotunda, thus giving her several precious moments of a head start.

"Come on," she told him, grabbing his arm. "I'll get you away from them." The arena was less crowded now, the cops having gotten their checkpoint techniques operating more or less smoothly. Solomon guided Caprice away from one of the exits where they were sure to be cut off by the story-hungry sharks.

"Yo, hold up," she heard someone yell.

"Juno, Juno, it's Bobby C," a voice yelled.

Solomon and Caprice rushed toward the private entrance to the skyboxes. The guards were gone and the door was locked. "Shit," she cursed. The pack was getting closer.

"Need help?" Victoria Degault was suddenly at their side.

"Yeah, I—" Solomon started to say.

Degault had already punched in the combination on the door's electronic lock. A pair of National Guardsmen had also appeared, demanding to see acceptable identification.

"How about you keep them back first?" Solomon requested, pointing at the press who had arrived. A few of them sucked air from running. Others surged forward to get at Caprice.

"Back up, folks, back up," one of the citizen soldiers said.

"Hey, you can't stop us from asking our questions," one of the press retorted. Solomon recognized her as a sports commentator from ESPN.

"And you can't stop them if they want to leave," the Guardsman replied.

As those gathered blathered their questions in staccato bursts, one of the Guardsmen confirmed that Degault was who she said she was, and so too were Solomon and Caprice. That established, the owner of the Riverhead got the door open and they were allowed to pass through. The horde voiced their discontent but weren't allowed entry.

Inside the passageway, Caprice told Solomon, "Okay, you've earned your interview."

"Yeah, baby." Solomon made a fist and jerked it down in a celebratory manner.

"Come on," Degault said, leading them toward the monitor room entrance and out into the casino proper.

"You wouldn't want to tell me what you have Chainey up to?" Solomon asked Degault as they started off.

The dark-haired woman smiled sweetly and kept walking.

Pronounced vibrations surged through the walls as they went along. It seemed as if large machines were moving into place over the whole of the Strip.

CHAPTER FIVE

The left fender of the classic ragtop 1963 sky blue Jaguar X-KE crumpled under the treads of the Abrams tank. The mechanized mammoth continued over the hood of the decimated vehicle. This tremendous weight caused the struts of the British beauty to collapse as the front end pancaked onto Twain Avenue. The driver of the car was so astonished at the destruction of her prized chariot, she went into a dead faint sitting behind the steering wheel. The silver and purple wig she wore fell off her head and tumbled out of the convertible. Since there was no chance of the car ever functioning again, let alone driving wildly out of control, the fact that the woman was no longer conscious didn't matter.

Chainey watched transfixed as the tank turned the Jaguar into scrap. It was a nice, shiny, clean tank that looked like it had recently been washed and waxed. She recalled trying to plow through one of those techno-thriller novels once. That was, until the testosterone level and the hapless role for women in the book got on her last good nerve. But there were plenty of references in the work to inferior Russian T-60 tanks and gear ratio, and how U.S. battle wagons were part of what made our armed forces formidable.

The camouflaged, decorated thing had stopped, and someone was emerging from a hatch in the top of the turret. Even the gambling-weary populace of Vegas was stunned by the sight they'd just witnessed. The driver had somehow slipped past the K-rails that the Guard had been putting into place to block off the streets from vehicular traffic. The tank's operators, riding high and wide, hadn't seen the Jag coming until it was much too late.

As the soldiers revived the car's flabbergasted owner, Chainey continued, threading her way through the gaudily garbed masses. A wail of trumpets suddenly blasted, and three young folk in baggy pants, with bandanas on desperado-style, had jumped on the tank. They quickly whipped out spray cans and graffiti-bombed the symbol of the military-industrial complex with fluorescent emblems of peace, love, and brown rice. The Guardsmen who'd gotten out of the tank started to climb up for the young folk. Check that, Chainey corrected herself; both sides seemed to be in the same age range.

The anarchists, unencumbered by the bulkier gear of their opposites, managed to sprint away as some in the crowd cheered and clapped. The tooting of the trumpets carried after the brigands from a recording played on the boom box one of them had strapped on, bandolier fashion.

Chainey trudged on and was passing a corner of the Treasure Island Casino and Resort when her cell phone rang.

"*Chica,*" the syrupy voice said over her instrument.

"Mooch," she replied warily.

"I was wondering when you were going to call me, Marta," Ira "Mooch" Maltizar intoned, thickening his Cuban accent and purposely dropping the *h* in her name. His patois got richer when he'd had a few Habana Club Cuba Libres—rum and cokes—and puffs on his *puros,* his cigars.

"How'd you know?" Unconsciously, she touched her ears. She'd worn her good-luck-charm, solid silver horseshoe earrings to provide the luck for her fighter Jeffries, the one she'd bet on to win. Now she had a heightening awareness that she was the one who was going to need it. But her talismans hadn't done the champ any good.

She could hear Maltizar sipping. "I know something's been,

come se dice? absconded with. Otherwise why is Victoria making discreet calls to a few known-to-associate-with types?"

"One of whom called you. I guess that's why you've been in business so long, Mooch."

"Uh-huh," he said, ignoring the proffered compliment. "But how come you haven't called me during this *gran circo* we got going on?" He laughed heartily at his turn of phrase, describing the Felinniesque nature of the Strip under martial law.

I've been busy, as you've probably guessed." She'd purposely not called Maltizar because she was determined to find the thieves herself. The aging angler was her boss; he ran Truxon, Ltd., the courier firm servicing the Vegas players and hustlers. Maltizar was of Jewish extraction, born and, for the first eighteen years, raised in Cuba. He'd gotten his start in the gambling game as a courier for the Sam Giancana crew when the dictator Batista ran the island nation. This, just prior to Fidel and Che organizing their guerrilla movement among, of all things, Masonic lodges, and eventually riding down from the Sierra Maestra Mountains to seize power in 1959.

"Busy with Victoria's problem?"

Chainey smiled. The old wheeler was trying to push in on her action. But he did have the clout to glue ears to the ground and get tongues wagging to unearth information. "Why don't you ask the owner of the Riverhead?"

"Marta, for such a beautiful, capable woman, you have such a distrustful nature," he responded, an amused lilt evident.

"Look, Mooch, I'm not looking to negotiate anything at this moment."

"I'm simply offering to help." He sounded so grandfatherly.

"For the right percentage."

"This is Vegas, darling. We wash each other's backs in this town. And let's not forget you got other bendejos out there gunning for you. Somebody planted a bomb in your place when all that shit went down with Frankie Degault. You still don't know who that was or why."

"I know, but I'm dealing with this situation right now. If I get jammed up, I'll let you know." She was walking again, heading toward a specific destination. Overhead the whoosh of the spinning blades of an Apache helicopter—she recognized it from a "60 Minutes" report—swept by. Whatever Maltizar was saying was lost in the whooping of its backwash.

"What did you say, Mooch?"

"All information is useful." He could be heard blowing smoke.

"I got to go, Mooch."

"Don't forget, you won't have these *gajinas* in this cage too long, *chica*. I understand the National Guard will be gone by dawn and the emergency order lifted. Then they will be free to fly the coop . . . if they haven't already."

Dammit, he was right. "Like I said."

"Okay, okay," he placated. "I'll keep my phone on, huh?"

"Thanks, Mooch," she said insincerely.

"Anything for my number one, my dear," he retorted.

"Sure you alright." She told him good-bye and disconnected. Chainey clipped the phone to her belt and checked her watch as she proceeded. Given the emergency situation, she was banking on finding Moya Reese at the Treasure Island. The underground courier remembered that was where the receipt that had fallen out of her friend's purse in the skybox was from. And Reese's words, something like "They meant it," as she dashed out of the suite, had been dredged up from her subconscious.

The phrase hadn't quite registered on her initially. But it had hit Chainey standing in the hidden safe room. There might be nothing significant at all in what Reese had said, nothing at all.

As she crossed the plank bridge after exiting the pirate fort gateway, the Buccaneer Bay show was going on full bore. Chainey cautioned herself that she was probably attaching too much significance to the words, desperate as she was for a lead. But what else did she have?

The British man-o'-war rose up on its hydraulics, cresting a huge wave as two pirates swung over on ropes to Her Majesty's ship from the enemy ship, the Hispaniola. Cannon fire popped, and plumes of wet smoke laced with yellow pyrotechnics gushed all around the sea battle. *Oohs* and *ahhs* went up from the kids and adults watching the spectacle. In this town, Chainey theorized, the show would go on even as a sortie of bombers strafed Las Vegas Boulevard.

Getting closer to the entrance, she felt air rush into her suddenly open mouth as Frank, Dean, Sammy, and what the hell was that actor's name? strolled out onto the bridge from the opposite direction. True to their public personae, each were sharp in sharkskin suits and black shoes so shiny they gleamed white in reflected artificial light. As part of the moving tableau, each had a drink in one hand and a burning unfiltered in the other. Okay, she was hooked.

Chainey and many others stood still as the quartet, laughing and goofing with each other, got closer. As they did, she recognized the Sammy impersonator, had seen him as part of a legends revival revue that included Roy Orbison and Marvin Gaye doppelgangers at the Rio.

"Henry Silva." She shook a finger at the familiar actor anchoring one end of the pretend Rat Pack. "I just saw you in *Ghost Dog* on tape." Silva, part Puerto Rican and part Italian, had played everything from Asian detectives to Mexican revolutionaries.

The man she'd finally put a name to smiled and gave her a partial wave as he put the cigarette to his lips. "Thanks," he said, the fingers holding the smoke brushing against the side of his perfectly quaffed hair. The other three, the stand-ins, the phonies, were dragging on tobacco. The authentic one, Silva, the guy who'd been in the original *Ocean's 11* with the authentic *tres caballeros*, was puffing on a sweet-smelling clove stick—a prop cigarette used in movies and TV. The four marched on, old school merry pranksters becoming part of the frenetic proceedings.

Chainey got herself back on point and went inside. She passed through the Caribbean-themed town square, with its shops, and got to the hotel lobby. She avoided the desk because she didn't want them calling upstairs to Reese. Her instinct was to show up unannounced. Chainey went to one of the bars and eventually got the bartender's attention. He was burly and blond, and the sleeves of his billowy pirate's shirt were rolled up past his elbows. He must have seen an ad in an Iowa State college magazine and couldn't wait to come on out and make his fortune in the big city.

She asked him, "Do you know if Angela is on duty?"

"She's working the main floor." He started to turn away.

"You better not let the shift manager see that," Chainey advised as she moved away.

"Shoot," he blared, half-turning back to her, "you're right, thanks. I keep forgetting." He quickly began to unroll his sleeves to button them back in place. Vegas liked to maintain its illusions when it took your money.

Navigating the main floor, Chainey spied a couple of "rocks" she knew by sight in one of the eight-table poker rooms. Rocks was casino slang for poker-room regulars. These two—and they tended to be older folks, retirees—she'd seen here or at the Riverhead. What made them stand out was that apparently they'd been into body piercing way before it became a fad. The tender, grandmotherly visage of the woman was in jarring contrast to the ring inserted through one of her nostrils and the array of studs in her lobes.

Rounding a bank of video slot machines near the sports book section, Chainey spotted her woman. "Angela." She raised an arm and her voice.

"Hey." The cocktail waitress finished serving the drinks and got her tips. Her wench costume had a hemline that would make a real wench, if you could find one, blush.

Chainey fell into step next to the woman as she continued her rounds. "I need the room number for Moya Reese." She slipped the woman a folded fifty.

"The boxer?" She accepted the bill under her tray.

"The same."

"Hang out over at the Steak House and I'll swing by in a few."

"Thanks."

"Ain't no thing." The woman showed her teeth, a gold front one with a diamond set in it gleaming. She moved off, and Chainey went to the Steak House, one of the five restaurants at the Treasure Island. She didn't look out of place, given the line queued up to get inside. It took less than three minutes for Angela to glide by and tell her, "Eleven-o-two," and take off again.

Chainey traipsed over to the elevators. Given the demands of her job, she carried a series of recycled electronic door cards for the casinos on the Strip, and some in Reno too. Working as she did, on the margins, had its uses, and Mooch Maltizar prepared his employees well. The cards couldn't open anything but could pass visual scrutiny. Casually she flashed the correct-looking card as she walked between the guards stationed at their podiums.

"You having a good time?" The guard was a young brother, mid-twenties, she guessed. He looked a little like Taye Diggs, but fortunately was taller. His pecs were nicely formed underneath the loose material of his short-sleeved shirt. His almond eyes were observant, and his burnished skin was unblemished.

"I am." She put on her showgirl wattage and put the card away.

"Say hi again when you come back down," he said, sneaking a quick peek at her breasts. Circumstances dictated that he couldn't spend a lot of time macking, and Chainey didn't have time to dawdle anyway.

"I will." A young man was good for the blood now and then. And there was still Mr. Kuwada to get to know better. She could feel the guard's eyes on her backside, and it didn't creep her out, so that was a good sign. She went into one of the cars as its door slid open to let out several families. One of the boys, about eleven, in shorts and a Triple H, the WWF wrestler, T-shirt, did two cartwheels over the floor.

Chainey rode up one wing of the Y-shaped hotel towers and stepped off on the appropriate floor. She got to the right door along the slant and knocked. "Moya, it's Chainey." She waited, not hearing any movement beyond the solid door. She knocked again, and again there was no response.

She looked around like David Niven in one of those Raffles movies she always fell asleep watching on TCM. Melodramatically, she took the electronic cards out of her purse. She was startled as she inserted the third one when an amorous couple suddenly appeared, making their way along the hallway. Each was dressed in matching leather pants and gold sequined tops.

"Oooh, baby," the woman moaned with pleasure as the man's hands roamed over her breasts.

They barely noticed her as their hands probed each other, and they moved on to take care of their needs. None of her cards keyed the lock open. If Reese was inside, wouldn't she have heard the attempted lock picking and opened the door? Or was she sitting inside, in the dark, waiting for whoever was trying to sneak into her room so she could bust them in the jaw? Or simply put a slug in their head.

Chainey went back downstairs.

"That was quick," the cute guard remarked.

"Just had to pick up something. But I'll be back." She beamed at him; no sense not keeping her options open. She went directly to the checkout desk and asked about Reese. She was informed that the boxer had cleared out less than forty minutes earlier, and no, they had no idea where she was going. Chainey thanked them and mentally slapped herself for going through all that subterfuge for nothing.

Back in the prickly night air, she considered her next move. What traffic there was involved military vehicles and cop cars. Civilian craft were definitely not out and about. To her left was the area where the taxis lined up. There was a raft of the motionless vehicles, their engines off and their drivers smoking and talking with each other as they waited for Godot in the middle of the big circus, as Mooch called it.

"What's up with the fleet, Cynthia?" Chainey had spotted a female cabbie of her acquaintance and went over. She was taller than Chainey, six-two or -three, with a blond dread ponytail and a lone five-inch silver cross drooping from one lobe.

"They got a checkpoint set up at Flamingo Road," she said in a bass voice as she jerked a thumb vaguely south. "We have to go that way if we want to take a fare to the airport. And they've got a lane open on the boulevard for emergency and transport use."

"What about around here?" Chainey did a loop with her index finger.

"Hit the bricks, I guess." She lifted her square shoulders.

"My dispatcher said the Guard is ferrying people around inside the perimeter," a nearby cab driver butted in.

To Cynthia, Chainey asked, "Have you seen Moya Reese coming out of the casino?"

Cynthia's horse teeth were big and blunt. "My dream girl for a threesome with you, me, and her?"

"Whatevah," Chainey deflected.

The other woman gave off a throaty laugh. "Yeah, I saw her. She was carrying a Louis V backpack and a matching suitcase. She took off walking southbound."

"Thanks. I'll buy you a drink next time I'm not on the go."

"We'll make it whiskey over a strip poker game." She laughed again as Chainey waved good-bye.

It made sense for Reese to have checked out. But she hadn't, it seemed, taken off for the airport. Though it was in a southerly direction, why not take one of the cabs if they were allowed passage? But maybe she didn't know that. Maybe she went to one of the other casinos to catch one of the shuttles. But their schedules would be off, what with the checkpoints and all, so it could be Reese was still waiting around.

Chainey walked along, stopping now and then to ask a cabbie or doorman she knew if he'd seen Reese. The assassination of Jeffries had already made it up on the betting boards, and there was a book going as to when and who was the person behind the murder. As she made a circuit through the Flamingo Hilton, there was another special news report on the bar's TV about the woman called Sub-Commandante Khali. She'd supposedly been seen over at the Convention Center, and there was a breaking report as a SWAT team and National Guardsmen descended on the facility. Chainey went back outside and kept roving. Some minutes later, she got a break.

"That Reese is one bad bitch," the one called Karla with a *K*— she always told johns—said. She bent the tip of her cigarette toward the lit match Chainey held.

"I'm not looking to have a match with her." Chainey tossed the spent match. Curiously, she examined the book, wondering where she'd picked it up. It was from a place called Yamashiro's, a swank Japanese restaurant in the Hollywood Hills in L.A. She'd been on a run to Los Angeles last month and had to make a drop there. She must have put the matches in her bag while waiting at the bar. She didn't smoke, but being able to light Karla's smoke afforded an opening.

"I saw her fight tonight when I was on a date." She had a hoarse, cheap Scotch and too many Salems kind of laugh. A weary whore's laugh.

"You had the TV on?"

"Shit, yes." She put a hand on her hip. "I had me one of those Hong Kong gentlemen that just love that exotic black pussy." She laughed again, showing multiple fillings and crowns. "I told him I wasn't going back to his room at the Strat unless he ordered the fight." The Strat was the Stratosphere, 112 stories of space needle to the north. "He was all bowing and shit, promising me yes, yes." She imitated the man's actions, chuckling. "So I gave him his extra-special blowjob while I watched my girl take care of that tramp Raven Kim."

"But my question was about now, Karla; you said you'd seen her now." The two women stood on Harmon, near the 15 Freeway. The Strip was just to their backs, yet it could have been hundreds of miles away. The never-ending phantasmagoria didn't glow as brightly here in the beginnings of West Vegas. This was a part of town not often ventured into by the turn-arounders.

Karla, like Chainey, was an outlaw, but that application had a different connotation in her world. She was an independent hooker; she had no pimp or service she had to split her fees with. She did use bookers from time to time. Bookers were usually young working women attending the University of Las Vegas or waiting for their next dancing gig. The booker scheduled the appointments. Karla also had an 800 number and a website to which outlaws paid a commission when selling their porno photos, personalized love letters, soiled panties, and what have you.

Karla'd tried to get Chainey to invest, and she'd been tempted. You couldn't lose money on the sex industry.

Chainey punctuated her repeated request with two fifties. One Grant would have only gotten a raised eyebrow and a cluck of the tongue from Karla.

"She strolled on to the Cortez, girl."

Chainey displayed a questioning look.

Karla bugged out her eyes briefly. "I see her as I'm at the Chariot coffee shop, right? I'm coming out the can and she's there, big as shit, using the phone in the alcove. I say hi and can hear she's on the horn to the joint, askin' about space." She took the two bills, folded them precisely in two, and dropped them into her clutch bag—right next to her polymer-framed, compact .40 CZ 100. She clasped the bag shut. "I'll see you, Chainey."

"Thanks, huh?"

"Any goddamn time." Karla walked away, stopping to talk with two soldiers posted next to their Jeep under one of the freeway's pylons.

Chainey went off toward the Azul Cortez Motorcourt, which was on Martin Luther King, Jr. Boulevard, near Bonanza Road. The Azul Cortez was a clean and neat establishment, if not overly endowed with amenities. In this part of town, black Vegas, it made sense to go to ground there. If Reese was indeed trying to lay low until she could get out of town, she was less likely to be found at that place, as it wasn't in any publisher's official guidebook. Reese might be avoiding the airport and bus terminals, assuming these venues were being watched by the ones who cut Jeffries down.

There was minimal car traffic and people out and about at the motel. Two Vegas PD cars rolled past. This time she eschewed the desk; she knew that would be a waste of time. The Azul Cortez was a good place to be, because the proprietors were circumspect. You paid your bill, you expected quiet and not to be bothered. The management was quite clear about that rule. Chainey had met the owner, an ex-pit boss, through

Maltizar, but he wouldn't be around anyway. And if she called on her boss to put her in touch with him to get Reese's room, she'd have to cut him in for a share. Damn that.

Chainey considered strategies while eyeballing the place from across the street. Assuming Reese was in there under another name, how could she find out? She could go creeping around from room to room, trying to peek in between the window curtains. No, that would only get her arrested as a pervert. Idly, she tried to remember the last time she'd ever heard about a female Peeping Tom.

Okay, process of elimination. She's Moya on the run; does she stay on the first floor or second, off the open-air balcony? If it were she, Chainey reasoned, she'd want to be on the first floor. That way she'd have a better chance of getting away if something went down. The Azul Cortez was laid out in typical early-1950s' courtyard fashion. Chainey crossed the street and passed underneath the establishment's large glowing neon sign, curved over the archway of an entrance.

The motel's logo was that of an Aztec warrior driving a ragtop '51 Buick Cabriolet atop a lightning bolt that looked like something drawn by Jack Kirby in a Marvel comic book. On the trunk of the car facing the rear sat a woman Aztec warrior, her shapely legs crossed at the knee. The woman held a Ten Commandments type tablet that blinked VACANCY. The Triple A seal was beneath this. Over the car and characters was the name of the place in tall, thin letters that had nothing whatsoever to do with an attempt at Aztec design. The man and woman smiled brightly.

Chainey trod over the courtyard's gravel, anxious that each crunch would somehow give her away. There were various cars parked on the lot, and to her left the motel's coffee shop, called the Golden Ray, was doing brisk business. She could see several heads in there, all turned in one direction. The news must be on, she conjectured. But Reese, Chainey concluded, wouldn't be in plain sight.

Two of the rooms on the ground floor had the lights next to their doors shining. All right, you're hiding out, but you're on your J too, you ain't gonna be caught slipping. The porch light would reveal a sharp backlit silhouette of your pursuer should the door get busted in and he's blazing some rounds at you. That wasn't much, but what else do you have?

Door number one yielded a middle-aged, pudgy fellow in slacks and an athletic T. "Yes, ma'am." He snapped to his full height, his eyes level with Chainey's chest. "What can I do for you, my goddess?" He looked up and he looked down. He was one happy camper.

"Sorry; I was looking for a friend."

"You can come on in and wait if you like." He swung a palm toward his room, as if it were a suite in the Ritz Carlton. "Who Wants to be a Millionaire" was playing on the TV.

"Thanks, but I better get going."

"Well, if you get lost, you know where my room is."

"I sure do." Chainey had to walk away from the courtyard as the man stood in his doorway, watching her every step. She had to wait and then sneak back after he'd closed his door, his brief fantasy of her return having hopefully dissipated.

"Moya," Chainey repeated as she knocked on door number two, again with its outside light burning. The curtains were drawn and she couldn't see inside the room, but she had nothing to lose by being bold.

"Moya?" she said again, louder.

"Nex' doh," a raspy, country voice said from within the room.

Startled, Chainey stared at the door.

"She on the co'ner, the boxer, I saw huhr chec in, I bet on hurh, told hurh too," the voice said in a rushed, clipped manner. "Now leef us the fuck be. If'n ya pleeze."

"You tell 'em, Daddy," a female voice cooed.

Chainey grinned self-consciously and repeated her knocking on the door to the left, the corner location. There was no response, and Chainey jiggled the knob. The door was locked and there was still no response. Fortunately the Azul Cortez hadn't modernized its security, and the door had an old-fashioned key lock. She pried the lock open using a butterfly knife she carried in her purse.

Chainey took in the earth-toned room, the Aztec-styled wall-paper, the old-fashioned one-armed bandit on a table in the corner, and the crisp, made bed. Moya Reese, the ascending woman's boxing star, who'd recently been on the cover of *Sports Illustrated,* lay face up on the burnt-sienna-and-ochre-patterned bedspread. Chainey stepped inside, quietly shutting the door behind her.

There were two ragged holes in Reese, one in the forehead and the other off-center and high up on the breastbone. That must have been the first shot, the one to knock her down, followed by the head wound to finish her off. You couldn't punch a bullet. "I'm sure sorry about this, Moya." She closed her eyes momentarily, and in the bluish tint of her inner vision, Chainey could see the woman at the window of the skybox, vital and alive, urging Jeffries on less than two hours ago. And now both of them had been slaughtered.

CHAPTER SIX

Chainey removed her index and middle finger from Reese's neck. She knew there would be no pulse, but she was trying to gauge how long the woman had been dead. The neck was warm, the killing fresh. She gathered herself and began a search of the room. Through a gap in the curtains, she could discern the outline of the mountains against the soft black of night to the west, beyond the plate glass. Reese's bags were still around, and her makeup case was open in the bathroom. Chainey went through them and found nothing in the way of a lead, though she hadn't expected to. How the hell did private eyes do this?

She wiped off all the surfaces she'd touched—including the places she'd felt the corpse—and sat in a chair facing the bed and the body. The bags had all of Reese's clothes in them. There was nothing on the floor, thrown over a chair, or tossed onto a closet shelf. Had she just got in or, more likely, was prepared to go out at any minute? That would make sense; she'd want to be able to move quickly. Had Reese let the killer in willingly? Had it been someone she knew or was expecting?

Frustrated, Chainey hit the arm of the chair and stood, hands on hips. Now what? She looked again at her dead friend, and nausea spiked her stomach. Goddammit, Moya Reese was making something of her life. A woman of promise had been cut down, and it wasn't right to just walk away. Somebody you knew, somebody you've laughed with and had a drink with, is snuffed out, and the bastard who did it didn't give a damn. That wasn't right. Somebody had to give a damn.

Chainey looked around again and found what she presumed was Reese's cell phone. The thing had been stepped on and tossed into the tiny trash basket beneath the sink in the bathroom. The buttons didn't respond to her thumbing them, so there was no immediate way to activate the redial. She tucked the instrument into her purse anyway.

She took a final moment to view the once vital woman again. Chainey noticed that the necklace Reese had worn in the skybox was missing. A search through her bags didn't produce the item, nor could Chainey remember what the object on the chain was. A real detective would know. Shit.

Through the sliding window in the bathroom, which had been latched, the limber former–chorus girl easily extricated her body out of the room. After wiping down the frame she pushed the window shut, realizing that this was a further contamination of a crime scene. If she'd taken a chance and gone out the way she came in, the odds of being spotted would have increased. As it was, the couple next door would no doubt report talking to her when the police came. And then there was Pudgy. But Chainey needed any time she could cobble together to stay free to do her job, not waste valuable time playing twenty questions with Lambert.

Chainey made her way east, back to Bonanza Road, in the direction of the Strip. She wasn't sure what her next steps were going to be, but there was nothing to do but go forward. As she got closer, the congestion of bodies there was greater. More K-rails and mobile barriers had been set up, and there was a checkpoint with Guardsmen too. At a gap in the barrier there were two Jeeps on either side of the hole, facing one another. In the middle were two officers standing behind a long folding table. A tabletop lectern had been commandeered from the Belaggio and was set before them on the table. Other reserve soldiers were gathered around this section too. People were lining up to get back onto the Strip. Farther down, another checkpoint had been set up for those exiting.

"And what's your business tonight, Ms. Chainey?" The officer, a female captain with short black hair and light freckles, looked carefully at the driver's license before her. A laptop was up and humming near her elbow. To allay the citizens' feeling that the heavy hand of the state was upon them—and it was—she wore a name tag. Just in case you had to remember her when you sued the bureaucracy, Chainey gathered.

For a quick moment she considered concocting a story as to why she just had to get back on the Strip. But Chainey simply said, "This is Vegas, and I like to gamble. And the off-the-main-line places aren't bringing me luck." She made a thing of fingering one of her horseshoe earrings.

"Yes, that seems to be the only thing people do around here," the officer sighed regretfully. She handed the plastic back to Chainey. "Don't shoot your load at one time, hear?" There was a reddening around the freckles.

Chainey smiled sweetly and passed through the checkpoint into the cordoned-off area. A man in crisp black jeans, heavy boots, and a white T-shirt, the sleeves rolled up '50s greaser style, stepped past her. He suddenly stopped and turned, a sheaf of flyers in his hand.

"Read this." He jammed one of his papers at her face and marched off even as he let it go, the sheet floating on the humid currents.

Curious, Chainey picked the paper up and read it as she went along. Essentially the communiqué, produced in black and red via graphics software, warned that the martial law imposed tonight was the signal of a takeover by the secret cabal running the United States. The screed went on to alert the reader that there would be further incidents to provide an excuse for these covert plotters to abrogate the Constitution. That already the silent helicopters were flying sorties out of Nellis Air Force base. And that right now there were trucks hauling lumber and sheetrock out to the Big Smokey Valley for the erection of concentration camps.

There were several groups listed as co-sponsors on the flyer, but it was hard to tell who was the actual producer of this doom-

and-gloom. Chainey did notice that Sub-Commandante Khali was said to be a pawn in all this.

Chainey smiled. When you got outside of town, the rest of Nevada slapped you in the face with its off-kilter reality. It was a big, open state peopled by rednecks, Mormons, snake worshipers, cowboys, tribes, hermits, old hippies, nuclear labs, secret vaults, broke-down dancers, survivalists, busted-out strippers, neo-Nazis, UFOists, rock climbers, midnight radio show hosts, Area 51 fetishists, soothsayers, and miners still lusting for that one big gold or silver strike.

Some of the craziness was bound to leak onto the playground now and then. Chainey threw the flyer away in a city trash receptacle. She was looking nowhere in particular and spotted Kuwada and Tosches diagonally across the street. They stood out because all around them people were moving, and these two stood still. Each man was shaking a finger at the other, and they were definitely involved in a spirited discussion.

She started to walk over to them. If nothing else, she'd flirt a little with Kuwada. But midway across Flamingo Road, two men and a woman came at her swiftly from her right. Chainey swung about, tensed and ready to defend herself, when she recognized Haulsey as one of the people.

"What is it?" she demanded. Something about the ex-Ranger itched where she couldn't scratch.

"Naomi would like to have a talk with you." His flat expression was belied by the hardness behind his eyes. He wanted her to object. He wanted to exert his will.

Men like Haulsey expected a lot, particularly from women. Chainey wondered how he balanced that macho outlook with taking orders from the head cheese. His adherence to Nymnatism must hold the answer, she concluded dryly.

"Why not?" she said. Forward motion was forward motion.

Chainey went with Haulsey and two of the FON to the Venetian, erected where the Sands once stood. The duo who'd come with Haulsey weren't glass-eyed automatons, as she expected the followers of Naomi to be. The two made facial expressions and took in their surroundings. One of them, a younger man with dirty blond hair and a single discreet silver loop tagged onto part of his upper ear, even cracked a joke with his older compatriot. It was Haulsey, the ex-army Ranger, who maintained the grave expression and frozen demeanor. Chainey imagined the big stiff was probably chanting to himself over and over how great the Nymnatists were, how great it was to bask in the love of the high mother.

She almost laughed aloud and had to clear her throat to avoid slipping.

"Ma'am." Haulsey unnecessarily indicated the walkway ringing the Grand Canal fronting the Venetian Hotel and Casino. There were several gondolas sailing past with couples, and one with rowdy frat boys. The gondoliers all wore distant expressions as they effortlessly plowed the waterways.

"Aw, girl," one of the inebriated frat boys yelped. He stood in the boat, grabbing his crotch as he caught sight of Chainey. "Come on and take a ride, huh?" His friends roared, and the one who'd spoken fell back down. He wore oversized shorts and a stained USC T-shirt. His baseball cap was set backward on his head. Ghetto chic by way of Nebraska, Chainey surmised as she gave her would-be suitor the finger.

"I don't know how you live in this." Haulsey shook his head reproachfully.

So they knew about her. Naomi no doubt had an intelligence and research apparatus. If they figure some of your hand, make sure you still keep a couple of cards tucked away, Wilson McAndrews had told her more than once. But how did you do that in the age of the Internet and fiber optics, which made privacy an archaic word?

The quartet moved across the magnificent vaulted lobby of the Venetian. It was like something out of a big-budget movie, complete with CGI effects. The grouping walked past a photo of the Italian icon Sophia Loren as she christened a gondola.

"That's a little more like it," Haulsey mumbled.

Off the lobby was the Doge's Palace, the 120,000-square-foot casino. Apparently, the Palace was a replica of the real thing from the old country, circa the eighteenth century. There were

2,500 slot machines of various denominations, single zero roulette, and 122 gaming tables, offering the initiate everything
from Pai Gow to Caribbean Stud Poker. And of course there
were the off-limits lounges for the whales to really throw some
coinage around.

After a silent elevator ride, the four arrived at Naomi's suite
of suites. Every room in the 700-room Venetian was called a
suite, but if one spent the required amount, there were some
suites that were more equal than others. And Naomi's expansive
chambers were just a notch or two less fancy than the Sultan of
Brunei's crib, Chainey imagined.

Authentic Berber carpets and Strauss crystal chandeliers
abounded, and a fifty-two-inch plasma screen was anchored to
one wall. There were seven phones scattered at different points,
and the suite even had its own concierge.

"What would you like?" the leader of the Nymnatists asked.
She was seated in a wide club chair covered in green felt and
languidly fluttered a hand at a wet bar.

"Tonic water, if you don't mind."

"By itself?" Naomi's voice had a radio talk show host's quality
to it—at once direct yet practiced in its modulation.

"Yes." Chainey sat in a striped, padded bergere chair and
waited; let the guru think it was her show. It was one way to pos-
sibly learn whether the Nymnatists were up to something.
Crouching in the back of her head was the idea that it wasn't a
coincidence that Haulsey had stopped her as she returned from
Reese's room.

One of the FON who had come over with Chainey handed
her a tall glass. Chainey took a sip, her dry mouth feeling invig-
orated by the bitter, lemony drink. She set the glass aside on a
silver coaster on a stressed end table. Behind an array of vases
with huge sprigs of larkspur and gladiolus, a door opened, and
in stepped a serious-looking woman in a serious-looking business suit.

"We'll be a few, Davis." Haulsey didn't turn his box of a head
to look at the woman. He kept a cold gaze on the courier.

The other woman's jaw tightened, and it was clear she was considering several rejoinders. But she settled with saying, "Very well." She closed the door and sealed herself off from whatever was going to be said or done in the main room.

"I think you need to get straight with us on a few matters, Chainey." Haulsey had his hands clasped behind his back, chest out, chin up like a wet dream for the armed services. "We need some answers."

Unhurriedly, Chainey plucked her glass from its coaster and took another drink. "I expect some answers too, Haulsey." Never let 'em see you sweat.

"Now you look—" he began, taking a couple of steps toward the summoned woman.

"Wilfred," Naomi interjected, "I'm sure a more positive sensibility will garner a more conducive atmosphere, don't you think?"

Haulsey was unfazed by this gentle reminder from his leader. He'd already halted his advance, and his body language was more relaxed. "You're right, of course, Naomi."

It was their version of good cop, strange cop. Chainey crossed her legs and waited. She was on a deadline, but she wasn't going to let it show.

"I understand you're assisting Victoria in the search for the lost wagers."

Chainey lifted her hands halfway off each chair arm and let them flop down again. "That's a quaint way of putting it." No sense trying to stonewall her; she knew what was up.

"And you must know I bet against Tyler."

Chainey watched for a reaction from Haulsey, but there was none forthcoming. "Kind of a lack of faith, wasn't it?"

"Please don't misunderstand, Chainey. I had very wonderful plans for Tyler's advancement in the Nymnatists movement. We wholeheartedly believe in goal fulfillment."

"Wasn't Tyler's goal keeping his crown?"

Haulsey moved his lips but said nothing. The other two FONers were sitting on a mammoth couch in the rear quarter of the big suite. One of them leafed through a magazine while his pal talked on one of the numerous phones. A Jacuzzi bubbled nearby.

"We try not to confuse romantic notions with concrete solutions." For a brief moment what might have been an ironic smile animated one side of Naomi's face and then it vanished. "The bet Captain Haulsey made for me was just that, a wager."

Odd how she interchanged *we* and *I,* Chainey noted. She was the Nymnatists and they were her—or was it that they were nothing without her? "So he was useful as a prop to advance the cause of Nymnatism only?"

This time Naomi allowed the annoyance to settle on her features. "We're not having a dry run of a 'Sixty Minutes' interview, Chainey. What you are here about is working together with me to find the ones who perpetrated this heinous crime against a true benefactor of humankind."

She managed to make it sound sincere; you had to give her that. "You already know what I'm after."

"You believe those efforts weren't coordinated? That it's just coincidence that the champ was murdered at the same time the robbery went down?"

Chainey's mouth was starting to feel like the desert again. "I know Victoria believes there's a connection. But it's also not too much to believe that the thieves planned the robbery because there was all this other stuff going on. It was a perfect time to pull off the heist."

Naomi nudged her head toward Haulsey. "What do you think?"

"You know the theory I subscribe to."

Chainey finished taking a gulp of her tonic water. "Why did you bet against Jeffries? What did you know that no one else did?"

"That's not your concern," Haulsey piped in.

"Whatevah." Chainey rose. "Thanks for the pick-me-up, girlfriend."

Naomi didn't stop Haulsey this time as he and the other security people came toward Chainey as she headed for the door. They crowded her near the exit.

"You can't half-step with me, Naomi," Chainey said, talking past the grimacing trio of hard boys. "If your wolf pack is gonna snarl, they better bite." She wasn't anxious to get a beat down, but she weighed that against the bad press Naomi wasn't looking to generate.

Quiet dragged on for several seconds until Naomi said, "Let's start over, shall we?"

The three let air circulate around Chainey again. She didn't move.

Naomi had remained seated. It was as if all this drama with the Nymnatists had been orchestrated to pull Chainey in several directions at once, to keep her constantly off-guard. "You know the lay of the land, Chainey. We want justice for Tyler. Not only is it the right thing to do, but yes, it will show the world we took care of our own."

The phone the FONer had been using rang, causing the glass top of the coffee table to tremble to a low note.

Chainey remarked. "If you expect my cooperation, then surely the Shackle of Dreams must say something about the intersection of interests."

That got a crunched eyebrow from Haulsey.

"Very good." Naomi dipped her head slightly, acknowledging Chainey's skewering her on her own precepts.

The phone had continued to ring and the woman in the other room had opened the door again. "Has everyone lost the use of their legs?" she asked irritably. She'd no sooner stepped across the threshold when the ringing ceased. "Argh." The woman clenched her fists at her sides.

Naomi had continued speaking. "I want you to know, Chainey, that my betting against Tyler was," she paused, searching for the right phrasing, "a reality check, if you will."

"You told Jeffries?" It was Chainey's turn to raise an eyebrow.

"Of course I didn't," Naomi said, with the proper amount of indignation in her voice. "I was in his corner to aid Tyler and provide psychic sustenance. It was the least I could do for the troubled man."

Chainey was about to inquire exactly what that meant when a pounding on the door cut her off before she began.

Haulsey glided quickly to the door, his two shadows flanking him. "What?" he barked.

"Lambert," came the equally terse reply.

Haulsey tried to stall. "What do you want?"

"Guess," Lambert shot back.

Ex-Army opened the door, a low sigh of exasperation floating from him.

"Hello, everyone," the sheriff announced affably as he strode into the room with two of his deputies, a man and a woman, right behind him. "How the hell is everyone?" Lambert purposely stood near Naomi, who remained sitting.

"We're just fine, Chief," the leader of the Nymnatists answered. "What can we do for you this evening?"

Lambert's spidery fingers fooled with the brim of his off-white cowboy hat, his eyes drifting toward the female deputy, then back to Naomi. "Just want to make sure we're operating off the same page, if you will."

Haulsey's body tensed but he didn't speak.

Naomi smiled beguilingly. "I'm not sure what you're driving at there, Chief."

"Snatching citizens off our public thoroughfares, for one." Lambert pivoted to take in the ex-showgirl.

"She's here of her own volition," the woman who'd been in the other room snapped.

"Is that so, Ms. Chainey?" Lambert tilted his hat up onto his head. "Is what Ms. Willoughby is saying accurate?" He didn't sound serious in his question. This was all just to show who was running the show.

"Of course," she concurred. "We were simply having a conversation about current events."

"Oh, I see." The chief massaged his chin between index finger and thumb. "Well, I guess someone who does the kind of work you do for Maltizar and his Truxon, Limited, is used to dealing with sharpies."

"The freight business is demanding," Chainey said, straight-faced.

"Is there something you need, Chief?" Haulsey folded his arms.

"Like I said, seems to me we should have a meeting of the minds before things get complicated." Lambert did a quick motion with two fingers, indicating seeing eye to eye. "I will not have your security force acting as de facto police, Mr. Haulsey. I will not have you traipsing all over town seeking to intimidate people and contaminating an ongoing investigation."

"I would think," Naomi began, "that any help you received in identifying and capturing the person or persons responsible for the murder of Tyler would be an added benefit."

The female deputy snickered. And she did that cop thing of putting her hands on her squeaky leather belt while simultaneously twisting her upper torso to its full extension.

"That's what we're gonna get straight." Lambert gripped the crown of his hat and removed it from his head. His thinning hair was slicked to his head, as if the strands were painted on his skull. "You can go, Chainey."

"I don't mind hanging around an air-conditioned room." She was hoping to learn more information in this probably heated exchange. The woman the chief called Willoughby had moved farther into the room, her stern face etched with a fighter's anticipation.

"Very amusing, you are." Lambert was holding his hat before him as if it kept him from doing damage with his long fingers. "But I'm sure you have plenty to occupy your time, and I wouldn't want to detain you any longer."

"It's your world, Chief."

"Now that would be a fate I'd wish on no man or woman." He set his hat atop a rococo lamp shade. He turned his lanky body to face Naomi, Haulsey, and the other proponents of the wondrous and ever-elastic way that was Nymnatism.

Chainey left, assembling what pieces she had or guessed of this heist as she descended in the elevator. The crew that made off with the table money had to be no more than four; better if it was three. One too many mouths to feed also meant one too many mouths yapping. Of course, there could be a corpse cooling in an alley off the Strip right now. But the odds still favored a small, efficient bunch who wouldn't attract attention and who, as a cohesive unit, would move fast. Get in, get out, wasn't a good adage in lovemaking, but it sure went a long way in the thieving game.

The first notion she'd formed, that Tosches might have had a hand in the doings, hadn't shaken loose from her. Maybe it was sexist, but pillow talk had tripped up many a head of a corporation in other walks of life. A reel of Victoria Degault and Dean Tosches knocking boots played in her head, and Chainey was very grateful when it ended as she set foot outside again. She had to talk to the owner of the Riverhead to settle this disquiet she had about the owner of the High Chaparral.

Like anyone who had risen to some level of prominence in Vegas, there were stories about Tosches. How this Italian American kid from Union City, New Jersey, had reinvented himself several times since dealing stud in dives along the Jersey Shore and playing Jeeves for the *machers* on vacation in the Catskills.

Tosches hadn't built the High Chaparral. In fact, the original location had been downtown in the '60s and moved uptown in the '70s. By the late '80s the place symbolized a kind of creaking je ne sais quoi eclipsed by the newer, flashier, and bigger models. He'd been a partner in the holding group and had taken over after the former owner, Treat Carlyle, had contracted liver cancer and had to step down.

There was plenty of juicy gossip about the way Tosches came to be a partner in the holding group. Appropriately, as befits all Vegas legends, there were conflicting tales. But the story Chainey clearly recalled was the one she'd heard several old-timers recount, and Maltizar had alluded to its veracity as well. Essentially, Tosches had grifted his way into the holding company. He'd arranged to videotape one of the partners engaged in sexual acts with underaged boys and had used that as his ticket to ride.

Whatever that said about Victoria Degault being involved with such a man, Chainey reflected as she dialed, she saved for ruminating on later.

"I need to know a couple of things," she said after the line connected and they'd exchanged greetings. She could hear traffic and wondered if the other woman was driving.

"Yes?" Degault said, betraying neither wariness nor testiness.

Two women in blue latex jumpsuits that adhered to their every crevice, each hoisting a fringed parasol, sauntered past Chainey. Amazingly, in all the other phantasmagoria, they merely blended in.

"Chainey?"

"Sorry, I'm here. You said Frankie had the special room done up?"

"That's right."

"But was it in the original plans?" A military Jeep sped past on the street. "Khali, they've got Khali," one of the Guardsmen on the vehicle bellowed into a portable radio. The Jeep made the corner and screeched away.

Degault had heard the commotion and waited until it had subsided. "In fact, now that you bring it up, no, the room, or at least what it's used for now, was added afterward." Victoria paused then continued. "It was a few months, about half a year, I guess, before the incident happened." Her voice had lost all its vitality. "It was when Frankie was making his plans to take off that he had the room changed from the original plans. There was already a hidden safe in our offices on top of the Riverhead."

The incident Degault referred to was her brother engineering a theft of some seven million in cash that Chainey had been hired to transport. The two who'd received the delivery had been killed by the shooters, but she'd survived. In the end, Victoria Degault had had to kill her own brother—not to save Chainey, but to save herself. Her brother would have come after her at some point.

"What was the room supposed to be?"

"Climate-control backup machinery that had to then be put on the roof. What are you getting at?"

"I'm not sure, but maybe watching all those reruns of 'Columbo' was good for something. Plus you knew Frankie, always keeping a back door open." She felt awkward referring to him in the past tense with the woman who had done him in.

Degault was quiet for a time. Suddenly three other people were standing near Chainey, activating their cell phones. It was as if by standing still the courier had somehow signaled the area as a gabbing zone.

"I see what you mean," Degault finally drawled. "I'll see if I can find the plans among Frankie's things. I—I never did throw them out," she stammered.

"Get back to me as soon as you can." She said good-bye and, with nothing to do but kill time, Chainey went back into the Venetian. She was doubling down on two kings and a ten when her cell went off.

"Card," the dealer said.

Chainey was dealt a nine and turned over her cards for half the pot. She took her chips and answered the phone.

"He was, indeed, full of odd and strange quirks," the conversation began.

"How do you mean?" Absently, Chainey shook the chips in her hand.

"I found the name of the contractor he used to convert the room to its present purpose." Uncharacteristically, Degault giggled. "I didn't find the plans, though."

"So what's funny?"

"He had a woman contractor do the work."

Given the fact that her deceased brother wore his sexism on his sleeve, Chainey said, "She couldn't have been his first choice."

"You wouldn't think," the owner of the Riverhead responded. "But you could never tell about Frankie. There might have been some reason for choosing her."

"If I find her, I'll ask. Hold on a second while I get my pen and paper." Chainey signaled to a passing waitress and plucked a couple of napkins from her tray to write on. Degault gave her an office number, fax and pager.

"Let me know what develops," the other woman said.

"I will." She was anxious to ask about Tosches but didn't know how to get into it over the phone. *Say Vic, has the guy you're bangin' also been getting into your business?* "I'm sure I'll need to talk to you sooner than later, anyway. This goddamn curfew, or whatever the hell you call it, isn't gonna last forever."

"I doubt if I'm going to sleep tonight anyway," Degault replied. "I'm way too wound up."

"I'm off." Chainey severed the connection and then dialed the pager number for the contractor and left her cell number at the beep. Her name was Gihan Varzagas, which could mean any-thing in terms of her ethnicity. Not that Chainey expected that, if the woman was black, there'd be some instant bond of sistah-hood. But as Vegas grew, so too did its black population, diversi-fying into the strata represented in town and the surrounding areas. There were still no blacks on the city council or in state government, but she expected that to change in the natural progress of things. Then again, there was nothing natural about Las Vegas, as this night of a thousand dramas reminded her.

Chainey was sipping a seven-and-seven when her cell rang.

"This is Chainey" she answered.

"I know you, darlin'?" a pleasant voice asked.

"Not directly, but I was a friend of Frankie Degault's." Which, in bizarro world, was true.

"You in the business?"

"I work for Truxon, Limited; heard of them?" She couldn't tell by the woman's inflection what her race was. Why the hell was she obsessing about it?

"Oh, yeah. So what can I do for you, Chainey, was it?" There was a clatter of indistinguishable voices also coming over the phone.

"Listen, I was hoping I might ask you a few questions. But not over the phone, and I can make it worth your time."

Off the mike of the phone, there were the muffled murmurs of Varzagas talking to someone. Then she came back on. "Sorry, what were you saying?"

"I need to ask you a few things about some work you did for Frankie at the Riverhead. If you like, you can check with his sister Victoria about me."

"No, no, that's cool," the contractor said. "I know the street rep of Truxon. When I hear what you have to say I'll decide if I'll tell you anything or not." She laughed heartily.

"That's fair. Where can I find you?"

"You know the Block Sixteen nightclub? Near the Algiers?"

"I can find it."

"That's where I am."

"How will I know you?"

"What do you look like?"

Chainey described herself.

"Six foot in bare feet?"

"Yes," she admitted.

"Damn. I'll look for you for sure."

"Won't be long, but I'm on foot; getting around inside the perimeter by car is a pain." Chainey took in a breath and marched off to do her duty. Block 16 was a lesbian bar. Not like Chainey had anything against anyone's lifestyle, provided it was consensual adults making the choices. Whatever floated one's boat was down with her. But it did seem of late that a lot of her chasing after money and the people who took the cheddah invariably brought her into the orbit of alternative lifestyles.

Was it some vibe about her, or was it just the way things were in the modern world? Actually, she was flattered anyone took notice of her. And, she admitted, it wasn't like she hadn't thought about it now and then. Women, she noted to herself as she walked north, had more latitude in the sexual territories than the opposite sex. Straight men certainly found it a turn-on to watch two women making love; that couldn't be said for women watching two men doing it.

In front of Chainey a wedge of people parted, and four figures dressed like the psycho killer in the *Scream* movies burst through, riding big aluminum tricycles. On the shoulders of each shrouded psycho was a multiracial variety of blond Venuses in black thong bathing suits, yelling and laughing. The young women had sacks strapped around their bodies, and they threw small objects pulled from the sacks.

A colorful plasticine packet fell at Chainey's feet. Inside it was a sample of a new white chocolate chip cookie with the tag line: "You'll just scream for more Gooey Louies." The living billboard moved along to spread the high-calorie goodness.

Since the normal rules didn't apply, Chainey ignored her diet and picked up a couple of the packets. She snacked on the delicious cookies on her way to the bar—she figured she'd need the energy.

CHAPTER SEVEN

Block 16 was a split-level establishment that catered to both the lowbrow haute Benetton crowd and to flannel shirt and torn jeans wearers too. In keeping with its bifurcated construction, the ground floor contained the sedate conversation section, with its polished maple bar and leaded glass mirrors. Up the fire house–style metal stairs was the dance floor and more aggressive meat market. Naturally that was where Chainey was directed to find Gihan Varzagas.

As she walked up, she passed a photo of the original Block 16. That had been the red-light district of Las Vegas, located near First and Main in the first part of the last century. Post-World War II the district was cleaned out and shut down as Vegas blossomed and illicit activity was brought under the control of the mob.

"Hey," an Asian woman in a leather mini greeted as she descended the stairs.

Chainey nodded self-consciously and continued up. It took three tries, shouting into dancing women's ears, until she got directed to the right person. She approached a muscular woman throwing darts with two others.

Chainey introduced herself as a Joan Armatrading number ended.

"You didn't lie," Varzagas said, extending a hand. She glanced up at the top of Chainey's head.

"Why would I lie, yet?" She returned the handshake. Varzagas was tanned in a Speedo tank top and tight stone-washed jeans. Her arms were corded and her hands like that of a large man's. The legs in the jeans were deftly formed and her wide face was pretty in a contained, alert way. Chainey was still stumped as to the woman's ethnicity even after meeting her.

"So, what exactly is it I can do for you?" Varzagas upended a bottle of Beck's Dark.

"It's somewhat touchy, but it'll only take a few." Chainey smiled weakly at the two women with the contractor.

"It'll give you a chance to get even, Sherry."

"Shit," Sherry sneered affably and took the darts.

"Come on." Varzagas led the way to a relatively quiet spot toward the rear, near a large linen scrim.

It had occurred to Chainey that the theory she was now pursuing might easily include Varzagas. Who knew the layout of that room and its construction better than the one who'd built it? And in just the few moments they'd been together, Chainey could tell Varzagas was self-confident, hard charging. But then again, she'd have to be in the male-dominated world of construction.

It was gut time. "The safe you installed for Frankie Degault in that room in the Riverhead was hit tonight."

"This have anything to do with the Jeffries killing?"

"I don't know."

The contractor blinked hard. "Hold on, will you?" She went to the bar and leaned across it. The bartender, a willowy Latina in sweats, handed her a phone from underneath the scarred top. Varzagas dialed and talked into the instrument.

She could be alerting her accomplices, Chainey thought, her senses suddenly kicking into higher register. Her eyes flitted toward the two women who were still playing darts. How long had Varzagas been here? Was this where she stashed the money after the heist? This might not have been the brightest idea. But getting jacked was one way of flushing out the culprits. Assuming, she warned herself, she lived to recover the money.

Varzagas finished with whoever she was talking to and replaced the handset. She strolled purposely back to Chainey.

"What's my end if I help you?"

"Five thou, if I get the money back."

"You must be pullin' down more than that. How much was in the safe?"

"Take it or leave it."

"But I got what you need." She tapped a thumb against her sternum. It sounded like a knuckle against a barrel full of water.

"Then you go after the dough." Chainey guessed the tough woman had a business to protect and couldn't or wouldn't take the chance in being involved in a matter that might jeopardize her contractor's license. That was why people like Chainey were useful—someone had to move and groove in the territory between the law and the underworld.

Briefly, Varzagas worked her tongue on the inside of her cheek, then said, "Let's dance." Jimmy Scott's version of "Angel Eyes" had just begun. "It'll look more natural." She slipped an arm around Chainey's waist. "I don't need everybody to know my business. Anyway," she admitted, "I want to see if you can move that body of yours."

"Lovely." The two drifted onto the dance floor, where several couples were holding each other tight and swaying to the hypnotic sound of Scott's tremulous voice.

"That call I made," Varzagas began, "was to the woman who runs this on-the-fly labor hall I use from time to time. Normally I have a steady crew of people I call on, with an emphasis on getting more women into the trade."

"I see."

Varzagas pressed her hips in close, and Chainey stiffened. "Don't worry, I'm not trying to convert you," the woman laughed. "Just flirt a little."

"Good thing you can't tell I'm blushing. Now, about the job for Frankie . . . ?"

"It was one of those last-minute things, as far as I could tell. I'd been brought in as a subcontractor to do some concrete finishing, and Frankie Degault cornered me, all excited about this brainstorm of his to do the space as his secret safe room." She laughed again.

"He was impulsive like that."

Varzagas brightened. "Of course, the real reason he used me and not the main contractor on the gig was to hear stories of 'lesbian love'." She pronounced the last word in an exaggerated manner.

"He liked his jollies too," Chaincy said. "So what did you learn in your call to your friend?" Scott's contralto stretched out the lyrics, and a pair dancing near them kissed. Chaincy felt exposed but tried to go with the flow.

"Well, like I said, he was all hot and bothered to get this thing done, so I had to bring in some people I don't normally use."

"And one of them is a likely candidate for the score?" The couple next to them were now humming as the song wound down.

"Yeah. Of all people I shouldn't play into stereotypes, but one of the guys I had to use had a record, B and E stuff." The song ended, and there was light applause. "I remember, because I made sure only me and my friend the jobber knew. I didn't want to raise any hackles. I mean, the money was good for what really wasn't that much work. But it had to get done right then, you know? I would have used one of my regulars, but they were all tied up."

Chaincy wanted to get out of the grouping of women; she wanted anonymity. What if somebody she knew saw her here? Then she checked herself; so what if someone did? And what would they be doing here? She got back on track.

"So who is this guy?" Chaincy and the woman had taken up residence at the bar. Varzargas's friends were now out on the dance floor, boogying to a Melissa Ethridge cut.

"We square on my end of the money if you get it back?"

"Absolutely." Chaincy stuck out her hand.

"I guess that'll have to do, unless you want to seal it with a kiss." Varzagas showed good teeth and took Chainey's hand.

"This'll have to do for now, honey."

"Never hurts to ask. The man's name is Eddie McDaniels. And look"—Varzagas made a slicing gesture with her hand—"I hope I'm not giving this guy grief. He did his work and didn't once beef about working for a woman. I only thought about him because of his past, but like I said, I'm not one to throw stones." She paused, assimilating the import of her own words. "Maybe I shouldn't be so greedy," she said regretfully. "Maybe you should just forget I said anything."

Chainey leaned closer to be heard over an Ethridge guitar riff. "I'm not a cop, Gihan. I'm about getting back the loot, that's all."

"You should see your expression," Varzagas said, her brows bunching.

"Your friend got a phone or address for this guy?"

"I got the phone." She retrieved her purse, on a table near the darts, and consulted her Palm Pilot. She wrote it down for Chainey. On the back of the scrap, she put her home number.

Chainey read the slip. "Thanks. I'll be in touch either way. Oh, what's he look like?"

"About your height or an inch taller, white, kinda wiry."

"How about something in the way of distinguishing him in a crowd?"

"His hair, at least then, was dyed very blond, and he's got a piece of overgrown skin on his jaw." She put a finger on the back of her jawbone, below the ear. "I guess he'd been in some kind of accident or fire years ago and had a small chunk of his hide taken out."

"Hopefully he hasn't grown a beard."

"Should I wish you good luck?"

"There's never enough to go 'round in Vegas, right?"

The other woman laughed again and the two parted. Outside, Chainey tried the number, but it only rang; no answer, no answering machine. If Varzagas was bullshitting her, she'd done a good job of it. For all Chainey knew, this was just an elaborate lie and Varzagas was going to book any minute. What would a PI do? she wondered. Would she stake out the Block 16, figuring the prime suspect would make a run?

Conversely, Varzagas had seemed genuinely reticent about sending her in McDaniels's direction. And if it was a ruse, she certainly wouldn't have supplied a valid phone number. Although now she was going to have to work to find the guy, assuming he actually existed. Okay, she berated herself, let's get one thing done at a time.

At a twenty-four-hour RiteAid, Chainey found a Vegas phone book. She searched for McDaniels's listing. As she expected, there were several, but one of the McDaniels listed matched the phone number. So far, so good. The address was in Henderson, and that meant wheels. There were a few cabs roaming about, like metal beetles in search of the perfect dung heap. She hailed one and rode out to the address, getting stopped twice by roving patrols of soldiers.

McDaniels's abode was a cookie-cutter apartment box called the Tahitian Breeze in the middle of a working-class block not far from Arroyo Grande Park. It even had ratty netting drooping off one corner, fish silhouettes, and one of those metal sunburst artifacts stuck off-center in the front.

The intercom box was set next to the apartment's legend. But many of the red Dynamo-lettered names had cracked and broken off, or were partially missing. There was nothing to indicate which apartment might be McDaniels's. Fortunately, the tag for MGR had been replaced recently on a piece of index card cut and taped into place. Yeah, you could never tell when there'd be a run on rooms in a joint like this, Chainey reflected sarcastically.

She dialed and waited. No response. She repeated the ritual.

"What?" blared through the cracking speaker.

"I got a delivery for Eddie McDaniels."

"So?"

"So his apartment isn't listed out here, ma'am." She wasn't

entirely sure it was a woman she was talking to, the voice harsh and virtually sexless through the ancient device.

"He didn't tell you that when he ordered his shit?" she barked acidly. The TV could be heard playing loudly in the manager's apartment.

" 'Fraid not."

"Oh, for the love of . . . just leave it out front," the pitiless voice snapped. "I'm missing 'Survivor Meets Temptation Island, dammit."

"I need to deliver it personally." Chainey almost cracked up; this was too good, bothering the most incredibly put-upon woman in the world.

"Twelve, okay, shit." This was the limit of the largesse of her patience. The line was disconnected. Chainey dialed the apartment but got no answer. Okay, that maybe made sense if he was the man. He and his crew pull the job, then everything falls apart after Jeffries's shooting. The cops and Guard clamp down on everything. Moving five-million-plus around without being conspicuous wasn't easy. They wouldn't want to take a chance at being stopped and searched.

Chainey walked around in front, going over what she'd do if she were McDaniels. You'd have to ditch the money, then blend in, waiting for things to die down. She stopped and looked at the building. Would there be a clue to his whereabouts in his place? But how to get inside on the DL, the down low, as they say? Though that tactic might burn up too much time and not yield anything. Nesting in her mind was the less than 100 percent feeling she might be chasing a ghost. McDaniels might have nothing to do with this at all, but it wasn't like she had a lot of other prospects.

Chainey walked away and found a few cabs drifting up and down Atlantic. One pulled over when she signaled, and she had him drive her to the Truxon offices. The headquarters of the service Mooch Maltizar controlled was located in a prosaic strip mall sandwiched between West Vegas and the Strip. The second story of the mall was given over to the enterprise's offices and cubicles for the euphemistically titled freight handlers and a few assistants. The ground floor contained a Chinese food and doughnut shop called the Chocolate Chopstick, a nail salon, Video Vivian's Video Shoppe, and a U.S. One check-cashing outfit.

Chainey was one of the few people who worked for Truxon who had earned their own tiny office, and she was the only woman. The male couriers in her world were no different than in the straight world of clock punchers. Some of Maltizar's guys had been muscle for the old crews, pit bosses, and a couple had been cops back east. But to the man they all thought only their gender could do the heavy lifting. And no matter how much shit she did, and how much business she took care of, there was always some backhand comment or ogling of her body meant to put her back in her place.

"Fuck 'em," she suddenly blared.

"Excuse me?" the silver-haired woman driving the cab said.

"Sorry," she said. *Pace yourself, Chainey.*

She tipped generously to compensate for her outburst when the cab deposited her at the office. She'd expected to see a light on in the corner, indicating that Mooch was ensconced in there with his bottle and his memories. But the place was dark and quiet. Though, as usual, there were patrons in the Chocolate Chopstick.

Upstairs, after pressing in the proper codes in the alarm system, Chainey sat before the new Pentium gigahertz hooked into its own DSL line. She typed in her requests on several search engines and then gathered information on the Nymnatists and the activities of Sub-Commandante Khali. Before she got back to the hunt, she thought it was best to be as prepared as she could be.

She studied her printouts, making mental and written notes of the flotsam and jetsam of data. She checked the time; it was past 2 A.M. and the getting was good. Fast Eddie had to be found. She ditched her purse and strapped on an ankle holster and piece. Then it was back out on the bricks.

Forty minutes later Chainey was hitting her third possibility, at an off-the-Strip joint called the Floating Deuce on Warm Springs.

It was a grade B bump-and-grind place that also housed an escort service in the back. She talked with one of the bookers at her desk, a part-time actress named Mandy who'd been the dead hooker, the screaming blind attendant, and the frightened waitress in some direct-to-video fare.

"Yeah, Chainey, I'm up for a part in *Reanimator IV: The Return of Dr. Phibes's Ghost*. The rapper Jay-Z is starring." The line buzzed, and she held up a hand. "Hold on." She slipped on her headset and made an appointment for one of the stripper/escorts who went by the name of Jenni Boston.

"You get any dialogue this time?"

"Hell, yes," she said excitedly. "I've got five and a half pages, my goddamn debut." Both women laughed. "So what's up, eight baller?"

Chainey explained who she was after, and gave the description she'd been given of the man.

"No." Mandy shook her head, "I don't know him, but I got a guy who might. He's a regular, and he does construction; plumbing, I think. I know he did some work on the Belaggio." She used her mouse to open a file on her computer.

"Won't he freak, you calling him like this?" A leggy woman dressed only in a leather sarong and stilettos came out of a side door. She had a black bra draped over her shoulder as if it were a shirt, and she marched through the room without a care in the world.

"No, he's cool. Plus he's got a crush on me. Lemme see." She dialed and got him on his cell phone. Mandy made small talk and flirted and then asked him. She listened, then told him to have a good time, and that she looked forward to his call next week. She took the handset off. "He was partying with some friends in Reno." She tapped the side of her nose to indicate the kind of controlled-substance gaiety the pals were having. "So I caught him in a good mood. He says he knows a couple of guys like the one you mentioned, but the chunk missing from the jaw sounded familiar. He thinks this Eddie hangs out at the El Morocco 'cause he went with him there once or twice to unwind when they did a job together."

"Close enough." Chainey handed over a fifty. "Be cool."

"It's your world, player." Mandy didn't have time to laugh as the line rolled over to her and she answered the call.

Chainey waved good-bye and walked back through the club. On stage a woman in a G-string grasped a pole between her muscular thighs and inched herself upward. She held herself aloft and bent backwards from it to appreciative hooting and hollering. The pursuit, the watching, the wanting, the needing, and the obsession of sex was something to behold, the one-time chorus girl pondered, and not for the first time. She had vivid memories of men's and, as society's constraints loosened, a few women's, eyes searing her sweating skin with intensity. There she was, going through the choreographer's elaborate number with forty or fifty pounds of spangles, beads, feathers, and headgear on her, a living hood ornament, the object of fantasy.

But then, what was the job of these women working nudie joints or escort services but to sell the fantasy that any man, for the right price, could have any woman do any number of things to him or with him? And when it was over there were no entanglements, no having to call and listen to her feelings, her problems. And now what better than downloading hardcore pics and videos off the Internet? You didn't even have to get off your wheezing ass and actually rent a bang tape from the neighborhood video store. Hell, you might be spotted by your son's coach or teacher, fer chrissakes.

But then, maybe sex and satisfaction had nothing to do with it at all, she considered as she stepped back into the early morning. Power had a lot to do with it too. In this modern world, men found themselves adrift. Women doctors, women pilots, women CEOs. Sure, for most of the world women were still coming up short, but there were enough examples of females getting over it here that had to make men nervous. How better to make things like they used to be, or always wanted them to be, than by paying for a blow job or being able to order the chick to do exactly what you wanted for a price? And even better, you didn't have to reciprocate. Yet, paradoxically, men always wanted that

fake-ass dream they'd seen in some flick one late night. The one
where the prostitute somehow fell madly in love with him and
reformed. Chumps.

Chainey got to the El Morocco at twenty past three. The
casino was on Industrial Road, trucks and cars humming by on
the 15 Freeway not too far away. It was one of those places the
natives frequented, with its semi-Moorish trappings, flocked ox-
blood-colored wallpaper, and drink servers in belly dancer outfits. The casino was of intimate size and exuded a friendly,
unhurried atmosphere. Given the hour and its off-the-beaten-
path quality, Chainey could actually hear the spin of the roulette
wheel and the marble bouncing around.

Walking past a section with shops done up as a bazaar, she descended a series of short steps into the bar called, appropriately,
Rick's Place. The stools were plentiful, and she sat on one so as
to take in the open-air bar and part of the casino floor. She or-
dered. As per the inverted logic that operated in Vegas, Happy
Hour had started at two this morning and would go on until ten
A.M. If her boy was waiting until the state of siege lifted, he might
be drinking. Or he could be shacked up miles from here in
Laughlin or Reno, or he might even have driven to L.A. by now.
Her cell phone rang, interrupting her second-guessing.

"Hello?"

"Martha, where are you?"

She told Rena Solomon where she was. "So . . . ?"

"So, like whatchu doing?"

"Don't be a cutie."

"Can't help it. I picked up a rumor that the Nymnatists bet
against their golden boy."

"Why you telling me?" she deflected.

"I know you were summoned to have an audience with her
highness."

"We talked about this and that." Her gin martini arrived.
She'd figured she was entitled to a bracer.

"Come on, throw me a friggin' bone here," her friend whee-
dled.

"Okay, I've heard that too."

"And that's connected to why you're running back and forth across town now, right?"

"Maybe."

"Good enough, honey chile. I'm off to see Joaquin Muhammad now. He's convinced this group calling itself the Black Jihad is after him and got Jeffries by mistake."

Chainey stopped in mid-sip. "There was a guy handing out flyers earlier. I think this group you just mentioned was listed on the thing. You know, one of those ultra-conspiracy things."

"You still have it?"

"Naw, pitched it; sorry. But I'm sure you'll find plenty of them littering the Boulevard."

"I'll see. You gonna be able to talk to me later?"

"If I'm successful."

"Aren't you always?"

"I wish."

"Catch you later, gotta bounce."

"Right, right." Chainey thumbed the instrument off and got up with her drink. It wouldn't be long before her friend dug up what Chainey was up to, and that might also get back to the people she was supposed to be tracking down. And now there was this bit about some kind of collection of militants that Muhammad was worked up about. What happened to the old days of a snatch-and-grab as just a simple robbery?

Chainey was making her circuit of the casino when she passed within three feet of Eddie McDaniels. He was leaning over the craps table and throwing his point, shooter's point. He was muscular, dressed in a loose T with the band Everclear's logo on it, khaki pants, and worn work boots. He wasn't bad to look at and hadn't grown a beard, though his hair was now jet black. But the section of flesh missing from his jaw was easy to spot. It was an oval-shaped area, about two inches around. The depression was toward his ear, as Gihan Varzagas had indicated. But what really nailed it was that one of the waitresses squealed his name as he tossed the dice.

"You're red hot, Eddie, red fuckin' hot." She bounced up and down, the tops of her breasts jiggling in her push-up bra.

McDaniels laughed raucously as he made his point, five. "You're goddamn straight, Sandi," he said. The ones who'd bet on the shooter on the line also beamed. Everyone likes a winner as long as he's making them money. Two of the three dealers made the payouts. The stickman, in this case a thick-bodied woman with green eyeliner, shuttled a pair of dice back toward McDaniels.

McDaniels indeed had the arm for a time and made his point more often than not. Even when he crapped out, he was still ahead, thanks to shrewd betting on the pass lines. And several times he rolled seven or twelve in his come out, his initial toss. This went on for another forty minutes, until he started to get cold. So she wouldn't be conspicuous, Chainey had left the vicinity of the table a few times and played a few hands of black-jack or fooled around with the slots, always keeping him in sight.

When she got back to the table, McDaniels was ready to cash out. He gave four chips worth a hundred dollars to the cheer-leading waitress, and she gave him a peck on the cheek. The courier hung back, but there wasn't that big a crowd in the casino, whose main room could fit inside a church hall. She was aware that he'd been checking her out when she'd stood near the craps table.

She watched him go to the cashier and turn in his chips for a check. Then he went into the bar, and Chainey had to decide whether to follow him in there or not. She could plop herself down beside him and strike up a conversation, make McDaniels think she was interested in him. Winners drew certain kinds of women to them like ants to sugar, so it wouldn't seem out of place. But she didn't think she could put the vamp on him to make him babble. She knew some men found her attractive, but that didn't mean she was vain enough to believe she could put him under a spell. But she would stick out just standing around. She went in and sat on the far end of the bar.

Her mental contortions were for naught as Sandi the waitress veered in from her rounds and dive-bombed McDaniels. Either she was on break or, given the paucity of customers, she could afford to set out the hook for the fish. She flicked a quick back-off glance at Chainey, then concentrated on her mark. They laughed and talked and touched foreheads, and laughed and talked some more. Chainey nursed a glass of seltzer.

When the shift supervisor stood by the archway, hands jingling change in his baggy pants, Sandi finally had to get back to work. Chainey drifted away to not be so conspicuous and still keep the bar in sight. A minute later McDaniels was on the move, studying his watch and heading out the door.

Chainey wasn't practiced at tailing anyone; that wasn't a skill required in her line of work. But the clamp down and the usual whirl of nightlife ensured a good amount of people out and about, even in the early morning hours.

He went in a southwesterly direction, but he wasn't wandering; it was clear McDaniels had a specific destination in mind. Tracking got to be trickier for Chainey as the crowds thinned. Some Guardsmen were bivouacked to the rear of Binion's Horseshoe, and the neon reflected hazily off their dull rifle barrels. On Cheyenne, McDaniels threw away the cigarette he was smoking and crossed the street at an angle toward Las Vegas Boulevard. Chainey, half a block behind him on Cheyenne, kept walking, along with two other women on the stroll. Her quarry ducked into an all-night laundromat, and she had to fight the urge to dash in there after him. Appropriately, the wash place was called the Shady Lady. If he'd made her, he was going to run out of the back. If he hadn't, he damn sure couldn't have an urge to get some washing done now.

One of the women said, "Naw, girl," and the blonde white prostitute, in a butt-hugging black slit skirt, returned, "You know the most kink I'll do is a golden shower. Shit."

"I'm telling you, Roe," her Filipina friend, wearing tight tiger-striped pants rejoindered, "all you got to do is hold the handle and pop that sweaty ass with the cat o'nine tails now and then.

Bitch, you gonna make five hundred dollars. I'll do all the real work with the studded dildo."

"Lemme think about it, okay?"

Chainey walked behind the pair until the end of the block. By then Roe had accepted her associate's offer to expand her repertoire. Chainey doubled back and walked on the other side of Las Vegas Boulevard, where the laundromat was located. There wasn't much in the way of cover. The best she could do was tuck herself into the recessed doorway of a motorcycle shop. The cyclopean headlights of sleek Kawasakis and blunt-nosed BMWs blindly looked out at her through the plate glass, behind the accordion grill. She didn't have long to wait; McDaniels did have an appointment to keep.

Four shapes were moving purposely toward the Shady Lady from the east along the Boulevard. Chainey slumped in the doorway, as if she were drunk, and mumbled to herself.

"What's this shiznit?" one of them said in hip-hopese.

Chainey kept doing the act.

"Fucked up, but damn she's fine, yo," another one uttered.

"Keep your mind on business," a third one, a woman, declared. All four were young. "Let's go, he's waiting," the woman ordered.

The quartet trooped into the laundromat. Chainey counted a few beats, then got up and chanced to ease closer. If she was spotted, she'd do the drunk dodge and see if it got her over. If not . . . well, if-nots didn't get the job done. She pushed up against the storefront of a closed copier place just beyond the spill of light from the laundromat's doorway. The elevated voices were sharp on the quiet street.

". . . damn that, Eddie. We have to move now, while the cops are concentrated along the Strip."

"Now look, I know a little something about this shit, okay? This ain't like disrupting the Democratic Convention you rookies did in L.A. You go down for this, it isn't a hand slap and a notch on your little red badge."

"Fuck you, man," the man who'd said Chainey was fine swore. "You couldn't have pulled this off except for us."

"It's the other way around, from my way of thinking," Mc-Daniels replied edgily. "I'm the one who hooked up the technical—"

"You performed a service, and like any wage slave you'll be taken care of." The woman's voice was low key but had a no-nonsense tone. In some ways the confidence of her inflections reminded Chainey of Naomi. The heisters continued talking, but her attention was now on a car gliding in from the west. The vehicle's lights had been cut as it rounded the corner from Sandy Lane. The creeper had its low beams on, the front end drooping down, hovering over the asphalt.

Chainey finally assigned a name to the silhouette; it was a lowered Chevy Impala, probably a '63 or '64. Like a submarine in enemy waters, the car silently coasted to a stop at the curb, parked the wrong way. It too was just outside the cone of light from the laundromat's door, on the other side from Chainey. She was walking away, pretending to be passing by so as not to focus undue attention on herself. But the hurried exit of the group in the Impala indicated that they could have cared less what she was doing. As one, four men rushed into the building. In the lead was King Diamond.

"Whaz poppin'?" a voice bounced off the walls of the laundromat. Chainey had resumed her post.

"This is none of your concern, King D." The young woman was clearly in charge of the other crew.

"Tyler gettin' smoked is my business, Khali."

Well, well. Chainey chanced getting even closer.

The woman snorted derisively. "You a pig now, D?"

"I wouldn't go there if I was you, homegirl. I ain't the one sellin' out the movement."

"Fuck you know," a new voice put in.

There were some sounds that Chainey interpreted as jostling, and she could hear a body being shoved against something solid.

"Hold the fuck up," Kind Diaomond shouted. "We need to get straight on some shit here, Khali. Thas why I had my peeps out, lookin' for your conniving ass all goddamn night."

"Look—"

But she was cut off as a Bradley—Chainey recognized the craft from the description she'd read in the high-tech novel—rumbled onto the thoroughfare.

"Motherfuck," someone swore.

"Chill, chill," another voice counseled.

"Move the whip, man, move the whip," King Diamond's voice urged.

Like an elephant grazing, the Bradley took its time coming down the street. A body jumped into the Impala and waved at the soldiers as he started the car and parked it correctly on the street. The vehicle stopped and deposited two Guardsmen, who went into the laundromat, M-16s at the ready. Chainey had returned to her drunk pose in the motorcyle shop's doorway. She wasn't sure whether the soldiers had seen her, but it was the wisest course of action.

From her post she could hear only muffled conversation. There were two other Guardsmen in the idling Bradley, and they joked with each other as their compatriots grilled the people inside the laundromat. She supposed if they wanted to they could arrest Khali and King D's forces by virtue of the state of emrgency. Though there was no curfew per se; that would have been unwieldy to enforce in a place like Vegas. Minutes passed and Chainey yawned, the overdrive she'd been on starting to wear off.

She came alert as the two Guardsmen came back out, got in the Bradley, and took off. Apparently the charisma of King Diamond extended to many levels of society. The Guardsmen looked hard at her in the doorway, then got to the end of the street and kept going straight, due north.

Chainey was about to get closer again when the two posses rolled out onto the sidewalk in front of the Laundromat.

". . . all I know"—King Diamond was pointing a finger at Khali—"is you is crooked as a motherfuckin' corkscrew."

"You hardly can question my motives," the young woman huffed. "You ain't all that jus' 'cause you sing about the homeless and striking janitors. You sure livin' large."

"I do some shit with my money, baby girl." King Diamond placed his burly form in front of the smaller woman. She didn't flinch. "And I ain't no murderer."

"Neither am I, ass head." She shoved him and it was on, fists and feet and "your mamas" flying. King Diamond was sucker-punched from behind by one of the anarchists, a kid in loose jeans and a cap with Limp Bizkt monogrammed on it. He countered with an elbow to his attacker's gut. One of the King's crew, a brother at least six-four, had thrown Khali on the hood of the Impala and socked her hard in the jaw. But she was tough and thanked him with a knee to his groin.

"Skank bitch," he wheezed.

Sub-Commandante Khali was off the hood and onto the doubled-over man's back. She wailed on his head with her tiny but obviously effective fists and he went over like a demolished skyscraper. So far no one had produced any iron. Must be, Chainey mused as she moved in, that the King forbade his boys to pack.

McDaniels, where was McDaniels? She was grabbed and spun until she was looking into the eyes of a red-haired man with wildly braided hair sprouting like Busta Rhymes's.

"What you think you doing?"

"Working." She shook him loose.

"Hey, you were the one in the doorway." He grabbed for her again.

She swatted his hand away and kept stepping.

"No, who are you? You've been spying on us, haven't you?" He came after her as she went into the laundromat.

Ignoring him was going to be futile. Fortunately, everyone else was busy with his own skirmishes; that gave her a few moments of latitude. "Back off," she said, turning and leveling a twisting punch that sent him up against a washing machine. He looked more emotionally pained than physically hurt, and she regretted reacting violently. She went on through the back, the young man running outside to no doubt tell Khali.

Out back there was an old '53 Mercury on blocks with a tarp partially covering it. Beyond that she could see the outline of a fleeing McDaniels, and she ran after him. Discretion was now re-placed with necessity. He heard her footsteps and picked up his pace. At the end of the alley he went left, and Chainey did too.

Behind her, she could hear voices. Great; she'd united the warring tribes to go after the stranger. She stepped it up, gained the corner, and kept pumping. McDaniels looked back.

"Watch out," she yelled.

The bumper of a screeching green Checker cab made a sound as it met the lower half of McDaniel's leg. This briefly slowed the man, but then he continued on as other cabs in the street, like electric toys suffering a power loss, also came to a halt at various angles. Chainey took off and slid across the car's hood on her belly, then rolled into a standing position on the other side of the fender. She straightened and got her legs and arms in sync. *Come on, Chainey, you didn't do all those miles on the road and the treadmill for show, did you?*

As she bore down, she heard someone cursing behind her, and a pair of arms suddenly wrapped around her waist. She lost her footing and went skidding into one of those metal mesh city trash receptacles. Without waiting for an introduction, she sank her knuckles into the guy playing London Fletcher. He grunted, and Chainey fought her way loose and got herself upright. The others had now caught up and McDaniels was jetting.

"Who the fuck are you?" Khali, now that Chainey saw her clearly, was a young olive-complected woman. She wore ill-fitting cotton pants and paint-splattered boots. Incongruously, she also had on a buttoned-down light blue oxford-cloth shirt. Her face was neither pretty nor plain, but the seriousness of her resolve was evident in her eyes even in this half-light.

"I'm after McDaniels for nonpayments."

"Goddamn, you sure can hit." The man she'd socked was gripping his stomach, his lips in an *O* as he sucked in air.

"For a girl," Khali jibbed. "Now, what are you talking about?"

"I don't have to tell you shit." Chainey breathed deeply, puffing her chest. She too needed oxygen after her fevered run.

"She's got to be a cop." The man who'd spotted her stabbed a finger at Chainey's face. "We got to do something about that."

"Like what, genius?" another one put in. "We gonna beat her shitless?"

Chainey readied herself, picking out who to attack after she decked Khali with a kick to the midsection.

King Diamond said, "Y'all awfully bloodthirsty for a bunch of tree-hugging yogurt lovers."

"So you a cop?" Khali squared her shoulders, as if ready to take a blow.

"If I was, wouldn't I have a truckload of cops here by now? I'm after McDaniels for a marker he has to make good on."

"A fuckin' gambling debt," one of Diamond's crew declared.

"That's right." Chainey nodded her head in the affirmative.

Khali wasn't buying it. "You got some ID?"

"How about you?"

"Look," King Diamond interjected, "if she was heat, she wouldn't carry on with this bullshit. Let's bounce and settle our squabble peacably."

"Un-huh." Khali got in Chainey's face. "You're lying."

"Better step off, shorty."

"Or?"

"Let's find out." Chainey saw it coming before the smaller woman had it unwound. She blocked the blow and did an overhand thrust that caught Khali under her right ear.

"I told you she could rumble," the one she hit said.

Khali followed up with a blow to Chainey's gut, but the courier hadn't been doing crunches for nothing. She barely went off stride, gritted her teeth at the pain, and drilled the anarchist leader with a solid overhand right. The sub-commandante dropped to the asphalt, stunned but not out. As these things went, the once deserted streets were now populated with a small gathering of denizens, and somebody was calling out odds.

"I got a hundred on the tall one."

"Shit, that's a sucker's play, man."

Chainey and Khali mixed it up as the audience enjoyed the female fisticuffs.

"The cops," a third voice cried out suddenly.

Chainey had just elbowed Khali in the throat as she rushed her. The younger woman's technique was for shit, but she compensated with a fierce determination. But having her wind cut off made Khali gasp and reach for her vocal chords. Chainey had an opening to drop the woman, but the lights from the squad cars were already bathing them in reds and blues.

There was no place to run as several LVMPD cars screeched to a halt, fencing the group in. During the brief fistfight, King Diamond and his boys had faded. Cops with guns pounded onto the street and delivered specific, clipped orders.

"On your knees."

"On the ground."

"Spread 'em, goddammit, spread 'em."

A military Jeep also roared into view. The captain with freckles who'd been on duty at the checkpoint rode in the vehicle. She was standing up, General Swartzkoph–style, a Valkyrie in green at the wheel.

The cops roughly patted her and Khali's bunch down. The five stood in a semicircle, the lights from the patrol cars backlighting them on their knees. Their shadows stretched into dark corners.

"You got her, Chief," the captian announced joyfully.

"It would seem." Lambert came from around his troops to better survey the arrestees. "Ms. Chainey," he drawled. "I can't say I'm that surprised to find in you in the midst of my investigation again." He adjusted his hat against imaginary sunlight. "Nope, not surprised at all."

"What can I say, Chief, it's been a hell of a night." She didn't have time for this; she had to find McDaniels.

"That it has." He stood before her, his frame partially blocking the headlights. "Now, just how is it that you and the submariner, or whatever the hell she calls herself, wound up going a few rounds?"

Chainey tried the good-citizen tact. "I was walking along and spotted her. I was trying to collect the reward for her."

"There isn't one."

"My error."

"A-ha." he turned toward Khali. "And what do you say, Ms. Ashford?"

Ashford, aka Khali, didn't say anything. A blow from Chainey had closed one of her eyes. Her gaze smoldered, alternating between Chainey and the lawman. But what could Khali do? Chainey reasoned. She couldn't go on about McDaniels because he had the money she wanted. Anything the revolutionary said about him was bound to implicate herself. Khali needed McDaniels on the loose too. She was wanted for questioning in Jeffries's death, but not Chainey.

"Gonna play it tough, huh?" Lambert rubbed at the stubble on his chin. "Put cuffs on Ma Barker and her gang," he told his officers.

"What about this one?" A cop popped the barrel of his shotgun on the back of Chainey's head, making her wince.

"Stand up, Chainey," the chief said by way of an answer.

She complied.

"I better not find you a third time during this emergency period, hear? I don't for a hot second believe any of your bullshit, but it's Kahli I'm interested in, understand?"

"I'm going to make like yesterday."

He pointed a dirty-nailed finger. "Just remember what I said, smart ass."

Chainey bit back a rejoinder and walked away. The sub-commandante and her rogues were loaded up and carted off. As she went past, Khali glared malevolently at Chainey, willing her to drop dead. But when the captain passed her, she winked.

Chainey marched on. What a night, indeed.

CHAPTER EIGHT

"Hello." Chainey pressed the muzzle of the light and tight Springfield into McDaniels's kidney. According to the brochure that came with the gun, this .45 weapon could make a swell two-and-a-half-inch-across grouping of bullets at twenty-five yards. She wasn't the best on the range, but this close was no sweat.

"Fuck," he bleated. He stood at a locker in the El Morocco. One of his arms was inside the cavity, the other resting on the rim.

"Go ahead and take it out, honey."

Eddie McDaniels did as ordered. The construction worker held tightly on to the canvas bag, and he seemed to be considering flight. But he couldn't be sure the woman aiming the gun at his waistline wouldn't let off a couple of hot ones. Actually, she wasn't sure either.

"How about a two-way on this; Chainey, right?"

"What do you think?"

"I think"—he started to back away while facing her—"you won't blast my guts all over this nice tile." He swept his free hand at the floor and walls. "I think I'm going to walk out of here with this grip and out of your life forever."

She purposely spoke in a lower register and slower manner than her natural voice. "Who do you think I work for, Eddie?"

That put a skip in his step.

"You think I don't have anybody to report to? You honestly believe it ends here? The money is not the issue, sport. You don't fuck with these people and expect the rest of your life to go on like it was some sitcom on NBC."

He'd halted, taking in her every word.

"This is make-or-break time, Eddie."

"It wasn't my idea," he copped.

"That right?

"Okay, me and Rhonda."

"The sub-commandante?"

A couple conversing in German came in. Chainey nodded at them, and they returned the gesture. She had her hands clasped before her, obscuring the pistol. Fortunately, the tourists went right to their locker and didn't block the view she had of Mc-Daniels. She stepped closer to him as the tourists completed their task and departed.

"Yeah, that sorry-ass excuse for a revolutionary," he went on. "I should have known those fuckin' tofu lovers couldn't pull this off."

Chainey didn't point out that he'd apparently willingly involved himself in this scheme. "How'd you two hook up?"

"My goofball younger brother," he snorted. "He's a turtle head."

Chainey frowned at the reference.

"You know, clean water, trash all the cars and buses, that kind of shit."

"So through him Rhonda Ashford engineered the robbery tonight?"

His shoulders notched up, then down. "It seemed like a smart time to pull off the heist. It made sense, since everybody was going to be at the concert and the fight. Then there'd be the partying afterward; who'd be looking for us? I sure didn't figure on tripping the alarm from below. And that Jeffries would go down." He put the bag down, as if it were now a cursed object bringing only pestilence and plague.

"What about Moya Reese?" she asked.

"Who?" His blank look seemed genuine.

"Never mind. You entered the safe through the bottom. There's some kind of crawl space underneath, isn't there?" She'd suspected that was how they'd done the deed. And whoever helped install the thing was a natural for the boost. "How could you not have set off the alarm, Eddie?"

"The fuckin' thing was designed by that nut Degault," he whined.

"You mean Frankie wanted it to open from below?"

"Yeah," he said. "Listen, the box was in place and I get a call one morning. He was kind of blabbering; he told me he'd been up all night snorting and doin' his strippers, and the notion came to him in a brilliant cloud, he said." A crooked smile plastered itself on the thief's intense face. "So he called me 'cause he'd found out about my record, but he said that was cool. That I would appreciate his fuckin' vision."

"He intended to rip off his sister and anybody else who put money in there, didn't he?"

"That I couldn't say." He grinned. "Since he knew I was a welder he had me come in that Sunday morning and rig the bottom to unlatch into this little sub-basement that had been there in the original plans."

"How the hell did you swing that section back into place?" Chainey picked up the bag, testing its weight. You move enough cash around, you get a feel for it. The heft seemed right.

"He had someone come in later and put in a hydraulic system. That's how I got it to go back up earlier this evening." He flexed his shoulders again. "Or morning, or whatever time it is."

By now the two were moving out of the locker area and into the passageway leading back to the main part of the casino. Chainey had stationed herself behind a pillar to stake out the lockers. There had been no other place to go, and the El Morocco was as good a way station in which to hide the swag as any other joint. And this was where she'd encountered McDaniels marking time until his meeting with Khali.

"How come you two were getting into an argument?" They stood under an archway lit with green neon script broadcasting the room's function.

He snorted again. "The funny thing is, I didn't trust her. We were supposed to meet alone, and she rolls up with her Three Musketeers. I was worried if I took them back here they'd jump me and cut me out of my end." He halted. "And now I ain't got shit."

"You got your freedom, Eddie. I got what I came for." She tapped the bag, now slung over her shoulder by its straining strap. The gun was tucked beside it and her body, her fingers sweaty against the cold frame. "You won't need to look over your shoulder."

"I guess beggars and what not."

"I guess."

A couple of beats, then, "See you, Chainey."

"Could be."

With a decided air of defeat, McDaniels turned and walked away. Chainey waited for him to go and then re-entered the locker area. She put the bag in another available space and removed the key. An older woman wearing clothes intended for someone younger was leaning against the lockers, a cigarette dangling from her made-up lips as she touched up her mascara. Finished, she departed, and Chainey replaced her pistol in an ankle holster.

She'd assumed McDaniels wouldn't make a direct line to the casino to make sure the cops or one of Khali's bunch weren't tailing him. So now she'd done her job and was set to collect her substantial fee. But there was the matter of Moya Reese lying belly up, her eyes seeing nothing, that wouldn't leave her head.

Chainey wasn't entirely sure what to believe about McDaniels and Khali. Chief Lambert was of the opinion that she had killed the heavyweight champion of the world and was doubtlessly vigorously pursuing that line of reasoning.

But it didn't make sense, since theoretically the crew had a better chance of slipping out of town without all the hub-bub accompanying Jeffries's killing. Or she'd done it to prove she was down. By taking out the champ, the symbol of corporate marketing, was she proving to all doubters that she was the one?

This only reinforced the necessity for Chainey to do what she could to find out who had killed her friend. It wasn't like they'd been close. And it wasn't as if the earth would open up and swallow her if she did nothing to find out who did Reese in. But she couldn't pretend it hadn't happened either.

"If I was a snake, girl, you'd be bit."

Startled, the ex-showgirl exclaimed, "Rena."

"I've been busy; what about you?"

"Likewise. Glad we ran into each other."

"Me too. I have to tell you something, but this isn't for publication. Not yet." A gender-mixed group of "National Guardsmen" marched by. They were having a good time of it, arms around each other, laughing, carefree, and one of them was carrying a bottle of Jim Beam. Not only that; the women had their shirts open past the breastbone, exposing the upper portions of lacy black bras. A closer look revealed that the guns they carried were plastic replicas, and their purpose became apparent as the group passed the two friends.

On each one of the fake soldier's backs was a bold block letter of Day-Glo vinyl. Altogether the word spelled out was HANK'S. At the base of each letter was the address of the advertised bar. Chainey pulled Solomon off to the side, near a statue of Aphrodite in a pond. The Greek goddess of love and beauty was bestride a surfboard. Chainey told her about finding Reese's body.

"The cops must not know yet, since Lambert didn't detain you," Solomon said when her friend was through.

"They don't know either of us knew her," Chainey countered.

"I'm not sure about that. The cops were interviewing a lot of people when they clamped down at the stadium. Someone was bound to mention that they saw her with you when you went downstairs to fetch her after her bout."

Chainey nodded agreement.

"So what you were up to for Victoria has to do with Moya and Jeffries's deaths?"

"I don't think so." Chainey explained what she'd learned

from McDaniels without mentioning specifics about the missing wager money. "Now Lambert's sweating Khali, but I think that dog's barking up the wrong tree, as Uncle Hiram used to say."

The women walked and talked. "Check this out," Solomon said. "As you may know, the good King Diamond has been producing other rappers' music videos and has done a couple of direct-to-video B efforts."

"And those have blown up, as they say," Chainey added.

"Right. Low budget, plenty of gats and some hotties, and Blockbuster can't keep 'em on the shelves. But pertinent to this discussion, the King has branched out into sports management."

"This is where Watson always looks openmouthed at Holmes, isn't it?"

Solomon did a brief bow. "No, please, you'll turn my head," she cracked. "Down For It Enterprises, the King's firm, was one of the promoters of tonight's undercard. Reese had just signed a week ago to be rep'd by him."

"No shit."

"I shit you not."

"Was King D trying to sign up Jeffries too?" Portions of the confrontation between Diamond and Khali replayed in her mind. The rapper too seemed to believe she'd had a hand in the champ's death.

"I have no direct knowledge of that," Solomon offered, "but it would seem logical that King D would have pursued him. I do recall a couple of times when I've seen photos of the rapper getting all chummy with Jeffries at charity auctions, things like that."

"Let's ask him," Chainey suggested.

"If we can get past his barrier of bodyguards and his entourage. They're thicker than fleas on a mangy dog, Chain."

"Maybe Victoria has some sway with him."

"Can't hurt to ask."

Chainey called around for Degault on her cell phone and left messages. Within ten minutes the owner of the Riverhead called back. Chainey and Solomon stood in the shadow of the Arc de

Triumph at the Paris Casino while she talked to her. Several tourists stood around the replica snapping pictures or taping a smiling spouse or girlfriend. Ten years from now there'd probably be a full-motion 3D hologram backdrop of cars and people to complete this quaint Parisian scene in the desert. Soon one would be able to take holidays on holodecks like in "Star Trek" and never have to deal with cramped plane rides or uptight foreigners and their irritating ways.

"Looks like we're gonna get some steam." Chainey thumbed off her phone.

"We are. It's ninety-five goddamn degrees of humidity now." Solomon grasped the material of her blouse and shook it for emphasis.

"What can I tell you, Rena, the lady says meet her at the Hard Rock Athletic Club Spa. Apparently they've opened the facility just for her."

Solomon glanced at her watch. It was almost five A.M. "The rich are strange and can afford it."

"Very true." The two started for their new destination on Paradise Road. Chainey hadn't told Degault about finding the money. Partly it was to keep the information from Solomon, at least for now. The other reason was more devious. She wanted Degault to get them in to see King Diamond, and she might not work hard at it if she knew her stolen cash had been found. Nothing like providing incentive, she reflected as they crossed the street.

A Bradley armored vehicle went by, two National Guard troopers sitting on the outside, holding on to part of the machine. One had on a helmet and the other a bright orange sweatband. That certainly couldn't be regulation, Chainey thought. Were they actual troopers or some other advertising gimmick? It was getting harder to tell the legit from the fake.

At the Hard Rock the women asked for Maurice, whom Degault had said would lead the way. The man was tall, caramel-colored, and filled out his sky-blue shawl-collar jacket quite nicely.

"By all means, lead the way." Solomon made a lustful face as

Maurice turned and marched along a hallway outside to the main restaurant. Passing by one of the glassed-in booths, the two women nudged each other. They'd simultaneously spotted members of the JBs, the famous R&B instrumental band that was part of the James Brown family. Maceo Parker was saying grace as the others bowed their heads over their plates of food. Collectively, the gold jewelry on their fingers, wrists, and around their necks would be enough to fund a small protectorate.

Maurice took the pair up in a private elevator whose buttons were stenciled with various musical notes. They were let out into a darkened lobby of smoked glass and large standing vases of willow sprigs and lush fronds. All the way up, Solomon and their guide played visual tag.

"I do hope to see you back here again," he said to the reporter as he unlocked the entrance door.

"I might need to talk to you for this article I'm putting together." Solomon handed him a business card.

"Let me give you this." Maurice also produced a card and scribbled a number on the back of it. "That's my cell." He handed it over, his gaze steady on the woman. "I always return my calls."

"I'll be in touch."

"Enjoy." And he departed.

The women entered the spa proper, each grinning and laughing at the other. "Damn, could you be any more obvious?" Chainey ribbed her.

"I'm just doing my job as a journalist. I don't know what you're talking about."

They giggled and went along past Cybex and Precor exercise stations. There was a light on, giving off an amber glow at one end of the exercise area, and like moths the women headed for it. They were surprised to see four female attendants down the passageway, who led them to a locker room where Chainey and Solomon stripped and wrapped themselves in big towels. From there they followed two of the women deeper into the place to a rough-hewn wall of dark rock shot through with yellowish stone.

In a room that was like a hothouse for humans, Victoria Degault rested on a wooden shelf. A towel was draped over her lower body and her torso was bare and sweat-drenched. She had her hair wrapped up in a towel, and her head rested back against the golden-tinged wall. Her eyes were closed.

"Ladies," she murmured in a voice thick with fatigue.

"I keep winding up in these joints," Chainey remarked. While chasing after the money that led to Frankie Degault's demise, she'd run down a lead that had taken her to a woman's bath house in San Francisco.

The two women sat down on either side of Degault. A sonata played softly via hidden speakers.

"We need to—" Solomon began.

Degault held up a hand and made a hushing sound. "I find if I allow myself to be pampered, I can surge into the next set of my most pressing endeavors." She hadn't lifted her lids, and she breathed in deeply.

Solomon shot Chainey a look and Degault, who must have guessed what her expression was, crinkled her lips slightly. "I know you must think it's decadent, but what can I say? What works, works, right?"

The reporter was about to mouth off sarcastically, but Chainey cut her off with a finger to her lips. The atmosphere and music was calming, so why not roll with it for awhile? She too rested her head against the warm but comfortable tiles. Soon her eyes dropped closed.

"Yo, Chain," Solomon said. "You with us, home-grown?"

"Damn, how long was I dozing?" Some drool had collected in a corner of her mouth.

"You were sawing, homie."

Solomon and Degault chuckled.

She could feel her cheeks flush. "Okay, okay, I'm awake now, dammit."

"Victoria was saying," Solomon continued, "that she'll see about getting us to the King."

"For a square white girl, I guess I should be flattered I have his number." Degault had fetched her phone and was powering it up. "I'm'a blow his number up, isn't that how they say it?" She smiled, flicking her now loose, wet hair out of the way of her ear.

"Yes, that's right," Degault spoke into the instrument. "Tell him if he doesn't see them, there's going to be some accounting delays issuing the check." She glanced at Chainey, a mischievous glint in her dark eyes. "Uh-huh," she finally said when whoever she was talking to came back on the line. "There's no reason for that kind of language, ah, Big Shorty, is it?" It was as if Degault were a therapist trying to soothe a distraught patient barricaded in the bathroom with a straight razor. "I'll hang up on you if you're going to start talking about lawyers, Big, my man. Then how would you explain that to Mr. Lawson?"

Solomon whispered, "You're enjoying this too much."

Degault was on hold again and was about to respond when Big Shorty returned. "Ah, now we're talking. They'll be around in about an hour. Thank you," she said sweetly, signaling her phone off. "You're set; he and his posse are staying in the Thunderhead suites at my casino."

Solomon got up. "We better get going."

"Wait a bit," Degault said. "Recharge, get the stress levels down some, huh?" She let her head fall back again and wet her lips with the tip of her tongue.

The two took Degault's advice and chilled out for about twenty minutes, letting the steam invigorate them. Then Solomon rose again.

"I'll be right there." Chainey gave her friend a nod.

"Okay, but no more sleeping on the job, honey." Rena sauntered off to get dressed.

"What's on your mind, Chainey?" Degault rubbed at the underside of one of her breasts. Then she wiped the flat of her hand on the towel over her taut legs. Degault was a bicyclist and had been in several marathons.

"What's up with you and Tosches?" She wanted to be convinced that Eddie McDaniels's hanging around the El Morocco was just happenstance.

She arched a well-defined eyebrow. "If Mama was alive, she'd ask a question like that."

"Do you trust him?"

"Can any man really be trusted?"

"You know what I'm talking about. You know the stories that are out there about him."

"Like everything else in Vegas, Chainey, if you come away two percent ahead you're doing good."

"That means you settle for what you can get?"

"It means I know the business I'm in." As if she suddenly realized part of her body was exposed, she folded her muscular arms across her breasts. "I'm not fooling myself that my hands aren't dirty either." Her contemplative stare bore into Chainey.

"I'm not questioning that. But you of all people, the only woman owner on the Strip, have no choice but to always keep both eyes on the business. Men have the luxury of thinking below the belt; we don't."

"You better get going, you're going to be late. The sun's almost up."

"I'm not scared of the sunlight."

"Neither am I."

"I'll let you know what we turn up."

"I appreciate that." Her body relaxed again and she resumed the pose she'd been in when the others had come in. She added, "I'll let security know you're coming up."

Chainey caught up with Solomon in the locker room and they changed back into street clothes and walked over to the Riverhead. As they did so, the duo passed yet another new construction site, this one on a lot to the east of the casino, off the main line.

"What's that supposed to be?" Chainey asked Solomon, referring to the steel skeleton looming some twelve stories into the air. She'd noticed the construction before but as there was constant jettisoning of history on the Strip, she found it hard to distinguish one project from another unless it was relevant to her work.

In an off-hand manner, Solomon said, "Oh, that's the first dot-com financed casino. It's not that big, as you can see, but it's going to have all the bells and whistles. Each room will have a media center, and you see that corner there? That's where they're going to have a four-story arcade like no other, with giant screens and what have you. There's also going to be a wrestling superstar–themed restaurant and a virtual gallery where you can wrestle buffed beef like Chyna and the Rock in cyberspace."

"What's it going to be called?"

"Zardoz."

"Huh?"

"I don't get it either. It's some kinda geek joke, I guess."

The weak light of near-dawn cast everything in a violet-gray pall, as if the people and buildings had survived a biological attack. The density of the crowds had thinned somewhat, but there were still a number of police officers and the Guard out. But they looked listless, like gamblers pulling an all-nighter and coming up bust too often, yet too wired to stop.

In the Riverhead's lobby, which resembled a massive loading dock into a jungle adventure, Solomon turned to Chainey. "So the Thunderhead Suite is on the tiptop?"

"Two floors down on the forty-first, so the guests can walk up to the moon deck in their own mini roof garden. Nothing but the best reserved for the whales and steamers."

"Let's hit it, then. King D awaits." The two walked toward the elevators.

Neither woman had paid any particular attention to the five hotties in the lobby area in various degrees of revealing attire. The troop of young, natural, and augmented women had been searching for some hours for the rapper and his entourage. Collectively they were known as the Furious Five and had burned a self-made CD of their R&B-flavored raps. The CD had done moderately well, given the boost it had received when the five did a suggestive video to accompany the title cut. The vid got a lot of hits on their Web site.

But they weren't tramps like those three showing their titties during the King's concert. That was hood rat shit. The Furious Five were a class act. Sure, they used what God gave them to their own benefit, and it wasn't their fault that sex sold. They were simply acceding to the demands of the marketplace.

And now, as one, they were charged anew upon overhearing that the King was indeed in this hotel/casino. They'd been following up one rumor after another all night and had started out in the Riverhead, as it was a logical place to begin. The women had been all around town and even over to Floyd Lamb State Park, on the tip that the King was staying in a tour bus parked out there. The quintet were on a mission—after much footwork, persistence, and luck, they'd been rewarded. The Five grinned knowingly at each other and marched toward the elevators. Getting past security should be a no-brainer.

CHAPTER NINE

The Thunderhead Suite was a series of interconnecting rooms taking up two levels and five-thousand square feet of the forty-first floor of the circular story of the casino. The suite was outfitted rustically, with knotted exposed beams, furs tacked to the walls, throw rugs, electric fireplaces made of rounded stones set in concrete, and many other accoutrements of roughing it in climate-controlled splendor. There was a spiral staircase leading to a second tier. Upstairs was a leather couch occupied by two barely clad women—part of the trio that had exposed their breasts at the concert—playing a video game that involved growling, screams, and machine-gun fire.

Someone had opened the heavy drapes on the main cathedral window, some six feet across at its base. The milky gray dawn frosted the room in its cold light, belying the eighty-plus degrees heat outside. And this was the cool part of the day.

Galileo Lawson was playing chess with Desmond Lee, the band's blistering bass player. Lawson had changed clothes since Chainey had seen him last. He was clad in oversized cotton shorts and a T with C.L.R. James's face silk-screened on it, and his dreads had been pulled back in a ponytail.

Through a door to the right, and up a rise of slaglike steps, a man and a woman were getting frisky in the Jacuzzi.

"You're Chaney and she's Solomon." The King had just captured a bishop and pointed the piece's head at the two women.

"Why do you think Khali had Jeffries killed?" Chaney let her gaze settle briefly on a large brother in overrun boots and a 5X extra-long shirt. He sat at a glass table toward the back of the room on another rise, near a Roland piano. Quietly and conscientiously, he peeled an orange with a knife. The blade was big enough to give a rhino pause.

King D scrunched his features as his opponent moved his knight to rook four. "I don't think she actually planned the deal. She ain't that connected." He moved his queen to protect the knight.

Chaney took a seat in a director's chair. Solomon dropped down onto a bean bag in front of a cylindrical lava lamp that she moved aside to get a better view. "But you think she's an opportunist and was used in the hit?" Chaney crossed her legs.

"Again, exactly, why is it that Victoria is on my jock for me to talk to you?" King D captured one of Lee's pawns.

"Because I'm going to get your shit back, the benjamins you put down on your boy. Why do you think I was there when you showed up?"

King D blinked and bobbed his head up and down, then held his mouth open in a silent laugh. "Oh, why didn't you say so?"

Chaney held her arms open. "Now that I have your attention for a few minutes?"

"No doubt." King D's knight was taken and he countered with the move he'd been setting up two plays back. "Check, homie."

"Fuck," the other man muttered.

"Heh, heh. Now what up, tall and firm?"

"You want to talk about it privately?"

"It's some of their bling-bling too." King D swept a hand in a semicircle, taking in those gathered. "Besides, we don't roll with that chief-and-crew shit."

"Not much, at least," Lee cracked. He got his king out of check but had to expose his own knight.

"Fine," Chaney responded. "This all have to do with Jeffries and your sports management firm?"

King D looked up from studying the board. "He was getting shuck of that bullshit soon; did you know that?"

"How do you know this?" Solomon put in.

"How you think?" The rapper moved his rook but didn't take his hand off the piece. "I'm not using a medium around here, Chainey. My man and me had a couple of meetings, that's why he came to me in the first place."

"Came to you?" Solomon was making notes.

"More or less." King D put the rook back in its original position and moved his knight instead. "What matters is that Tyler was trying to figure out the best way to get out from under the high heels of Naomi. Again, he was grateful for all they'd done for him, but he'd done shit for them too. What really went down was, they made each other, like a weird-ass version of Ali and Cosell."

Solomon wasn't sure that analogy held up but said, "So where does Khali fit in?"

"She and the Nymnatists worked this together?" Chainey blurted.

"You know what a gut check it would have been for the Numb-Nutters to have Jeffries bounce from their camp?"

"You sure you're not letting your dislike for Naomi project all manner of bad things on them?" Chainey questioned.

"You tell 'em, Des." King D winced as the guitarist took his bishop.

"The word is that Khali is a stone media ho. I got some peeps who are sho' nuff fo' real with the anarchist-syndicalist thing, right? Like these dudes, and I mean some hardcore women too, who don't just do their thing for the cameras in Seattle at the WTO and whatnot. They get all up in corporate America's face, civil defense, all that on the regular."

Chainey looked at Solomon, who said, "Civil disobedience."

"Right," Lee went on. "These are the ones who do the grunt work, the meetings, the back and forth arguing, organizing, sacrificing, and don't look to get their names on the lips of Arianna Huffington at the next coffee klatch she's throwing to help out Mumia."

"But your girl Ashford, the self-appointed sub-commandante, pimps on these good folk to build up her name like she was the bomb. You know she sold the rights to her life story to New Line Cinema?"

Solomon put in, "You've financed some direct-to-video gangsta joints, King."

"True, true," he acknowledged. "I won't pretend we don't wrestle in the capitalist pits. It's not like we're purists, but, again, we understand that shit. But we damn sure stand on our thing, not on somebody else's and call it ours." King D's eyes gleamed with glee and his queen swooped on Lee's rook, putting his king in checkmate.

"Ain't this about nothing?" Lee knocked his king over in defeat.

"You think they call me the King for sport, huh?" Lawson was up on his toes, swaying to and fro as he taunted his friend. The breaking light of the sun spilled across his back and spread over the thick carpet like spilled luminescent paint.

Chainey asked, "What about Moya Reese, King? She in the mix in this too?"

He danced closer to her.

Then it seemed as if the sequence was simultaneous, but in hindsight Chainey recalled with absolute clarity the order of events. The question was just out of her mouth when the door to the suite banged open. In poured five young women. They were either in short shorts or miniskirts, but they all had on platform shoes. One of them, Chainey's color with straight pressed hair, was holding a CD jewel pack aloft like it was a sweepstakes ticket.

"King, King," the pretty young woman was yelling vociferously, "You've got to hear us. Just let me play the title cut and—"

Chainey was up and had taken a step toward the newcomers. King D was laughing, enjoying the tableau as he moved and swayed. The double-wide brother who'd been peeling his third orange was, like many men his size, faster than one would assume at first glance. He was within range of the Furious Five when the plate glass boomed inward. A jet of red and bits of flesh erupted from King Diamond's chest and he fell to his knees. His handsome face was sunken, as if strings were pulling at it from inside.

Chainey spun around and bent down, grabbing at her ankle and the gun.

"King, King," Desmond Lee wailed as he leapt on top of his fallen comrade like a soldier during a firefight. But his words were lost to the chorus of screaming the Furious Five were performing.

Chainey had her piece. She and Solomon crawled and reached the curtains at the same moment. Deftly, they pulled the drapes shut over the jagged hole where the glass had been.

"The ambulance is coming," someone shouted.

"What the fuck, what the fuck?" one of the Furious Five was muttering. She walked back and forth on a small area of the rug.

Chainey peered out through a sliver where the drapes came together. The shot had most likely come from the Turnberry Towers, the luxury twin condos across the way.

"See anything?" Solomon said hoarsely.

"No." She kept looking. "There, maybe. I see an open sliding glass door on the—I don't know—fortieth, forty-third floor. Tell Lambert when he gets here, Rena."

"Let me guess, you're—"

"That's right," Chainey said, already sprinting for the door.

"Hey, wait, goddammit," the very big man shouted, reflexively reaching for the ex-showgirl.

Chainey easily eluded him and vaulted into the oddly deserted hallway.

"Aw, hell no, it ain't going down like that. Your ass got some answers to my questions to deliver." The freight hauler of a man was rumbling steadily down the corridor. Chainey considered shooting him in the knee, but unfortunately there was no way her insurance was going to cover that.

She bounded off a wall and went left. He was gaining ground. Chainey got to the stairwell and yanked the door open. She went up, not down. Home Fries could probably bench press four and a half, but he damned sure didn't push himself doing a set of stairs. Conversely, Chainey's workout last week had included several rounds up and down the bleachers at the University of Las Vegas track. Plus factor in a certain amount of beer and Courvoisier he might be imbibing. She was on the forty-third floor, the top, and could hear his puffing echoing a floor below.

Chainey ran into the hallway and got lucky. She could hear an elevator door ping open and followed the sound around a corner. She stepped into the car, joining a couple dressed in running shorts.

She'd put the ultra-compact back in its holster. Breathing through her mouth, Chainey punched the button for the second floor and dabbed at the sweat on her forehead with the palm of her hand. The joggers pretended she wasn't there. The car made another stop, but there was no one there. Chainey tamped down the anxiety worming into her stomach as the elevator got going again. Finally she calmly walked out onto the mezzanine, and the car's door started to close, the early-morning exercisers bestowing a bewildered glance on her.

From where she was, Chainey could look out on the main entrance below. So far, no cops. She got to the ground floor and out through a side entrance. Three police cruisers had arrived, their sirens blaring through the morning breeze. She assumed Lambert was behind the wheel of one of the cars. An ambulance also wheeled to a halt, and the ex-showgirl disappeared into the throng that had gathered. People were looking in many directions, up and down, like a thousand-headed beast.

She worked her way through the bodies only to find the front doors of the Turnberry locked. Guards were posted in the lobby, and one of them shook his head at Chainey, pointing at the release bar. All right, presumably the shooter hadn't come that way. And the guards certainly didn't act like they thought the shot had come from their establishment anyway.

She zigzagged back through the gathering crowd. Everybody seemed to have a theory, and some even claimed to have been eyewitnesses. What the hell was it about groupthink that so often led to brain damage?

She went along a walkway bordering the grass to the right and saw a familiar figure. Damned if it wasn't the man who'd been handing out flyers earlier. Was he her Lee Harvey Oswald, like in that *JFK* movie she'd seen with Kevin Costner? Or was he the real deal, his cover the whack conspiracy nut hiding the whack conspiracist willing to carry out his paranoid notions?

Passing within easy reach of him, she discarded the idea. This clown was busy trying to convince passersby that the shot was the signal for the silent Blackhawks to move in. The guy still had a bunch of flyers and was trying to give them away. He'd have about as much success as he would giving away nude pictures of Tom Arnold, she thought. If he was a cold, calculating assassin, he was a damned good actor.

There were two service doors that Chainey found didn't open from the outside. She looked around. At the red curb on this side of the street were a phone company truck and a plumber's pickup. The killer might still be in the building; he might even be a resident. But the odds were that the guy simply came down an elevator and blended into the terrain of the populace. And no doubt he'd stashed his rifle or just dropped it in plain sight, wiped clean and untraceable.

Something disturbed the crowd behind her and she whirled to see two cops rushing forward like linebackers.

"You're under arrest," the first one said. She had a runner's lithe form, and her hair was pinned behind her head. The arm that held her nine-millimeter gun steady on Chainey was dotted with freckles.

"I was trying to—" She'd halted and was holding her hands above her head.

"Save it," the partner blared. He was thick-bodied but moved with the ease of someone used to putting his body through its paces. He jerked Chainey's arm down and around and propelled her against the side of the condos. "Spread," he commanded.

The woman officer stepped forward to pat her down.

"I've got a piece in a holster on my ankle. I've got a permit for it."

The woman cop, covered by her partner, took the rig off and continued patting Chainey down. They handcuffed behind her back and marched her toward the Riverhead.

"That'll teach your jackrabbit ass." The very big man smiled gregariously as he stood outside the casino, enjoying her plight.

Chainey was taken back to the suite.

Chief Lambert was standing on one side. The drapes had been opened about a foot. The sheriff glared at Chainey, then returned his attention to the wounded rapper. Two EMTs had stabilized the King, who had been secured to a collapsible stretcher. For a moment the people in the room watched the rhythmic rising and falling of his chest, and the oxygen mask attached to the man's now ashen face. Solomon wrote frantically. One of the other cops in the room nervously picked at an invisible scab on his forearm.

"We're going to get him to surgery over at Desert Springs, but his signs aren't bad for a man who's been greased with a high-powered round." The EMT who'd spoken took the lead and, with his partner, carried the wounded man out of the room. The very large man went along, as did Desmond Lee.

"Ramos, you go with him and stay there until you hear from me, hear?" Lambert addressed the cop who'd been absently plucking at his arm.

Ramos left without a word. Lambert raised his Motorola portable radio to his mouth and talked into it. "Stevens, DuPree, talk to me, over."

"We're on the floor now, Chief," a voice crackled on the receiving end.

"Call back when you've got something. Be careful, out." Lambert's arm descended slowly from his face, as if it were operating on half-power. No one said anything, but the video game continued its mayhem. "Chop him, tear out his guts," was heard over and over from the upper tier.

"Somebody shut that fucking thing off, please," Lambert asked politely and pointedly.

One of the women who'd been playing the game went double

time up the spiral stairs and did as requested. She flew back
down and stood at alert next to her equally scared friend.

Several minutes passed, then one of the cops reported in over
the radio. "Chief, this was the room all right. It was the twenty-
first floor, like you said." The chief's colorless orbs swung over to
Chainey, then back to the window he'd been looking out of as
he stood stone still. "The shooter was a pro; there's a spent shell
from a bolt action here. That means he wanted more punch,
that's for sure."

"The gun isn't there?" Lambert asked.

"No," came the reply, "but that doesn't mean he waltzed out
with it. There's too many people out on the street."

"Could have broken it down on the way out; stick it in a backpack and he'd be off to the races again." Lambert paused, a sour
taste seeming to have gathered in his mouth. "I'm sending
Clemmons and his bunch over with their kits."

"You don't want us to begin sweeping the building?" the police officer on the other end said.

"Captain Williams of the Guard and some of her squad
should already be in the lobby area. They're gonna work their
way up with some of the K-Nine crew. You two stay where you
are."

"Okay, out."

Lambert talked into the radio once more to send the evidence person to the Turnberry. Then he replaced the device on
his belt. "I can't say I'm particularly surprised to see you didn't
pay attention to my warning about the third time, Ms. Chainey.
You've had quite the merry-go-round ride these past few hours."

"Just trying to be a good citizen, Chief."

"Is that so? That why I found you kicking Khali's ass?"

"I subdued her, yes."

"I didn't then or now believe that bullshit about you looking
for her because you'd heard about some price on her head." He
was about to comment further but instead plucked his radio off
his belt and walked out of earshot. He talked into it and listened
to whoever responded to him on the other end. Then he came
back toward Chainey. "Take her bracelets off, Dave."

Dave was the athletic, thick-bodied one. He showed no emotion as he removed the handcuffs. Obviously they'd run a check on her conceal-and-carry permit and found that it was valid. She was sure he'd also found out more about her employment—or at least what it was rumored to be.

Lambert wiped a hand across his tired face but managed to dredge up a warm expression. "Unless you want me to put you in jail until we feel like taking the paperwork over to the courthouse, you better make good this time on what the fuck you're doing. I wanted Khali last time so it didn't matter what you told me." He twitched a nod at Solomon. "Her, it's obvious. But your story is what I'm interested in hearing. And I don't need to remind you, or anyone else in this room," he added, raising his voice, "that the period of martial law has been extended due to this latest incident."

All eyes were on the chief.

Chainey knew she couldn't talk about the missing cash she'd found. She also couldn't mention finding Reese's body as, apparently, the police hadn't yet. "I'm working with Riverhead Sports and Entertainment Enterprises in a professional capacity." If she glanced over at Solomon, she was going to crack up, and that would blow it for sure.

"Capacity?"

"Find out who stole a shipment of merchandise related to the fight."

"You're not a PI, Chainey."

"No, I'm not. But Truxon, Limited, my employer, is a licensed and bonded courier service, and I'm in charge of sensitive freight matters. Fortunately for us, the shipment wasn't handled by us, but that's why they called us in to take over."

Both of Lambert's eyebrows went up until they were almost touching the underside of his Stetson. "And I suppose Victoria Degault will verify this? That you're flitting here and there on the hunt for a box of baseball caps and T-shirts?"

"It's more involved than that. But, yes, of course she will," Chainey bluffed.

"I'll hold on to that for awhile," he said. "And this somehow brought you here to Lawson's suite?"

"He's got a sports management arm," Solomon said. "He was set to sign up Jeffries, who was looking to make a break with the Nymnatists."

"That's right," one of the crew responded. "King and the champ had a couple of meetings about the shit. I mean, deal."

Lambert hit the brim of his hat with a flick of his index finger. "We'll have some coffee and sweet rolls, hell, even a little fruit, sent up. This is Vegas, after all." He grinned to himself. "Everybody will be . . . chatted up, and then we'll see what we're going to do next. I suggest you cop some squats until we call you." He marched into one of the other rooms to have some privacy while he made his calls. The other cops took up positions around the room, their demeanor and posture letting everyone know to settle in.

CHAPTER TEN

Two and a half hours later, Chainey and Solomon were back on the Strip. In the daylight, the state of emergency seemed much less pronounced than it had during the evening and early-morning hours. That was probably how it was in real coup situations, Chainey reflected dryly. As long as the hot water worked and you could still get your 7-Eleven Big Gulp, who cared who was running the show? But threaten to take those creature comforts away and you'd have full–on insurrection on your hands.

They walked along until they found a coffee shop and were mildly surprised to find it sparsely occupied. They got a booth.

"So, which way to jump next?" Solomon said after the waitress took their order.

"I don't know, Rena, but we've got to find out how this all ties into Moya getting killed."

"You're not so tough sometimes, Chain," her friend said, poking fun at her.

"Who is?"

"Okay, from what King D said and what I've learned, it definitely doesn't seem like Khali and her gang would do something like these murders." Solomon rubbed one of her eyes with the heel of her hand.

"Let's go with that."

The waitress brought their coffees and plastic tumblers of water.

Chainey continued, "Lambert must also be figuring this another way, what with her and a few cohorts in lockup."

"Unless it's some stone-cold, hardcore, hope-to-die mufu that she's set in motion and can't be turned off. The Terminator of the Save the Dolphins set," Solomon opined.

"A hook-up with this Black Jihad?"

"Nothing is too crazy, Chain. But that reminds me, I still need to find brother Muhammad."

"You're gonna have enough for a book by the time this madness is finished."

Their breakfasts arrived and they waited until the server went away again to continue.

"Or at least," Solomon quipped, "material for one of those movies you always see playing on HBO Three at whack hours. Maybe they'll get Vivica Fox and Nia Long to play us." She forked in some eggs.

"I'll save the argument for later as to who plays who," Chainey snorted. "But you said you hadn't heard of the Black Jihad before." She had some of her oatmeal.

"Just 'cause I work at an alternative paper don't mean I'm any more on top of this shit than the reporters at the *New York Times*. In the world of MP3 and Linux, things change awfully fast."

"Or that you're getting over the hill and don't want to admit you may be out of the cool loop."

"Whatevah . . ." Solomon enjoyed her eggs.

"But Anson likes to think of himself as forever with it, doesn't he?" Chainey persisted.

"I get the drift." Solomon got out her cell phone and dialed her boss. "He got a cab back to the office to sleep it off. The lad knew he was drunk but kept insisting he didn't want to miss the action." She dialed and got the office answering machine. "I forgot it was Sunday," she said sheepishly and clicked off. Solomon tried another number.

Chainey gazed out the dingy window. "I know what you mean. It seems like we've been living inside a domed city or something." On the sidewalk a scuffle broke out between some grungers and several preppie-looking types. Onlookers were so inured to it all, they simply glanced at the participants and walked on.

"Yeah, like in one of those sci-fi Vertigo comic books my niece loves to read." Solomon held up a finger as the line connected. "Anson . . . sorry to disturb your slumber . . . uh-huh," she said, making a funny face as she listened. "That's what you get for drinking like you were twenty-three again. And you didn't even get laid."

Chainey sipped her coffee. It was pleasantly invigorating.

"Yeah, yeah," Solomon said, commiserating with her hung-over boss. "Look, me and Chainey are on to something, and if it breaks right, you're gonna love me more than you do already. You ever heard of the Black Jihad?" She bit off a corner of her toast as Hiss spoke. She made notes on her pad, then interjected several more questions. Finally Solomon ended the conversation with, "Okay, uh-huh, I understand. Thanks, and I'll check in later."

"Yes?" Chainey ate more of her spinach omelet.

"He says the Black Jihad first surfaced in Philadelphia during the GOP convention there. There were flyers around announcing the group, which claimed to be the shadows of the shadows."

Chainey frowned. "What the hell does that mean?"

"Something about making sure the pure stayed pure. And that pretenders to the cause would be excised. Anson kept a file on them and had a copy of the flyer that went around in Philly."

"I guess if they operate on that kind of logic, then going after Muhammad fits in."

"Or Jeffries," Solomon noted. "Anson also said that the activists in Philly pegged the Black Jihad to be a put-up job, a front for agent provocateur–type stuff, like the old days of the FBI disrupting the Panthers and the civil rights movement with COINTELPRO." She cocked her head and chewed. "There might be something to that; the cops in Philly and L.A. sprinkled undercover among the demonstrators."

"Have they shown up anywhere else?" Chainey signaled the

waitress for more coffee. There was going to be no rest today either.

"Supposedly the Black Jihad was responsible for some attacks against some Larouchites in Chicago and Boston."

"The whats?'

"Lyndon Larouche's followers. He's the nut who runs for president every now and then. He claims Henry Kissinger and the queen of England are behind the worldwide drug trade. He did time for securities fraud."

"Heh," Chainey snorted. "And now they're supposed to be after a guy 'cause he's adopted blackness?"

"I didn't write their manifesto. Now, nobody's ever really been able to ID who these people are, let alone the leader, club-house, none of that."

"The shadows," Chainey repeated.

"Exactly," her friend concurred.

"What did Anson say about them being here?"

Solomon nibbled more of her dry toast. "He'll check around, but he said it could be that the Black Jihad has cell groups that operate independently of each other, or this could even be a splinter group."

"Wouldn't they want a different name then, to differentiate themselves?"

"Maybe one faction is out to undermine another. Muhammad is popular in the black community. He's seen as a unifier between black and brown, but others criticize him for pimping on the black thang, ya heard me."

"Please." Chainey drained her coffee. "Shooting King was a desperation play," she conjectured. "Now the town is gonna be locked up tight until they find the gunman. But I don't think Muhammad is the mastermind behind all this."

"And I'm not sure King D was the intended target," Solomon emphasized.

Chainey's lips formed an *O*. "Me?"

She jabbed at Chainey with the blunt end of her fork. "He was doing his little victory dance, right? When the shot went off, he'd moved in front of you."

"Not directly."

"But we know the shot came from an upward angle. I don't know what that means in the dynamics of bullet travel, but I'll bet that's a millisecond or so slower than a shot at no angle. The sniper could be gunning for you 'cause he figures you know something."

"Like what?" Eddie McDaniels's face appeared in her mind.

Solomon moved a shoulder. "Could be he thinks you saw something at Moya's hotel room."

"Why not take me out then?"

"Who knows? Too exposed, didn't have the rifle handy."

"Moya was killed with a pistol."

"Okay, didn't have that around either. Or better yet, figured to play the percentages and see who and where you went after the motel."

"And I didn't go to the cops because I know they'd hold me and getting to the . . . well what I had to find, that trail would get colder and colder." She was starting to regret letting McDaniels go. And that she'd been selfish when it had come to doing the right thing about her friend's murder. Now she had to make it right.

"Following you around in this atmosphere"—she tapped the window pane—"wouldn't be hard."

"One step at a time, Miss Marple," Chainey remarked. "Why don't we hunt down your boy Muhammad?"

"Caprice was clear that wasn't going to happen."

"We're in the most expensive fishbowl there is, baby. If a couple of steppers like you and me can't find him, who can?"

"Sure you right." Solomon slapped an open palm against her friend's.

They left the coffee shop and hit the streets. The heat was climbing again, but it seemed to have little effect on the transient populace. Everybody had a destinaton in Vegas, Chainey mused. That was why they kept returning, looking for the one big, fabled score. In Vegas you could say anything and play any role; you had no past and your future was determined by chance. Vegas, at least the megabudget version, was the best drug there was. It consumed all your money, but the rush was instantaneous, and it occasionally kicked back a little, just enough to make you come back again and again. It was where great pugilist Joe Louis wound up as a greeter, and the Liberace Museum was considered sedate.

"Do we call our godmother?" Solomon asked.

"Might as well. I assume Muhammad and company were staying at the Riverhead too."

Solomon tried her numbers for Victoria Degault but only got voice mail. "We could try the spa," she conjectured.

"She must be gone from there by now. Let's go ask."

At the Riverhead, from a concierge who knew Chainey did work for Degault, they learned that Caprice had checked himself and his fighter out at around three A.M. And no, she didn't have a clue as to where they went.

"He's still on the Strip or thereabouts. I know he wouldn't be holed up in a second-rate place," Solomon observed as the two stood on the edge of the main gaming floor. "He likes the first-class life he's aspired to all this time."

"Yep," Chainey agreed. "But unless we're going to make like those hoochie mamas who busted in on us in the King's room, I can't see going from casino to casino, begging the staff to tell us if they've seen him."

Solomon poked Chainey's arm. "You know, like in those shows on USA cable where one of the characters says the thing that rings a bell for the other one."

"Girl, you trippin'."

"Could be." She began to check through her notes. "I did some background work-ups on both the fighters, figuring it would be useful in whatever story I came up with."

"And . . . ?"

"Muhammad's squeeze wants to be an actress, or singer maybe it was."

"How original."

"I know, but I talked to her some. Moesha, Malina . . . no, here it is, Monique LaVentura."

"Oh, please," Chainey retorted.

"This is important, shit." Solomon giggled, stil gazing at her pad. "She told me she once did some dancing around town."

"You mean stripping."

"I took her implication to mean yes, that was the case. She also said she did some booty shaking in a few music videos."

The two were walking again along Las Vegas Boulevard and passed in front of one of the newest and, even by the high Vegas threshold, most flamboyant additions to the never-ending panorama. The Titanic Hotel and Casino would be impressive even to movie special-effects master Stan Winston.

"Damn, that's big," Solomon remarked as their minuscule forms walked within range of the beautiful and pretentious offering to global capitalism.

The construction was a carefully re-created beached version of the fabled ocean liner that had been the subject of novels, documentaries, feature films, and at least one irreverent poem often recited by Vegas resident Rudy Ray Moore. Moore was an old school black comedian who'd come of age playing the "Chittlin' Circuit." He'd honed his skills in theaters and other black venues with peers such as Red Foxx and Moms Mabley, who also worked during the days of Jim Crow and enforced segregation. Moore had created a persona, Dolemite, a modern-day urban bad man who riffed on the folklore of characters like Stagolee, Desmukes, and Petey Whitestraw. Dolemite was the star of several low-budget films Moore had made, and he had appeared in several rap videos too.

" 'Captain, captain, don't you know,' " Chainey suddenly blurted, " 'there's forty feet of water on the boiler room floor.' "

" 'Git back, ya dirty black,' " Solomon added, " 'we got a thousands pumps to take care of just that.' "

They both cracked up as people looked at them askance. " 'Shine on the Titanic,' " Chainey said shaking her head. "My Uncle Hiram used to recite the whole poem now and then. Especially after he'd had a few blasts of Old Grand Dad."

The Titanic was built as a response to the ever-increasing competition the city faced in its pursuit of visitors' dollars. In particular, Vegas needed to hold on to the lucre from California residents, who represented a third of the people who came to gawk and spend in Vegas. Native American casinos in the Golden State offered Neveda-style slot machines and blackjack. The spectacle factor had to be amped up constantly in Vegas so as to ensure a steady stream of patrons.

The Titanic Hotel and Casino certainly was amazing. From the ship—which rested on a moat of fake ice floes—there was a passageway that led into an iceberg that was the main area for gambling. The body of the ship contained hotel rooms, and the quartet of smokestacks were time-share condos. The gift shops offered everything from hokey plastic replicas to genuine silver scale models of the ship. The whole of it, ship, iceberg, and the Ice Village of shops, boat rides, and restaurants was on a twenty-six-acre parcel of land.

"Why anyone would think this overgrown tugboat would be an attraction," Chainey remarked off-handedly.

"It's on land, so right there they're one up on the poor schmucks who went down with the original," Solomon pointed out.

"Touché. So, are we going to prowl the meat clubs and get eyeballed by the droolers looking for our girl?" Briefly, Chainey wished that Lambert hadn't confiscated her piece.

"I got something better." Solomon put a finger on a place in her notes. "I know a guy who's directed some music videos she's been in."

"A ha."

Solomon's cell was dying, so they entered the Titanic to make some calls. They could have used Chainey's, but they wanted an excuse to see some of the interior. The phones were housed in booths designed to look like mini-staterooms. After that the two got a cab outside the lock-down zone and found themselves in a housing development in the northeastern end of town. The tract town houses were still under construction and the place was a maze of wooden skeletons and unpaved streets.

"What was here before?" Chainey asked as she and Solomon walked away from the cab and toward people, cables, and lights. Over a portable radio, Toni Braxton sang "Deep in My Heart."

"This is the desert, baby; nothing was here. We're making it up as we go along, you know that," her friend quipped.

"No," Chainey muttered, "something about this place . . ." But nothing solid formed and she let it slip back into the recesses of her mind. A Panaflex camera was pointed at a Mission chair on a woven rug, a standing lamp beside it. These items were an incongruous part of a set that looked like it was a starship's bridge.

Off to one side were three women in Victoria's Secret bras and panties casually chatting and sipping bottled juices. Lazing at the feet of one of the women was a Rottweiler that easily weighed 130 pounds.

"Hey now," a tall, lithe black man with brown-colored dreads said. He separated himself from a couple of others staring into a playback monitor. "Good to see you." He quickly kissed Solomon on the lips and hugged her.

The reporter introduced Chainey to the director, who went by the name of France. The three walked a little distance from the others to talk.

"So, when you gonna let me put you in one of my shoots?" Playfully, France leered at Solomon. "I can make you the next Lil' Kim."

"I ought to slap the mess out of you," she flirted. "I don't show these to just anybody, you know." As she spoke, she quickly waved at her breasts with a hand. "And we came here to talk business."

"And Monique is gonna be mentioned in your article?" Someone yelled a question to France, and he gave them an answer. "Sorry; now, what is it I get out of this if I help you out?"

"You better stop foolin' around, France." But she didn't mean it; she was enjoying their back-and-forth. Chainey tried not to look too irritated.

"I guess we'll negotiate those terms later."

"That's right," Solomon said.

"I get a mention in this piece?"

"Boy, this ain't about your career."

"Come on now. You know I'm trying to blow up in the features thang and every little bit helps."

"I'll see. First your info has to work out."

France got a concerned look on his face. "This don't make me a snitch, does it?"

"Do it?"

Chainey was two tics from slapping Solomon upside the head.

"I ain't about getting anyone on the spot," France said seriously.

"I told you, we only want to talk to her to get to her boyfriend. This is just for my article," she lied.

"You know where she is," Chainey declared.

He slid his browns over her. "That's right."

"Then don't be stingy," Solomon urged.

"Maybe I should call her first."

Solomon stomped like a spoiled child denied a treat. "Goddammit, France, we ain't trying to run up on her. But if you warn her, she'll bounce." She grabbed his shirtfront and pulled on it, tilting her face upward, closer to his. "Where the fuck is she?" Solomon whispered sweetly. They gave each other a smack on the mouth.

Hormones won out. "She's staying at my sister's place. When all the shit went down after Jeffries was shot, Muhammad naturally freaked out. She called me and asked where she could take him to chill. Said he had to be away from the Strip, but she didn't want to be too far from the haps either." He made a noncommittal gesture, then said, "My sister and the family are out of town for a few days, so I figured why not."

"She mention the Black Jihad?" Chainey interjected.

Quizzically he said, "That a new rap group?"

"It's not important," Solomon said. "How about that address?" She grabbed his hand. "And the number?"

He told her, and Solomon promised to call him later that day. Once again they exchanged a kiss. France walked back to his set and there was a squeal from one of the lingerie girls. The Rottweiler was now energized, bounding after a squirrel.

Walking back to the cab they'd asked to wait, Chainey noticed a corner of something in the freshly graded earth. She bent and moved away dirt with the flat of her hand. Behind them, they could hear a group of people trying to corral the dog, and others egging him on to catch the squirrel. But the animal had safely climbed up a 4-by-4.

"Why are you digging that traffic sign out?" Solomon asked in a piqued tone.

"It's not," Chainey commented as she tugged the metal sign loose. Once upon a time the sign had been white with black script lettering on it, bordered by red and blue stars. Now it was dented and scratched, and paint had chipped away with age.

"*Welcome to Lost Acres, Homes of the Future, Today,*" Solomon read. "This place was developed in the past," she remarked.

"Yeah, it was built in the early fifties, not too long after Levittown. There were several housing tracts completed, and even a main street with a bank and a movie theater." Chainey recited the words as if they were memorized from a textbook.

"How do you know that?"

"It's, ah"—she stood up, studying her find—"it's, ah, some stuff I looked up after Drew was killed."

Wilson McAndrews, the former owner of the Rye Breaker nightclub, was the man to see when you needed a favor in black Vegas, a much smaller community in those days. Or when you needed an emissary, someone to intercede on your behalf, when it came to dealing with the Strip's heavies. But Drew also had dreamed of one last big score. And he did it; he and a crew he put together ripped off the King Solomon's Mines, a theme casino operated by Isome Brand. Brand was the last of the old-school gangsters in the gaming business. He made Capone look like a scout master. McAndrews and Brand had, in their younger years, been friends upon their arrival from Kansas City in the '70s.

In the end, each man killed the other. The Mines were closed and eventually torn down. The Riverhead was built over the old site.

"I'll tell you about it a little later," Chainey said, taking the sign with her. The two women rode quietly for a time in the back of the cab. The driver was an older woman with platinum hair, a lone chandelierlike teardrop earring dangling from one lobe.

"Well," Chainey finally exhaled.

"He's a good guy," Solomon averred.

"How good?"

"About this good." She held her hands apart several inches.

"Oh, my." Chainey fanned herself with one of her hands.

"Oh hell yes," the woman with the lone earring chimed in, looking in the rearview mirror.

All three laughed. Soon their transport deposited them at their destination, a tidy Arts and Crafts frame house not far from McDaniels's apartment in southwest Vegas. The abode was from another era, and in the odd quiet that had descended on this part of town, it seemed as if the two women were in a time warp.

"What if we call her and see if she and Muhammad come running out?" Solomon wondered aloud.

"Let's knock." Chainey was heading for the enclosed porch. "You're starting to think too deviously, you know that?"

"Must be the company I keep."

"Ha, ha." A busted-out recliner squatted on the swept-clean concrete of the porch. A gray-and-brown cat lazed on the seat. Indolent, the creature didn't deign to turn its head at the two interlopers. Chainey rapped the back of her knuckles against the door.

"Yes?" came a tentative reply.

The tall ex-showgirl explained why they had come to see the boxer.

"We don't want no shit," was the response after Chainey had finished talking.

"It's not going to be long before some other journalist or snoop"—Solomon winked at her friend—"hunts you down, ya know what I'm sayin', Monique?"

They could hear a muffled exchange on the other side of the

door; then it was snatched open. Joaquin Muhammad stood with a hand on the doorknob, the other on his waist. "Okay," he said. He was dressed in a silk robe, the Polo logo prominent over a paisley field. Underneath he had on only loose dark gray sweatpants. The sockets of his eyes were bluish and a fine growth of whiskers covered his chiseled jaw.

"May we come in?" Chainey asked in a finishing-school manner.

"You're here." But he stepped aside.

The two women entered a living room, where the smartly decorated furniture wasn't best in gloom. The shades were pulled down and the only light came from a rectangular side window with old-fashioned glass louvered slats.

"Might as well let some light in and set the table, honey," Monique's voice called from behind the kitchen's swinging door. The crackle and aroma of meat frying was present.

The fighter grumbled something and ambled into the kitchen.

"I guess he's not what you'd call a morning person," Solomon said out of the corner of her mouth.

"You might be funky too if you were the possible target of an assassin," she replied quietly.

"So we don't tell him about King Diamond?"

"Not if we want him to talk," Chainey answered.

The heavyweight stepped back into the front room, and it was as if he'd been given an injection of effervescence. "Excuse me for being all tacky and mush-mouthed, ladies." He displayed ideal pearlies and adjusted the belt of his robe. "Have a seat at the table while my girl gets the grub together." Muhammad whirled in a precise semicircle and then wagged a finger. "Now don't misunderstand"—he craned his neck around at them— "she likes to cook."

"We didn't think you were being sexist, champ," Solomon said, managing not to bug out her eyes.

"Good. I want my fans to know I ain't no dog, like some of those playaz out here." The more he was awake, the more easily he slipped in and out of urban inflection. "You know I ain't got nothing but love for the females."

"Right on," Chainey said evenly.

Walking into the dining room, Muhammad opened the drapes on a rear wall, revealing a sliding glass door. Beyond that was a compact landscaped garden with Yucca cacti and other succulents, limestone croppings, and arrangements of lilies and wheat stalks.

"Shit," Muhammad said appreciatively, "I didn't notice that last night." Absently, he scratched at his crotch as he faced the flora. Then he turned back and made a gesture, as if signaling the start of a foxhunt. "Please, please, sit down."

The two took chairs around a matching table. There was a glass on top of it that smelled of stale whiskey, and several pieces of unopened mail. Muhammad went back into the kitchen and soon returned with a pitcher of orange juice and three drinking glasses from the same set. He held the glasses with his fingers and thumb holding them together and set all of them down with a thump. He poured and finally sat down. Monique was half humming and half singing, off-key, a Rah Digga number as she went about her culinary deeds.

"Exactly what can I tell you? You both work for this *Las Vegas Express?*"

Solomon explained again how their objectives coincided.

Muhammad looked toward the kitchen, as if he was receiving inspiration via telepathy. That failing, he said, "So you wanna know who's tryin' to run up on me?"

"You think it's this Black Jihad?" Solomon had her pad out and had also produced a mini-DAT recorder from her purse. "You don't mind, do you?" she asked, jabbing a finger at the machine.

"Naw, quiet as it's kept, I like being taped. I tape myself, practicing my public speaking and shit. Don't want to come off as just another mumblin', stumblin' pugilist," he proudly proclaimed. "As to that business," he continued, leaning forward, interlacing his surprisingly thin fingers, "yeah, I gotta admit this shit has got me bugged, no doubt."

Solomon scribbled. "Besides the note on Monique's car, have you received any other threats?"

"Don't you think blowing the top of my man's head off was a fuckin' threat?"

Before either woman could respond, Monique entered the room with a plate in each hand. Piled on one, like a lopsided tower, was a stack of pancakes. In the other was a generous helping of eggs and sausage. "Don't trip, y'all, this is turkey and chicken meat." She set the plates down and kissed the boxer. "We can't be havin' no one named Muhammad grubbin' on that nasty-ass swine."

"I know you still sneakin' them pork chop sandwiches," her old man teased. "I can taste it on your tongue."

"That's not the only thing I've been putting on my tongue." She crinkled her nose at him and sat down. "Y'all better come on and dig in," she announced. The young woman stabbed at one of her magazine-layout golden brown hotcakes. "Way I was raised, ya gotta go for yourself when it comes to chowin' down." She raised the pancake on the end of her butter knife and deftly placed in on her plate.

The other two explained that they'd just eaten. After a few moments Chainey stated, "It does seem that Tyler Jeffries was the intended target, Joaquin."

"Look," he countered, a sizeable portion of pancakes on his fork, "I know something about these kinds things." He chewed on his food, then added, "This kind of death squad action ain't new to me, feel what I'm sayin'? I've had cousins and friends disappear—only to have their bodies show up in a field or floating down the Lempa River back in El Salvador."

"You think this is political?" Solomon asked earnestly.

"The State Department backed ARENA, the right-wingers in El Salvador, right?" Muhammad cut another helping of pancake for himself.

"But the government doesn't gain from Jeffries's death," Chainey observed. "Hell, he was a goodwill ambassador for them."

"See, see," Muhammad said over his food, "that's my goddamn point. I ain't." He swallowed. "This Black Jihad thing could just be a smokescreen to cover up the real forces out to chill my shit."

Monique let her eyes briefly shift to the ceiling as she ate. Apparently this perspective wasn't new to her.

"I'm not exactly following, Joaquin." Chainey had some juice.

"I speak for a generation, yo," he uttered guilelessly. "My coming on the scene has rejuvenated the boxing world not since Ali or the early days of Tyson. Nobody turned out for Holyfield or Lennox Lewis like they have for my fights. That's not brag," he proclaimed, downing his food. "The gate and ancillary fees for worldwide bear me out." He looked at Solomon for confirmation.

"I heard from a friend at *Sports Illustrated* that at least sixty million was estimated to be generated when you added in all the stuff coming off the fight." She continued to make notes on the pad next to her plate.

"Like for instance," Muhammad said, "King Diamond was supposed to use some live recordings from his concert last night and some studio tracks with me and Jeffries on a new CD. Regardless of who won."

"Really?" Chainey and Solomon exchanged a look as she sipped her coffee.

"Plus lunch boxes; I got two cameos lined up for TV shows set around the fight, all kinds of mad shit was on the line last night." As he talked, Muhammad held up a finger and counted off. "Now all that's shaky since Jeffries got blasted."

Solomon pointed with her pen. "So now you think it was he who was the target?"

Muhammad gave her a vexed expression, as if being made aware of his contradiction was sacrilege. "Again, it messes with me, now don't it?"

"Yeah, but he's the one who's dead," the reporter said.

"And they ain't gonna find out who did it, neither," Monique contributed. "They never do in situations like this."

Chainey informed them of Sub-Commandante Khali's capture.

"She's just a fall guy like they always have," Monique sneered. "You know, it took someone with sho' 'nuff connects to get the gunman in and out of that arena. They didn't jus' stroll up there with the rifle hidden in a blanket. Shit." She ate more of her food.

"We don't think she did it either," Solomon put in, "but it also seems it's greed behind this and not political motivation. No offense to you and what you represent, Joaquin," she added, massaging his ego.

"Yeah"—he rubbed his chin thoughtfully—"but who? If it was them Pneumatic motherfuckahs—" He and Monique cracked up before he could finish his sentence.

"You so crazy." She fed him a piece of meat with her fork. The two locked eyes on each other and would have skipped off to more private quarters if they'd been alone.

Monique finally said, "That silly-ass chick who leads them hummers may be nuts, but she damn sure knows how to read a balance sheet."

"Well, that's what I was gonna say, baby." The prize fighter put a reassuring hand on her knee. "They might have had a hand in this scandalous shit."

"Why do you say that?" Solomon eagerly wrote away. She, like Chainey, shared that opinion, among others, but was curious to hear his take on the possibility.

"You did notice that Jeffries's wife, the dentist, wasn't around?" Muhammad sat back, clearly enjoying his role of teacher/prognosticator.

Chainey and Solomon shrugged.

"That's 'cause him and the good doctor ain't been sharing no body fluids for a few months."

"How do you know that?" Solomon cut in.

"You come to me, right?" He spread his hands wide, the loose sleeves of the robe slipping down, exposing his sinewy arms. He was built like a painting by Italian Renaissance artist Raphael come to life. "I'm the one in the game, ain't I?"

"Yeah," Monique mouthed, "Joaquin knows what's what. Tell 'em about Moya, honey."

He smiled at her, the Burns and Allen of the hip-hop set. "I was just about to talk about that, baby girl."

Chainey suppressed the smile about to split her face. If she dared gaze over at Solomon, she'd lose it for sure.

"So the dentist and the boxer had been separated?" Solomon kept her face toward her notes so as not to even peripherally notice her friend's expression.

"You damn skippy." Muhammad plucked a sausage from his plate with his fingers and noshed on its end. "The way me and Juno heard it around was she was always the one who was the big-time numb-nutter. So them two having a split was also a way my man Jeffries could get out from under them fools."

Chainey tapped the rim of her coffee cup. "And Moya was in this mess?"

"She came up to see the champ at his training camp a couple of times. You did see that diamond pendant she wore, right?"

Alert, Chainey questioned, "How do you know I saw her?"

"Monique did." He jerked his head at his girlfriend.

She shook her head vigorously, finishing up a bite of eggs. "I saw you two walking up to the skybox entrance. Then when I saw you two roll up here"—she pointed to one of the front shades. "I peeked out and told Joaquin I'd seen you before and where. That's why we let y'all in from jump."

"Jeffries gave Moya that necklace?" Chainey asked.

"And not 'cause they liked to hold hands and go sightseein'," Monique amplified.

Chainey leaned forward. "And she knew he was looking to make a break with the Nymnatists?"

"The way I understand it, yeah." Muhammad had poured himself more orange juice and drained the glass in one motion.

"You should tell him." Solomon picked up her recorder to check the tape.

Chainey told Muhammad about the attempt on King Diamond's life.

"Could be that bitch really believes she's God or somethin'," Monique opined. "Looks like she's out to eliminate anybody who has anything to do with Jeffries."

"What I say," Muhammad exclaimed, standing and stretching. "I wouldn't be surprised that them knock-heads be all tied up with some secret branch of the CIA or what have you. Look how the U.S. supported the contras."

Irritated, Chainey growled, "The Nymnatists couldn't hardly be a creation of anything except Naomi's imagination."

He scratched his washboard of a belly. "Uh-huh. That cold-eyed bastard she got as her head of security. He was an army Ranger, right?" Muhammad didn't wait for a reply. "What if I told you the Rangers also made excursions into El Salvador and Guatemala on orders of the State Department in the Seventies and Eighties? Shit I know about since I was a kid."

"I'd say there would be validity to that," Chainey acknowledged.

"There is Haulsey's Panama connection," Solomon contributed. "It's not listed on his record that he qualified to be a sharpshooter, but I bet he knows which end of a rifle to point."

"If Naomi is behind this," Chainey argued, "then I'm betting it's more like Monique said. She couldn't have Jeffries make a break because that would be bad for business. She sends Haulsey or somebody after King Diamond also to teach him a lesson."

"And she kills Moya because she was encouraging Jeffries to leave the order," Solomon finished.

Chainey held up her hands. "People with egos like she must have do nutty things."

"And on that note . . ." Muhammad stood behind Monique's chair. "Me and my lady are gonna wish you all well in your search, article, et cetera." He waved a hand like the emperor in the movie *Gladiator*. His big hands began to rub his woman's shoulder blades. Obviously getting packed was not their first order of business after breakfast.

"When are you going to leave town?" Solomon got up too.

"I ain't gonna be here," he shot back. "I damn sure am not gonna be a target for the nitwits or whoever the fuck are poppin' high-velocity rounds into people."

"We appreciate your time." Chainey rose and stuck out her hand, and the man shook it vigorously.

Solomon inquired, "What does Jeffries dying mean in terms of your status?"

He grinned, shaking a finger at her. "That's one of them 'Matlock' kinda things, huh? See how I answer it, trip my scheming ass up, then I break down and confess."

"No, really, I'm just curious," she said innocently.

"I actually don't know. Juno figured it would mean the title is vacated, and me and probably Sugar Shack Harris would duke it out for the crown."

"But you'd get the bigger purse," Solomon remarked.

"Yeah, so I capped everybody to make sure that would happen."

"Thanks," Solomon reiterated.

"No thang. Make sure you spell my name right." He and Monique got up and walked toward the bedroom, murmuring to each other. He called from the bedroom door. "And, ah, I know both of you are gonna be cool about not saying where you found me?"

"Nobody will hear anything from us," Chainey agreed. She and Solomon went out into the sun. Across the street, several Latino children, too young for regular school, played with plastic tricycles in a yard going to dirt. Looking around at the modest homes and cracker box apartments, the two could have been in any working-class area in any city in the USA. It was as if the Strip was merely the stuff of urban legends told to amuse and entertain the struggling masses; stories to keep them distracted from the grind of their existence. That despite the fact that the illusion of promise was less than seven miles away, it might as well be a continent away in distance and availability.

Walking, Chainey couldn't shake the apprehension that the resolution of this business was going to involve more rounds in the chamber, more shots squeezed off.

CHAPTER ELEVEN

"What the fuck?" the man swore, barely an inflection of animosity in his throat. His green eyes were as serene as a frozen lake on the front of a Hallmark card as he listened to the party on the other end of his cell phone. The subdued man's pickup was atop one of the rises of Wilson's Cliffs. Below him lay Spring Mountain Ranch State Park. He'd left his car not far away, at the motel in Bonnie Springs.

"I have to be certain," the man responded quietly and assuredly when the speaker had let up. He listened again, his body language betraying nothing of his inner disposition. "I am doing my job. You wanted Jeffries taken care of, he was taken care of. You're the one who got excited and killed the woman boxer. That action necessitated the assault against Lawson."

The expressionless eyes flicked toward the sound of a fly buzzing near his head, then resumed their composed gaze out the windshield. The green-eyed man spoke again. "You're failing to grasp what I've been attempting to get across to you. It was not my intention to shoot the rapper, but to neutralize that woman. Chainey, you understand?"

More excited words from the other end. The man's mouth twitched into a sardonic grin, then went flat once more. "I did not have a clear shot at her. Let's remember, it was you who stationed me in that apartment of yours at the Turnberry. The ideal spot to keep watch and hide in plain sight, you said." For the first time emotion crawled into his voice. It had a mocking, self-absorbed quality. "I saw an opportunity and took it, that's all."

Behind the turnout the pickup was perched on, several carloads of vacationers and sightseers went by in their vehicles. Though he never turned his head to look back, the soft-spoken man was aware of each car and van, cataloging where it was at any given moment on the road.

"Oh," he went on, "I'm the first one to admit it was calculated, as I already told you, but you will see the results, of that I am certain. I would have followed her after she was questioned and let go but had to deal with your incessant yammering." The derision in his voice surfaced again. The man yawned silently as he let his titular employer talk on. "Because you should be of the opinion that I know what I'm doing, that's what," he eventually said.

"Yes, yes I realize this is not a game, for you anyway." As if he was bored while waiting in line for a movie, the man studied his close-clipped nails while the other person bleated harshly over the line. "I am not coming unraveled; do I sound like I am some sort of hand wringer to you?" He heard the response. "If you believe that, then why'd you bring me in on it in the first place? Ah, there's no reason for you to offer an excuse, you see? You sought me out because you needed the killng done, didn't you? You sought me out because people like you always get someone like me to do your shit duty. Oh, please, please," the man deflected, "let's not entertain such a notion. We are joined shoulder and hip like Siamese twins, my friend. You are hardly in a position to compel me to do anything but what I determine to be in our best interests."

The man with the jade eyes was tired of the conversation and tired of small minds with money. How was it that the most brash, the least sophisticated managed to amass fortunes in this world? What kind of balance of the universe was that? The speaker droned on until the killer cut the words off. "This discussion and your tirade are at an end," he announced with finality. "The course has been set, the bet made, if you will.

"I will take care of the situation. By nightfall this Chainey woman will be dead and you will have no more excuses not to pay me the balance of the money due me. And though I have made sure this communication is bounced through a landline receiver to avoid detection, this is our last direct talk." With that, he clicked off the cell phone and made sure to erase its redial memory. Later, when he was done with this current assignment, he'd destroy the phone, and the disguised truck he was riding around in too.

Turning the engine over, he estimated what the fallout might be should he also slay the one paying him. His employer was getting nervous, second guessing the man's moves and the plan that had been set in motion. Killing those with deep pockets tended to cut down on repeat business, but it did ensure your continued freedom if they were getting squirrely. The gray fuzziness bubbled up in his brain and soothed him. It didn't make him uncomfortable as much as it used to. He guided the pickup truck, painted and lettered to look like one of those Southwest Bell inspector vehicles, out of the hills. As he drove along he worked out the steps he was going to take to tidy up his loose ends.

CHAPTER TWELVE

"Hey, that's Simon." Solomon pointed toward a man across Las Vegas Boulevard. He was putting away his cell phone and yawning, putting a hand to his mouth. The two had returned to the Strip after leaving Muhammad's abode.

Chainey called out the man's name, and he gestured at the two women. A police car passed along the quiet thoroughfare, and Kuwada crossed toward them in its wake.

The two women were near the Circus Circus casino and amusement park. A pair of twins, not more than eight years old, were pestering their parents to get them on the Rim Runner, the water ride inside the casino's Adventuredome.

"Chainey, as you prefer to be called." Kuwada kissed her on the cheek as he clasped her hand. "And you too, Ms. Solomon," he added.

"You been up all night?" Chainey stared into the man's face. It was lined, and there were bags under his eyes.

"Who can rest in all this?" The co-owner of the Ichibhan Arena swept a hand around him. "I've just learned there was an attempt on King Diamond's life."

Chainey told him about their involvement.

"Je-zus, you two go in for a lot of excitement, don't you? Man would have a hard time matching such expectations, wouldn't he?" His gaze lingered on Chainey.

"The *go* switch isn't always flipped on," Chainey responded. "A quiet time with a glass of wine and Sarah Vaughn in the background can be enticing as well."

"Most definitely." Kuwada showed strong teeth.

"But at the moment," Solomon broke in, "the hunt continues."

"She's after a cover story." Kuwada jerked his head at the reporter. "But what's your angle in all this, Chainey?"

"I'm supposed to find the cash you bet on the fight," she blurted out. She needed information from him and wasn't going to get it by dancing around the facts.

Solomon and Kuwada both let their mouths hang open for a few moments. "Forget the *Express,* I'm going to sell this to *Vanity Fair,*" Chainey's friend said joyfully.

"If you do, me and Simon and a few others will wind up at least indicted, if not jailed," Chainey relayed calmly. "Besides, I'll tell all when it comes time for you to write my biography."

"Like hell," Solomon said. "You know Victoria would do everything in her power to make sure that particular parts of your story never made it to print."

Unbeknownst to Chainey, Solomon had a pipeline to the owner of the Riverhead. The two had found it advantageous to share information on a two-way basis on a number of occasions. Maybe, she'd reflected now and then, the arrangement bruised the precepts of a reporter's ethics, but this was the real world. And as far as Solomon could tell, she was never going to perfect a method of successfully playing blackjack, so she had to do what she saw as necessary to make a living. Conversely, Chainey was right and she wasn't in any position to sever ties with Degault—yet.

"But this also has something to do with Moya's murder," Solomon commented.

"Can we talk about this in a more private setting?" Kuwada hastily suggested.

The trio wound up at the Neon City Golf Range, a virtual driving range situated on the second floor of the WWF Hotel and

Casino. Kuwada hadn't eaten and got a breakfast burrito. Solomon had more coffee.

"You think I can help you recover this missing loot?" Kuwada said.

"Not so much that," Chainey said. "I was more interested in what you and Tosches were going on about when I saw you dudes last night." She took a swing with the electronic club. Her digital ball had distance but sliced to the right into the holographic bunker.

A troupe of acrobats in costume from the Cirque du Soleil's Mystere Show at Treasure Island strolled past them. It was a testament to the blasé mindset that overtook all in Vegas that hardly anyone paid attention to their colorful jester outfits. This was simply one more aspect of the living tableau that was the town. The acrobats found an open spot and also began to work on their drives.

"Why is he a suspect?" Kuwada ate his burrito with gusto.

"Because I know how the robbery was done and who carried it out. Or, I should say, who was put up to it," she asserted. "But somebody had insider information, and the list of suspects is getting shorter."

Solomon didn't make notes. Chainey and Kuwada had forbidden her to write or tape their conversation. And she'd promised to only obliquely allude to this business about the missing wagers in her article. That didn't mean, though, that she didn't pay close attention to their words among the whooshing of electronic golf clubs and the occasional grunts of frustration.

Kuwada bobbed his head quickly. "May I?" he asked, and Chainey handed him the club. It was a normal driver with a titanium head. The feel and weight of the club had to be like it would be out on the links. There was a sensor in the shaft that corresponded with a sister unit in the tee, which was hinged, to the floor. The golfer hit a hollowed-out golf ball and the sensor chip in the ball was tied into a computer that instantly calculated angle, speed, and trajectory. The golf ball hit the jumbotron screen across the room and became a red blip in the virtual fairway.

His swing took the ball left but had a smoother flight han Chainey's. The simulacrum of the ball came to rest in a good position for par to the green. "You mean it's one of us three who engineered the rip-off?"

"Sub-Commandante Khali is slick, but she'd have to be clairvoyant to know about the money being in the safe." Chainey took the offered club and presented it to Solomon, who held up her hands, indicating that she didn't want it. Chainey got herself in position.

"It was a sure bet, and she could have simply guessed there would be money in the thing, given this big of a fight," Kuwada said. "You said she had a connection to this guy McDaniels through his brother. Could be he had more to do with putting the heist together than he let on."

Chainey got the head under the ball, and it sailed in a textbook arc onto the pixilated emerald expanse. "But would the crew take such a chance on an unknown factor?" she wondered aloud.

"This is Vegas, Chainey," he unnecessarily reminded her. "Rumors get around awfully quick in this place, I've found out." He stepped up, placing another ball from their bucket on the tab.

"We're all friends here," Solomon put in, "no need to be coy on our account. This is just background, right?"

"Right," he replied. He teed off, and a satisfying smile lighted his face as he watched the ball's flight.

Chainey folded her arms. "Well?"

"You asked what Tosches and I were going on about." Kuwada leaned the club against a column. "He's got an idea to turn the Yucca Mountains into a resort area."

"That's a hundred miles from here," Solomon pointed out. "And the government keeps threatening to turn that area into a nuclear dumping site just to mess with the inhabitants."

"There's plenty of local and state opposition," Kuwada countered, "and if someone can come in and make the state a better offer . . ." He gestured forcibly with his hands aloft, as if haggling over the price of tomatoes.

Chainey screwed up half of her face. "And this somehow has something to he do with the sub-commandante?"

"It has to do with Tosches not being as circumspect as he should be. I may be the spoiled son of money, but I've been around enough to know the moist smell of desperation."

"Money desperate?" Chainey asked.

Kuwada raised his eyebrows. "I think he's hungry to make his mark, Chainey. I think he's reached a certain age and is not content to run a casino that very soon will just be a memory like the Desert Inn."

"So he's behind the heist?" Solomon asked again.

"No, I'm not saying that." Kuwada shook his head vigorously. "What I am saying is, he's been going around trying to scare up investors in this idea of his, and I know he likes to impress people with what a big man he is."

"You heard around about the heist?" Chainey asked. In the stall next to theirs, a woman in up-in-her-crack hot pants and a see-through top squealed with excitement as she hit the ball. "Oh, baby, baby, I stroked it, stroked it good," she bubbled to her aging sugar daddy, who was festooned in rope gold.

"People I don't know came up to me the day before the fight, asking to get in on the action," he confirmed. "The word was out, Chainey. This won't be as tidy as you'd like."

"It never fuckin' is." She and Solomon exchanged a knowing look, and Chainey added, "Simon, what we really want to find out is who killed our friend Moya Reese."

Kuwada was about to bite into what was left of his burrito but halted. "I've been worrying about who killed Jeffries." He gobbled up the food. "Of course, my father was on the phone to me last night as soon as he got the news in Japan." He swallowed. "First I had to hear about how this only proves the disorder that is genetic in American culture and the danger that, well—" He purposely didn't finish his sentence.

"The danger of associating with dark folks, Simon," Chainey nudged.

"Something like that," he admitted, his cheeks reddening.

"You have to understand, he's definitely old school when it comes to understanding different cultures."

"Well, tell him next time you talk that so far it's been three black people who have been the target of this sniper," Chainey said.

Solomon finally swung, teeing off badly as they'd talked. "You don't think these attacks have been racial in nature? What if Anson was right, and the Black Jihad bit was just a ruse? It could be a white hate group out doing these killings."

No one said anything for several moments, the implication of the reporter's words making them uncomfortable and awkward. The spell was broken when the hoochie mama next to them yelped again in pleasure.

"I don't know what to say about that, Rena," Chainey offered weakly.

"It's worth pursuing," she countered. "Our Little Miss Sell-out Khali may be the conduit, but just not the way we were figuring. What if she really was some kind of put-up? What if she was really a supremacist and her job was to infiltrate the progressive movement?"

The sugar daddy was holding a cup of soda to the lips of his excitable friend with a be-ringed hand. She sipped and held on to the driver.

Kuwada's rejoinder was, "That's either crazy or too goddamn devious. If the white supremacist movement is getting that sophisticated, that's not good."

"I don't know," Solomon conjectured, "the cops infiltrated the protestors in Philadelphia and L.A. during the two major parties' conventions. And Anson remembers back when the Symbionese Liberation Army was running around, there was talk they were actually the creation of some branch of the U.S. intelligence services."

"For what purpose?" Kuwada was enthralled.

"What better way to smoke out true revolutionaries than by manufacturing supposed allies?" Solomon scratched a clear nail against her cheek. "The Weathermen were big on the FBI's Most-Wanted list in those days for campus bombings, torching banks, and whatnot." She gesticulated with her hand. "If that had some validity, then could be this does too."

"Big ifs," Chainey advanced. "The SLA was burned up on a house on Fifty-fourth Street in L.A."

They both gave her surprised looks.

"I saw it on the History Channel," she illuminated.

"That could have been a way to silence them for what they knew," Solomon said. "Last night, after talking with Anson, I dug up a clip from one of the old alternative weeklies in L.A., *The Reader*, I think it was. The piece theorized that Cinque, the leader, and those white women who were his crew began to take their roles seriously."

"The actors become the characters," Kuwada noted.

"Exactly. You keep foolin' with guns, holding up banks and snatching heiresses, that shit goes to your head." Solomon leaned on the shaft like it was a walking stick. "There's something to this," she murmured to herself, making up her mind.

"You're determined to pursue this angle?" Chainey asked.

"I'd be remiss, as they say, if I didn't," her friend responded.

"And what are you going to do, long and tall?" Kuwada did a stage leer at Chainey.

"I could have you escort me around to some of the people who came up to you, mentioning the bet." She grabbed his lower jaw with a hand and gave him a peck.

"Or not go around at all and catch up on our rest," Kuwada suggested.

"Well?" Solomon asked.

Chainey said with a sigh, "I better keep at it. I'm going to have a talk with Victoria about her boyfriend. You'd be surprised what a man will tell a woman." She blasted Kuwada with a heartbreaking smile, the showgirl's dazzle.

"Isn't that the truth?" Kuwada endorsed. He slipped an arm around Chainey's waist, and she allowed him to pull her closer. Their noses touched, and each looked deep in the other's eyes.

"Ah, kids . . ." Solomon coughed theatrically.

Kuwada finally said, "Since I don't want to play Keye Luke to your Warren Oland—" Their quizzical expressions cut him off.

"Number One Son to your Charlie Chan," he explained. "Plus, I've got a few matters of damage control I'd better attend to or my dad will have my head. And who knows? I might turn up something useful."

"Where will you be later?" Chainey touched Kuwada's unshaven cheek. She let her fingertips do a butterfly dance on his skin.

"I'll be around; you have my cell number. Where am I going to go except, hopefully, heaven later on?"

"That's so corny, but cute." She kissed him again, this time letting her tongue probe for his. And this time even the hot pants Nefertiti and her banker looked on. Solomon teed off, and her shot took the ball right into the sand trap.

Outside, the three prepared to go their separate ways.

"I guess we don't need to synchronize our watches," Kuwada kidded.

"This being Vegas, I'd say let's lay a bet down to see who comes up with the first good lead." Solomon chewed her lip. "But would Moya find that in bad taste?" She referred to the dead woman in the present tense, as if she could see the trio talking.

"We'll make it a friendly drink," Chainey resolved.

"You're on." Kuwada shook each woman's hand, and he and Chainey held each other's for a moment till he walked away.

"I don't want to get you upset, honey chile, but your new sweetie could have been jivin' us too."

Chainey was watching Kuwada as he went. "I considered that," she said. "But I'll worry about it when the time comes."

Solomon was going to comment but let it go. Nothing like lustful anticipation to affect one's critical thinking. "I'll call you in a couple of hours and let's see where we're at."

"Okay." Chainey cast a thoughtful gaze on her girlfriend. "You be careful poking around those neo-Nazi nut fucks, Rena. They don't play."

"Neither do I, baby." She winked.

"I'm serious. You want to borrow a piece?"

Solomon was startled. "Hell, no, Chain, what the hell would I do with one?"

"Sometimes we need insurance, girl."

"I'll be all right. I got some contacts with those survivalist types." She aimed a thumb in the direction of the desert to the south, as if the ones she referred to were clumped out there in the heat, hatching fevered plans.

"You just make sure you don't start thinking you're welcome among them."

"Oh, you'd be surprised what some of these boys are like one-on-one," Solomon countered. "Some of 'em are quite taken with the dark meat, honey," she kidded. "You ain't the only one who can handle herself."

"I know that." The two hugged and parted.

Chainey tried reaching Victoria Degault at her various numbers but only got rings and recordings. She trudged on, reflecting on the money in the bag she'd left at the El Morocco. She should probably go ahead and return the scratch to Degault. It didn't seem like keeping it a secret that she'd gotten the money back was a hole card worth anything now. But she wasn't going to haul the bag around either until she contacted the River-head's owner.

She found herself moving in the general direction of the El Morocco when a group of Vegas cops and Guard personnel came trotting around the corner of the North African–inspired Aladdin—the El Morocco writ humongous. At first she started, believing the armed forces to be part of some new attraction rehearsing for its show. But the carbines and riot shotguns the uniformed joggers carried were real, and the shouts they exchanged were charged with urgency.

"Let's go, let's go," a beefy women exhorted her colleagues.

"Double time, goddammit," another one hollered.

The makeshift platoon ran across the street with little traffic to stop. Curiously, they broke off into two sets and got into civilian passenger vans that would normally have been parked illegally. On the side of one of the vehicles was a magnetic sign advertising a pest control business. The vans swooped down the street, the occupants heading toward their mission. Except for Chainey and a couple speaking French, it seemed no one else had paid much attention to them.

Chainey continued on, becoming engulfed in an agitation of people roaming over the sidewalk. The breakfast buffet crowd, she concluded from the satiated expressions on their faces.

"Yo, how you like it when it's you that's clowned?"

There was no need to visually identify what she knew to be a gun in her side. "Hello, Eddie."

"Hello, shit, Chainey. Get your tight ass over there."

There was hard liquor wafting about his sentences, and out of the corner of her eye she could see from his pinprick pupils that he'd either been on the pipe or snorting coke.

"Whatever you say, Eddie."

"Don't be conda-shending. I had a girlfriend tha' used ta do that shit, and I didn't like it."

He kept close on her, one of his hands clamped onto her upper arm. He was rank and sweaty, his breathing forced through cottony lungs. McDaniels guided Chainey through the India Gate on the side of the Aladdin Casino.

"You think I was gonna let that shit you did to me slide?"

"If you were smart you—"

He jabbed her viciously with the barrel of the gun. It was a revolver.

Chainey bit her lip, willing herself to remain centered. "I like a roughneck, Eddie."

"You can stop." They were now in front of a Seattle's Best Coffee Shop. A youngish woman with red streaks in her hiar viewed them through the window as she sat inside and sipped her drink. For her sake, Chainey maintained a neutral demeanor.

"Where's my money, you pretty black bitch?" He leaned his face in close and suctioned his lips on her cheek.

"I'll have to take you to it, Eddie."

"Fuck you say. I went home like a kicked, broke-dick dog, but I'm a thinker, baby, a thinker." He tapped his temple with the barrel of his gun, and Chainey smiled crookedly. He wasn't that gone and soon tucked the weapon away again.

"I can see you've been planning."

"That's right," he lisped, the sarcasm going unrecognized. "I've been lookin' for you 'bout an hour now." He grabbed her hair from the end and yanked.

"Be cool, Eddie," she warned. "There are security guards all around, you know." And security cameras. She knew.

"Yeah, you're right," he rasped, as if conferring with a peer. "The money." He poked with the gun again to underscore his query.

"If you blast me, you won't have squat."

"I'll have satisfaction," he said.

"But you'll still be broke." She gave him her best poker face.

He weaved, as if a stiff wind had suddenly blown through the area. Maybe it was Aladdin himself, passing by on his carpet. "Where is it, then?"

"At the vault in the Riverhead."

McDaniels went fish-eyed. It was an eerie effect, his marbles for eyes tightening in the red area where the white should be. "You're lying, Chainey." The two had drifted farther into the busy Desert Passage Marketplace. State of emergency or not, Ma and Pa from Abilene had to have that knickknack from Vegas for the relatives.

"Okay, I am. Shoot me and skip right to the joint penniless for murder in front of hundreds of witnesses." Of course he was high and pissed enough, he might take her up on the offer.

"Then how do I get what's mine?" He wheezed under his breath.

Chainey nixed a comeback and waited, hoping her nervousness didn't show too much on her face.

"All right," the indignant thief continued. "But you twitch a titty and I smoke your fine ass. You got that, girl?"

At least she'd moved up in the female ranking. "Hey, I want to live."

"That's better. Let's get going."

Another jab. The two walked back toward the exit in the

manner in which they had come, McDaniels pressed close to her, one of his hands latched onto her upper arm.

Chainey calculated several options as they paraded through the marketplace. McDaniels's attention went from her to his surroundings, then back to her. She could hit him with a backhand blow to the face and throw him down using leverage. He'd shoot, of course, but Chainey figured to be diving behind one of the many wooden carts or stalls about for decoration. That could also mean a tourist could get shot, and that would be hell to explain to Lambert.

They were nearing the India Gate, the entrance/exit opposite the way they'd come in, a straighter line toward the Riverhead.

"Take it easy, Eddie, people are staring," she said gutturally.

"Don't fuck wit' me," He let the gun slide up the side of her torso, lodging it just on the underside of her breast. "I got more than money to get straight wit' you, Chainey."

"That's great, Eddie." She was about to make her move, then stalled. If she dropped him here, security would pounce in seconds. That meant not getting away, getting detained. That meant spending time in jail and dodging questions she wasn't about to answer.

"Just trying to help you out."

"Right. Keep walking." Quickly he removed his hand from her arm and rubbed her butt. He grinned, happy with himself.

"You're all bluff, aren't you?"

The unexpected response made him stammer. "What? What'd you say?"

"You know." She lowered her gaze to where the pistol was hidden between her arm and her body. "I guess that's the only gun you're good with."

They were crossing through the Gate, a massive archway of Moorish origins given the Vegas heavy hand. "I ain't stupid. I know what you're trying to do."

"Really?"

"Yeah, really." He gritted his teeth and shook her angrily. "You can't fool me with that reverse psychology shit."

"You don't know what I like, Eddie."

Wary, he responded, "What are you saying?"

Chainey allowed her previous words to linger, letting his imagination supply the fantasy.

"You tellin' me you dig this kind of stuff?" He ground the barrel into the upper part of her torso, near the armpit.

She gave him the show. "You tell me, Eddie."

He started laughing deep in his chest until he hacked and had to spit on the sidewalk. "Well, let's get that money; then we'll see how agreeable you're going to be."

Chainey fluttered her lashes. "Sure. We better go this way." She pointed and he looked. Perfect. The six-foot woman clamped her arm down hard around his hand and the gun. Simultaneously she grabbed and wrenched whatever she could get of the front of the piece and twisted it toward the sky.

"Bitch, I'm gonna . . ." he began.

Chainey snapped her elbow around like the prow of an icebreaker. She plowed it into his Adam's apple and used her heel to dig into the instep of his foot, then pivoted her hips, carrying him partially around the front of her body.

McDaniels got off a round, and the bullet singed Chainey's hand as the steel of the muzzle heated up. She could feel the round pass through her hair. As his body was off balance, she cranked off a punch to the underside of his jaw.

He grunted and sputtered, his arms whipping about as the blows and substances coursing through him took their toll. McDaniels's body landed with a nasty smack on the sidewalk, the gun, incredibly, still grasped in his hand.

"You're cold meat, you sneaky ho," he vowed.

The two Guardsmen she'd noticed lounging across Harmon in Alexis Park were rushing their way, as well as security guards from inside the marketplace. Chainey spun on her heel back toward McDaniels. He was trying to sit up and fire the piece. She leaped and landed behind him. Chainey deftly used the flat of her foot to kick him in the back of the head, and he projectile vomited. The ex-showgirl was upright, doing her best to duck and run among the citizenry.

One of the Guardsmen was after her, but she called on whatever reserves were left her after being up nearly more than
twenty-four hours.

Deciding to lose the crowd as cover, she ran across Las Vegas
Boulevard in a diagonal to the New York, New York Casino. A
Guardsman had a sidearm and, she supposed, could cut her
down if he had a notion. But she wasn't rioting, and it didn't
hurt that people were everywhere. Luck hadn't abandoned her
yet, and she made the escalator heading up to the second level.
She landed, shoving her way past irate patrons already ahead of
her on the thing. As she hoped, the Guardsman also got on the
moving staircase, bulling his way to her too.

Her next play had to be accomplished without thinking about
it too much or she'd freeze. Halfway up, she vaulted over the
side as a man in leather pants decided to be a good citizen and
made a grab for her. The onlookers enjoyed the show. Chainey
did as the sensei where she studied martial arts had instructed
her and visualized her next moves, landing and rolling.

The impact with the ground jarred her more than she'd pre-
dicted, and her roll wound up with her flat on her stomach. But
her wind was intact and her mind clear. She was on her feet and
had a bout of momentary panic when one of her ankles collapsed from under her weight. There was no time to slow down,
and she was relieved to find it was only sloppy footing and not a
sprain. She was running away as the Guardsman ran down the
up escalator, barking for her to halt.

For now, she was still making shooter's point; he didn't fire at
her as she made the corner and was gone.

CHAPTER THIRTEEN

Chainey had to assume a report of her altercation with McDaniels would be conveyed to Sheriff Lambert within the hour. The question she couldn't answer was how much credence he would give McDaniels's protestations. That he was drunk and high might buy her some time. Cops liked their arrestees to be coherent and cooperative. She was hoping he'd continue to be belligerent, and still have the presence of mind to keep his mouth shut. After all, he'd only be implicating himself if he insisted on whining about the stolen money he felt entitled to getting back.

So screw him; whatever McDaniels told the cops, she'd have to deal with it when the time came. For now she had to maintain her freedom of movement. That meant a change of clothes and doing her hair differently. It wasn't much, but anything that would make a cop or soldier look the other way rather than bore in on her was all to the good. But getting out to her place in the northwest was time-consuming and logistically difficult at the moment. Then a wide smile erupted on her sweaty face as Chainey walked along Reno Avenue, parallel and east of Harmon. There was always credit.

Rather than go farther south, where there was a chance of being spotted, she doubled back north on Koval Lane. There were a couple of police cruisers out on the street, but they seemed listless in their duty, just going through the motions. Had Lambert been right? Was Ashford/Khali, the mastermind behind all this? Had she told all?

It was probably just the usual wired boredom that invariably took up residence in you even through the excitement of an emergency situation. Chainey knew homicide cops who one moment were burning hot with rage and testosterone—men and women—ready to take some asshole's head off. But once the situation had passed, there was this rebound effect, this kind of letdown that she supposed allowed the body and mind to stabilize. Otherwise, if you were pumped all the time, you'd stroke out.

All this went through her mind as one of the patrol sedans went past her. The problem with the guilty was how to appear innocent. Languidly, Chainey looked over at the car and the woman officer behind the wheel. The two's eyes locked momentarily, and Chainey nodded, then instantly regretted that she'd done so. Was it too much? Too obvious she was trying to look normal?

The cop twitched a wan smile and the car drove on, then braked. Chainey had to force herself not to stop and kept walking in the direction of the LVMPD. The reason for the brake lights became apparent as a man in a floppy hat rode across the thoroughfare in one of those electric carts meant for people with hip or leg problems. Attached to the car was a flexible shaft topped by a small triangular flag with a full house, aces over kings, embroidered on it. The cop driving turned to say something to her partner, whose upper body subsequently shook with laughter. The car resumed its torpid pace as the cart reached the other side and a driveway.

Chainey breathed regularly and reached her destination, the Sands Expo Center. There was a clothing shop there that carried her size. She'd get some new threads and then the proper protection for the modern girl, a gun.

CHAPTER FOURTEEN

"**H**aven't seen you in a while, slim," the manager chirped. She was a petite woman somewhere between her mid-fifties and -sixties. The woman wore her dyed blond hair swept back from a high, unwrinkled forehead. She was handsome and her makeup expertly matched her years without trying to hide the wear. She was dressed in a long silk blouse printed with a geometric design over black slacks and high heels.

"Always running." Chainey could feel her temples cool as she stood in the air-conditioned environment.

"So what's your druthers, today, hmmm, sweetie?" the manager inquired, flitting closer to Chainey, as if on roller bearings. Her voice had the husky quality of having been coated by whiskey and secondhand smoke for years—Vegas throat. "You still look like the perfect size ten; I don't know how you do it." Up and down and up again went her delicately mascaraed eyes. "You work out hard, don't you?"

"All this time." Chainey moved around the shop, afraid that if she remained still, she'd be spotted through the large plate-glass windows. "How about some bell-bottom pants and, I don't know, something loose for the top?"

"Let's see, shall we? We got in some delicious colors just the other day." She began to sashay toward a display table. "They're all the rage, the Silvertab line that would simply be heaven on a woman like you, with your"—she looked back to drink her in—"statuesque physique."

"Thank you," Chainey obliged. She made her selections and charged the goods to her account.

"What else can we do for you today?" The woman's hand, massive gold rings on three fingers, brushed the surface of Chainey's on the counter.

"This is great; thanks again, huh?"

"Anytime and for anything, you bronze Aphrodite, you."

"Oh, stop," Chainey teased back.

"Never," the manager promised.

Outside, in the broiling atmosphere, Chainey made her way to her next destination as her phone rang. She unclipped it from her belt.

"Rena?"

"No, it's Victoria." She sounded distracted.

"Glad you called back. I need to ask you a few questions about your friend Dean."

Victoria said something unintelligible, and Chainey had to ask her to repeat herself.

"What is it you want to know?" Degault's voice was well-modulated, as if she was consciously keeping it in a neutral tone.

"A few things I've heard about him, Victoria."

"I see"—the neutrality fading—"you get this from your friend, is that it?"

"Among others."

"Really?"

"Victoria," Chainey began, equally sharp in tone, "somebody had to put that fake-ass Khali up to the robbery. There's not a long list of people who knew about the bet, and Tosches is looking to make a score."

"So are all the other rollers in this town, Chainey."

"You know what I mean."

"Did Simon tell you that he'd made an offer to buy the High Chaparral?"

"No; no, he didn't." She had stopped to talk and was next to one of the ubiquitous twenty-four-hour wedding chapels of the city. A large woman in a too-short dress and a man some sixty pounds lighter than her went arm-in-arm into the establishment. In the display window the ends of a garter belt peeked out below a mini worn by a mannequin that also wore a veil and a train. "Is he going to sell?"

"That I couldn't tell you." Ice could be heard in liquid on the other end of the line. Chainey longed for a drink herself. "But," she added hesitantly, "he hasn't mentioned it in a while either."

"You mean Simon withdrew the offer?"

Nothing.

"Victoria, I have the money, you understand me? I've got it back."

"Then why the hell are you pursuing this . . . this investigation? You're not a detective. Because in case no one has pointed this out to you, you're a far cry from Jackie Brown, or even Angie Dickenson, for that matter," she snorted. More tinkling of ice.

"Little early to be getting your drink on, isn't it?"

"I've been up all night, like you. And I might need this bracer."

"Bad choices, Victoria?"

Another pause, and she wasn't sure whether Degault had severed the call. "It's hard for women like us, isn't it, Martha? We know our own minds, make our own ways in this precarious world, and who do we have to share it with? But who says we have to share it with anybody? Why now, even in the twenty-first century do women still have to deal with bullshit like a man to have around, as if that were a natural adjunct to being successful? Shit."

Chainey replied, "What do you want to talk about, Victoria?"

"You're too fucking dangerous to have those kinds of talks with, Chainey." Her mood shifted to wary again. "Men and women wind up with holes in them fuckin' around with you, don't they?"

She held back a cutting remark. "Come on, it's me, Victoria."

"Me what?" she rasped. She drank more. "Oh, this is all so weak, you know?"

"Weak how?" Come on, let's get to it.

"All of the shit we do to be the one, you know what I'm saying. I mean, I killed my own brother, Chainey. I killed him for you," she blurted out. "Well, me too, I guess," she muttered.

"This is not a topic we should be discussing right now, is it, Victoria?"

"I'll talk about whatever it is I feel like talking about; shit. Don't forget what I own and what I paid to get this goddamn bauble."

"The Gaming Commission, remember?" Chainey said, aware they or any adversary could be listening in at that moment.

"Fuck them," she enunciated succinctly. "I'm not scared of a bunch of wide-ass, tight-lipped bureaucrats or you, Chainey."

People strolled past, talking on their cell phones, including a Guardswoman who was having a jovial time with whoever was on the other end of the line. "What are you talking about, Victoria?"

"Bring me my money," she blared, suddenly sounding very tired.

"Sure. Where can I find your boyfriend?"

"I think you sometimes forget who pays your freight, missy."

"No, I never do," she responded with like ferocity.

"What do you want, Chainey? What the fuck is all this about? You're an outlaw, we both are. We're holding on till they get wise to us, you know that."

"All the more reason to find out now who's behind Moya and Jeffries's killings," Chainey reminded her. "I need to find out, you understand, Victoria?"

"Why do you care, Chainey? You don't make anything out of it on that end."

Until she'd said it, the courier hadn't been forced to articulate what it was about the murder that had gotten to her. But she knew, and was bothered by the answer. "When I saw her body in that economy room, Victoria, alone and far from home, two nasty holes in her, it was me.

"We were the same age and, like me and Rena, Moya had been on her own since her teens. For the first time in her life she was making the choices, not just having to scramble to do anything to get by." She stopped, tired of explaining herself to herself or any person. She did add, "And because she didn't have anybody else; isn't that enough?"

"It's hard being a woman, isn't it?" Degault offered.

A slight breeze blew past the courier, but it didn't refresh her. "Yeah, sometime we have to defend our men, even if they're not worth the defending."

Degault chuckled soullessly. "Very good, Chainey, very apt."

"Enough with the repartee, Victoria. What is it you know?"

Another gulf of silence, then the Riverhead's owner said, "Dean laid off bets on Muhammad too."

"How do you know that?"

"I inherited certain ... enterprises, let's call them, with Frankie's passing. One of them is a sports book across town."

"Offering more payout percentages?"

"Something like that."

"So Dean bets with this book you own?"

"But doesn't know that I own it. I'm not some silly, lovesick child, Chainey. I know the premium on circumspect pillow talk."

"And you only found this out this morning?"

"Dean's been around here a while too, you know. He made the bets through intermediaries, some aging soldiers now on the fringes, cruising around in their Bush Senior–era Fleetwoods with the balding tires."

They both chortled at the image.

Chainey's cellular beeped, warning her the battery was running low. "So how does he profit? With Jeffries dead, all bets are off; money is returned. No one wins."

"Not necessarily," Degault said. "Not if it was about maneuvering Muhammad into a title match at your casino."

"And Jeffries ... ?" Chainey wondered

"He was locked into us, the arena partnership."

"But not Muhammad."

"No. And I know from the COO who runs our sports arm that Muhammad was being wooed heavily by Dean."

"This could all be just business, Victoria. Dean's an operator, and he could have just been covering his ass like anyone would with that kind of money on the line."

"You're the one who wanted to nail him," she chided.

"I'm just working through the possiblities," Chainey amended.

"I know."

"It's time for the kicker, don't you think?"

"Unfortunately."

"He called you, didn't he?"

"A man must really be desperate if he turns to a woman for help, huh?" There was a pause and another audible swallow.

"I wouldn't know," Chainey said, wanting to remain noncommittal and not piss off the tipsy Degault.

"Right," she said churlishly. "He called me because he wanted the name of the hitter who took out Frankie." A hollow laugh, then, "That's irony, isn't it?"

"He didn't buy the official story?" The killing of Frankie Degault had been credited to Vernon Sixkiller, the chief of security for the Golden Horn Casino, run by the Agua Caliente American Indians in Palm Springs. Sixkiller had been acquitted, the verdict self-defense, given that Frankie had been wielding a rifle at the time. Only the three, Chainey, Degault, and Sixkiller, knew the truth.

"This town loves its legends, and how Frankie died is one of them. The rumors persist, and it's better to let them fester."

Like a sore—but she didn't express that vocally. "And did you give him the name of a hitter?" she inquired sweetly.

"Shit," Degault chortled. "You must think I'm in the bottle every goddamn morning. I stuck to the lie." The words came off bitterly.

"So what did he do?"

"I can't say for certain, Chainey."

"But you have a guess."

"A supposition, yes."

This game of semantics was getting on her last nerve. "Where would he go, Victoria? Who would Tosches turn to to find this hypothetical killer he needed?"

"There are a lot of people he could go to, you know that. You could waste a lot of time and wear out your *zapatos* trying to find that out in any kind of reasonable time." She yawned.

"Then give me his phone number, will you?"

"Like he's going to just tell you?"

"You never know, Victoria." What she really wanted was to rattle him, force his hand, if he was the real wheeler-dealer.

"You might want to put such a call in to your boyfriend," Degault sniped. "It isn't like you're all that hot on your choices either."

Any other time Chainey would have taken the bait, but she kept herself in check. "Whenever you want to tell me." She'd been walking along and had entered the lobby of the Luxor. She bummed a pen from a passing chiseled pharaoh. The napkin to write on she'd filched from underneath an empty soda cup perched on one of the video slot machines.

She could hear a glass being put down. "Fine, fine." After a few moments, Degault read off several numbers for Chainey. "Do let me know what you find out." She sounded weary.

"I will. Get some rest."

"Thanks, Chainey. All that's left is to keep trying, right?"

"Okay. Talk to you later." She clicked off and stood for several moments, watching and listening. All about her were people with lives and concerns of their own. Some were facing long odds just to make it month to month, and some could drop twenty thousand a pop and not feel it. Who determined the set of circumstances that made one person a comer and the other a chump? And how did it sometimes work out that even though you were a wheel, things could change; you could be on the outs tomorrow, scrambling to try and get your thing going again. And why was it some had it handed to them, or had the golden touch from the cradle to the grave? And others, like her, had to hustle and fight for every inch of ground they got. From somewhere in the vast casino before her, the unmistakable jangling of quarters pouring out of a slot machine could be heard. The winner whooped with joy. Chainey called Tosches.

"Holt?" came his terse reply on the third number she tried.

"No, Chainey. Hey you're a hitter?"

"Chain—what do you want? I don't have to ask how you got this number."

"Need to see you about a few things, Dean."

"Fuck off." Then he mumbled something, but she couldn't make out the words.

"Wow, is that any way to be?" she jabbed.

He hung up. She called back but got a busy signal. She tried several more times and got the same result. Chainey knew better than to call Degault back to ask where the number she called led to. Anyway, she had the feeling that Tosches, at least for the next few hours, was going to be the least of her worries. She headed for the office.

"Mooch available?" she asked the receptionist when she entered the front door of Truxon, Ltd. She could have used her keys and entered through the back, but his office was located in this direction. Maltizar liked his view of nearby West Las Vegas from the second floor of the strip mall the business occupied. That, and the always changing graffiti on the retaining wall. This week the urban hieroglyphics had been tagged by the Kingsmen Gang, crossing out some scrawl by the lovelies calling themselves Anybody's Murderers.

The receptionist gave the courier an empty look at the request. Her name was Jobeth and she was a pretty Latina with a thin jagged scar running from her hairline to her left eyebrow. In one of her previous incarnations, the receptionist has been a second-tier porno actress specializing in girl-on-girl action.

Chainey stepped forward and repeated herself.

"Oh," Jobeth said, bobbing her head, finally understanding. "Lemme check, 'kay?" Rather than use the intercom on the phone, she got up and walked into Mooch's office without knocking.

"Why didn't I think of that?" Chainey said aloud.

"What up?" A man called Marley, who occasionally did some work for Maltizar, stepped out of the boss's office. "Haven't seen you since that throw down we had in Indio."

"Still got the souvenir from that one?" They shook hands, their eyes staying on each other for several moments.

"Keep it right on the shelf in back of the Hennessy," he laughed. Marley was a medium-built, above-average-height black man somewhere in his thirties. He dressed well, and sported a premature shock of white zigzagging through his close-cropped hair. He and Chainey had been working for two different clients but got caught up in an incident in the California desert town. The only way for either to survive was by working together. There was nothing like the immediate threat of death to heighten one's senses. Especially when your comrade-in-arms was fine.

"I guess you're on your way out of town," she said.

He made a clucking sound with his tongue. "You know how it goes. But I'm hoping to be back through in a week." They still had their hands clasped together. He pulled closer to the woman who was taller than him by an inch. "You didn't throw away those silky red silk panties I bought you?" he whispered.

"Of course not. After all the trouble we went through breaking them in?" She was about to nuzzle his nose when Maltizar intervened.

"Marta?" he announced from the doorway, behind Marley.

"Day-um," the handsome man muttered. "I'll call."

"Do that."

He stepped past in his Zegna sharkskin suit. Jobeth drilled him with an inviting glare and he smiled graciously as he went out into the midday heat.

"I'd like to pretend I used to have that effect on the women when I was young, but even I can't bullshit that good." Maltizar had a smoldering cigar in his hand; a Cohiba, Chainey noted from its band as she went into his office.

"So what's doing on whatever it is you were looking for?" He closed the door and eased behind his desk. It was a heavy industrial green variety, a refugee from a truck parts company. In a rotting leather sheath tacked to the wall behind him was a machete Maltizar had used cutting cane as a boy in Cuba. There was also a framed photo of a Sephardic cemetery in Baracoa on the island nation.

Chainey sat and crossed her legs. "Hear of a shooter named Holt? A real pro, not the usual bang-bang clown."

Maltizar's tiny orbs got wide behind the lenses of his thick-framed glasses. "This the mook took out the champ?"

"Could be." He could also be Tosches' accountant.

"And this is at your door now?" He puffed thoughtfully.

"That's right." She felt certain if she didn't find the killer, he was going to find her. Solomon's conjecture about her being the target had been gnawing at her for several hours. She could mark it up to a lack of sleep and general edginess, but the memory of Moya Reese lying on that bed on top of stale sheets was very vivid to her. Amazingly, she'd yet to hear that the woman's body had been discovered.

Maltizar leaned back, the cigar slowly brought to his mouth as he contemplated several options—one of which was simply cutting her loose. If it was something the old survivor figured would endanger his operation . . . well, he'd miss her for awhile. "I'm sure I can make some calls, Marta," he said evenly. "He's not a name I readily recognize." He blew smoke. "But judging from the past experinces you've had, are you sure it's a man?"

"This one, yes." She couldn't imagine Tosches relying on a woman to do his wet work. His asking Degault for a lead was one thing, but to actually employ a broad, he'd have to be ready for the retirement home. He was definitely of the Sinatra generation on his outlook on women.

"Glad to see I'm worth some effort on your part, Mooch." She uncrossed her legs.

He spread his hands, as if desirous of a blessing. "*Mi belleza,* how is it you think these cruel things of me? Yes, I must be in this sparkling ocean of ours with the tiburons, but does that make me one?" He smiled his smile of crooked teeth.

"It makes you king of the sharks, Mooch."

He gave her a grandfatherly look of reproach. But his eyes twinkled, as if he was pleased with the backhanded compliment. He wagged a finger in the air, the cigar hanging from one corner of his mouth. "I would be offended if I thought you were serious."

They both had a chuckle. Then Chainey said, "Could be he's had military training."

"Or even one of those nut jobs running around out there in the desert waiting for the apocalypse," Mooch glumly stated. "It's not like the old days, or even the goddamn Eighties," he lamented. "But as I said"—he gestured with his hands, the cigar between his fingers leaving disconnected trails of smoke like an oil-burning biplane—"I can make a few inquiries, as this is now a matter affecting my associate and my business."

Chainey wondered if he believed half of what he said at any given time. "Thank you, Mooch."

"This so-far-unknown shooter have something to do with these locos, these Nymnatists?"

"Why do you ask that?"

"You mentioned the military angle. Doesn't that tin-plate Gary Cooper that's their captain of the guard or whatever have some sort of background in that arena?"

"True," she conceded, "but all sorts of people have been in the service, these maniac end-of-the-worlders you just mentioned as an example."

"*Sí, sí.*" He jammed what remained of the cigar back in his mouth. "So who is this hitter working for?"

There it was. She either 'fessed up or left now and dug up what she could on her own. But that was time-consuming, and she didn't have the array of contacts he had. "Dean Tosches. But I'm not a hundred percent on that, you understand?"

Maltizar moved the flat of his hand back and forth in the air before him. "But you have reason to believe he wanted Jeffries dead for some reason. Some reason you feel compelled to be involved in."

"Yes," she answered. "Money, of course, is at the heart of it." She wasn't going to elaborate any more than that. She'd be damned if she'd let him in on the money she was due to get for her recovery fee. Or tell him she'd seen Reese's corpse. It wasn't simply greed that made her withhold information, she convinced herself, but a certainty that keeping some secrets was not only prudent but insurance for the future.

"Always"—he waved the stump of his cigar about again—"it's the money, isn't it, *chica?*"

She was on her feet. "Give me a holler on my cell; I'll be moving around some."

He ground out the Cohiba. "You hear the news this morning?"

"No, what?"

"That woman, Reese—they found her body a couple of hours ago."

"Damn." She feigned surprise.

Maltizar sucked in one side of his cheek. "You knew her, didn't you?"

She had her back to him, her face set in hard relief. "I did, yes. Talk to you soon, Mooch," and out she went. Lambert could already have an APB out for her, but there was nothing she could do about that. Chainey hadn't gone this far to lay low now. If the man who'd been having fun and games next to Reese's room happened to take a peek and see her leave the motel, so be it. Maybe the pudgy man would lie for her, he'd been so smitten. But until some cop or National Guard soldier yelled halt—and even then only if they could catch her—she'd keep going.

Back on the street, Chainey decided to spread the wealth. Maltizar was the best and most reliable source of information but not the only one available to her. Plus, she needed another gun. She walked to East Bonanza Road, the part of Vegas of check-cashing outfits and twenty-four-hour pawnshops. Where the Donna Street Crips rolled past in their whips on their dubs bling-blinging for all to see and envy. Where the hotel and restaurant employees union members who are the janitors and room attendants come home after their shifts in the casinos to the singularly unspectacular but tidy houses their union wages have at least allowed them to purchase.

You could find out a lot here if you knew where to look and who to ask. But if you stepped wrong, getting a bloody nose might be the least of your concerns. On a street off the main thoroughfare that was more alley than avenue, Chainey edged past a dark-complected transvestite in platform shoes. The individual was showing way too much butt out of her Daisy Duke's. The she/he was arguing with a tall individual with twisted braids exploding from his scalp. The two stood on the corner near a wall where a chipped and faded painted sign announced MCPHEELY'S LIQUOR.

"Umph," the tranny harumphed upon seeing Chainey.

The ex-showgirl pulled on the latch of a metal door set in the wall. It opened outward to reveal a stairway, portions of the landing swathed in shadows. She started up, then stopped. Casually treading his way down from the top of the darkened staircase was a bull mastiff. A white orb glistened with mucus in its right eye socket. The mouth of the creature partially hung open and it panted softly as it blindly glared at Chainey.

"Ragnarok," she said, making sure no fear or hesitation trembled in her delivery.

The dog kept descending and she continued ascending. She stopped as the beast suddenly sat on its haunches on one of the steps. She held out her hand, flat and relaxed. The creature's head tilted toward the limb, the dead eye boring in, as if it were going to collide with her fingers. Chainey remained still. The mastiff sniffed her hand, then barked once.

"Good, Ragnarok." She patted the mastiff's head, hard as cement.

The tongue of the animal flicked out across its now gaping jaw, the teeth inside the maw like mini-stalagmites.

Chainey continued her way up, the dog walking amiably beside her. She got to the landing, which had a recessed doorway not visible from below. Inset in the doorway was the edge of another door, also made of metal. This one was three-inch steel, and nothing short of a square of plastique could blow it open when it slid into place.

The lithe woman stepped through and into a hallway lit in subdued azure, thousands of minute stars twinkling on walls and ceiling. Suspended and swirling from a short pole in the ceiling was a Seventies-era disco ball. A small spot, placed behind the glittering globe, lit it as the thing twirled slowly.

"What, no Hendrix or Jerry Butler? Those were the jams in you day, right, Sly?" Chainey announced to her unseen host.

"Look here, girl, I may be having a cameo in *Ladies Man, the*

Return, so be cool." Sly stepped into the hallway, his rangy silhouette seeming to shimmer before her. The disco ball stopped
its orbit, and his form solidified before her.

"Right on, my brother." She rasied her fist in the air in a black
power salute.

Hands on his hips, he asked, "What is it you need, Chainey?"

"Guess."

"Ha, ha." He stepped back into the room and she followed. In
here the light was soft yellows, originating from tastefully designed wall sconces. The room itself was lined with metalwork tables. There was also a bandsaw, a drill press, a lathe, and a
rollaway toolbox, one of its drawers half open. On one of the tables lay a street sweeper, a shotgun-type weapon that had a drum
magazine that could be packed with buckshot for explosive
loads. A section of the gun's casing had been removed, and it
was obvious from the tools laying around the piece that Sly had
been doing some work on it.

"What it be like?" Sly had to be fifty-five or sixty, Chainey estimated. He was dressed in tight, stripped Silvertab retro flares,
Dingo boots, and a hippie shirt she swore she'd seen Lenny
Kravitz wearing last week on MTV. The dyed hair at the top of
his oblong head was done in long braids that revealed their
graying roots. He'd shaved off his Fu Manchu mustache since
the last time she'd been to visit him, but he still sported his avia-
tor glasses with the gradual tint.

"Need some equipment and a face to go with a name."
Ragnarok wandered in and squatted before an oscilloscope on a
stool. His one good eye watched the ribbon of light go up and
down, back and forth on the monitor. She produced two hundred dollars in fifties. "This is a down payment, of course."

"Muscle or killer?"

"Sniper training. Goes by the name Holt."

"The fight."

"Exactly."

"Not the usual."

"Specifically?"

He made a face.

"Come on."

"I may dress like this, but my name ain't Rooster. I ain't no snitch."

She put the bills away. "Barter, then."

That got his interest. "You do a run for me. No questions, no limits."

"Let's not get silly."

"Okay, but we agree in principle."

"That's right."

"I got a call."

"Know the caller?"

"You askin' about him or the triggerman?"

"Fine."

"Okay. I say not interested, dig?"

"Dug."

He cocked his head at her.

"Sorry, got carried away. Go on, please."

"Now this call was from a third party, not direct."

"But you were told what for?"

"No, didn't like the vibe. The one on the other end shaky goods."

"Then how do you know this is what I want?"

"Don't, Chainey. But this happened four days ago, so you tell me."

"Okay, go on."

"I give this third party a couple of names, just to blow them off, dig."

"Yes." She bit her lips so as not to snicker.

"But this Holt, that's not one of them."

"Shit."

"We still got a deal?"

"Why?"

"Give you the third party. I'm not the only one they asked."

"Who?"

"We good?" He made the motion with his two fingers of seeing eye to eye.

"Yeah," she snapped.

"Ginger Salley."

"What? The attack palm reader?"

"Spiritualist," he corrected.

Ragnarok yawned.

"How the fuck could she be in on this?"

"Vegas," was his one encompassing explanation.

"Sly, I swear, this better not be bullshit."

"She's the one who called me," he insisted. "Hell, I'm the one giving her up."

"She'd give up her mama for a twenty," Chainey spat derisively.

"That's on you."

"She still got that walk-up place of hers downtown?"

"Yep, right in that building where the El Morocco used to be."

Now it was Chainey's turn to put her hands on her hips. Back in the old days, before Tosches's reign, the casino had originally been a downtown fixture. The former owners had seen the future and in the mid-eighties had arranged the financing to move and reopen the casino on the Strip in anticipation of its revitalization. Hell, ol' Ginger might have read the tea leaves for them. "I'll make good on our contract, Sly."

"I know you solid, Chainey. You always was. Ever since I met you with McAndrews." He got a faraway look, then went back to work on the street sweeper.

Making her selection, Chainey paid for her goods. Then she headed for the door. Ragnarok barked once and fell silent again.

She returned to the Truxon offices and stashed most of her stuff there and split again. Back in the heat, her cell phone rang.

"Chain," Solomon said breathlessly, "I don't know what you been doing, girl, but Lambert's got his scout troop out looking for you bad. They were just here pushin' up on me."

When Solomon got excited, she tended to go ghetto.

"Thanks, Rena."

" 'Thanks, Rena'? You better do sumptin'."

"I will, relax, will you?"

"Shee-it."

"Do me a favor? Check and see if the building where the original El Morocco was is owned now by Dean Tosches."

"I get to run with this?"

"If what seems to be falling into place does, of course."

"I'll hit you back in a few. Try not to get nabbed before then."

"You're a scream."

"Ain't I?"

Chainey hung up and walked till she spotted a cab. The checkpoint had been relaxed, and twenty-four minutes later she was deposited at the Lovecraft Spiritual Healing Emporium on Bridger Avenue. The first story, directly below the place, was a joint selling used DVDs and vacuum cleaners. The window display had a leggy mannequin in a cocktail mini watching TV and vacuuming at the same time. She had a martini glass in her free hand, and a DVD of Schwarzenegger as Doc Savage played on the television's screen.

Upstairs, Chainey halted at the pebble-glass door leading to the Emporium. She could discern no shadows on the other side and listened for sounds. There were none. She tried the door, and it swung inward. The compact front parlor was decorated in heavy drapes and upholstered chairs, muted in its tones compared to the brightness of the fluorescents in the short hallway. She expected to see the trappings of the all-knowing, such as crystals, ankhs, and the sort. But there were none present in this room—not even a crystal ball, she noted dryly.

"Ginger," she called. From behind a Japanese-style room divider, she could hear a radio playing softly. Beyond the divider was an archway to another area. She was about to call out the woman's name again when she heard another noise, like the scuff of a toe, below that of the radio. Chainey got prickly and bent down to retrieve the just-purchased Beretta from her new ankle holster.

Standing on tiptoe to one side of the screen, the tall woman could see part of a linolium floor and the cabinets of a kitchen beyond the archway. Subtly, the radio was turned down. Chainey craned her neck, hoping she wasn't making an instant target of herself. She could see part of an old-fashioned chrome bread box on a counter. Staring hard at its polished surface, she was sure there was a shift of a darker reflection in its surface. If it was a human form, that meant Holt was to her right in the kitchen, backed up against the corner.

Chainey stepped back and was startled when a kettle suddenly whistled. She kicked the screen, and two silenced gunshots from inside the kitchen tore apart its frame. Chainey had run back to the entrance and was crouched in the hallway, only her gun hand protruding into the room.

"Smart," came a flat voice.

Peep your head out, asshole. Chainey leveled her piece, her left hand supporting her gun hand and helping steady the gun.

"I take it you're not an officer?"

She didn't respond, just waited for her opening, like during her workouts at the dojo.

"So who could you be?" he said in a singsong voice, a thin playfulness to his tone.

Chainey took in several shallow breaths, her pulse rate normal, her senses attuned for the slightest sound of movement on the part of her unseen opponent.

"Chainey," he concluded. "You're good; I like that. I like it that this skirmish will challenge our skills and, naturally, one's resolve."

What a fuckin' blowhard, she reflected.

"I don't have the money you're after, Chainey. Were you aware of that?"

"That's not why I want you, Holt."

"Ah, she doth have speech."

For a killer, he sure liked to hear himself talk.

"Are you a pro, Chainey?"

"Stick your head around the corner and find out, champ."

"Oh, I'm sure you can shoot at me. That I don't doubt."

There was more sound and the rustling of clothes. Chainey got set.

"But can you make the shot? The one that counts no matter what?" Holt had stepped into the opening of the archway—a big, clear target. He was holding a terrified Ginger Salley in front of him. She was dressed in a multicolored peasant skirt and a black blouse, a Macy's window version of the modern soothsayer. The ensemble was marred by the fact that the sleeves of the blouse had been torn away, and there were fresh knife cuts along each of her forearms. Her eyes were red and she was sobbing from pain and fear. Holt was a real sport.

Chainey stood, keeping herself back from the doorjamb. The boiling water in the kettle kept screaming. Evidently the only way out was where she was. Otherwise he would have kept going past the arch with his hostage and out some rear exit.

The man had one arm around her waist and his hand held a pistol pressed firmly against her temple. He wasn't particularly big, and he kept most of his head ducked low behind Salley's. A green eye that looked out at Chainey was startling in its coldness. It was more like something that belonged to a predatory bird than a human.

"Good to meet you."

Chainey had sighted, but he knew better. There wasn't enough of his forehead exposed to risk a shot. Not that she had any sympathy for Salley, the woman who'd help set the events of the last twenty-four hours in motion. Chainey couldn't get too close or he'd shove Salley at her.

"You see how it is?" he taunted, inching himself and his prisoner forward.

"You're not leaving." She stepped into the room.

"Aw shit, Holt," Ginger Salley wept. "I told you, I didn't tell anybody anything. Please, let me go."

"How'd she get here?"

"How the fuck should I know?" she cried. "The two of you take this shit somewhere else. I'm not involved. I don't deserve any of this."

Chainey felt like shooting the self-centered woman on general principle.

"Shut up," Holt said. He couldn't gauge Chainey's resolve and couldn't guess. He knew too little about her, other than snippets picked up in the last few hours. Once again, as before,

in places like Nicaragua, improper intelligence had led to tacti-
cal deficiencies. But he'd taken the job, and he'd finish his assignment.

"Please, Holt, I'll do whatever you want," Salley started again.
"Come on now. You and me are on the same side." She tried to
sound pleading and seductive all at once.

He jabbed her quickly on the side of her head with the muzzle of his gun. She went back to being silent, tears flowing down
her cheeks.

Chainey was sure that if Holt's hand twitched, if the gun lifted
a millimeter from Salley's skull, she'd take the chance. She'd
have no choice but to blast away. If Salley got smoked, that was
one more item she'd have to explain to Lambert.

"What to do, what to do?" Ever so lightly, he prepared himself. He was going to throw Salley in Chainey's direction. She
would react, and he'd grind out several rounds at her as she
tried to get out of the way.

Chainey's attention was fixed on his gun hand. He was going
to shove Salley at her and pop off his rounds, she could intuit
his intent. Come on, come on . . . the goddamn bell over the
downstairs door jingled.

"Ginger? Ginger?"

The goddamn kettle kept wailing.

Salley looked about to faint. "Call the police, call them." But
she was so frightened, her voice came out hoarsely.

"Get the fuck out of here," Chainey yelled. More bodies led to
more confusion, and more chance of her getting hurt.

"What, what are you saying, Ginger?" the speaker asked. His
footfalls still approached. "Why are you talking like that? What
side of the bed did your grouchy self get up on this morning,
honey? And take that water off the stove," he joked.

Holt's emerald orb slid quickly in the direction of the arriv-
ing newcomer, assessing a possible threat.

Chainey used that nanosecond of distraction to leap at Salley
and Holt. She threw her body sideways, her knee bent so as to
drive it into the woman and thus upset the man's balance.

Holt shot, his round tearing through Salley's upper shoulder.

The bullet seared close to Chainey's torso as she made contact, and the three bodies fell to the floor.

"Oh my God, oh my God," the customer hollered. "What's going on up there?"

"I'm going to die, I'm going to die," Salley wailed, sandwiched between the combatants.

Chainey drove her knuckles in an downward arc and caught the edge of Holt's jaw as he trained his gun on her. His head snapped back, but he used his knee in Salley's back to knock her toward Chainey.

Anticipating that move, Chainey was already rolling out of the way and firing her semiauto just to the left of the wounded woman's head.

Salley's eyelids fluttered and she passed out. An off-balance Holt, on his knees firing and trying to also scramble away, missed Chainey, who now dove into the alcove as he returned fire.

"Police, police," the unseen arrival screamed from below. "They're killing Ginger, oh my God, they're killing Ginger," he bellowed, the bell jangling again as he raced out into the street.

Holt was up and moving toward the entrance. Chainey clipped off two and hit him somewhere in the upper body. He grunted and halted momentarily, then kept going, laying down some return fire as he banged against the far wall in the hallway and then fled down the stairs.

Chainey looked at Salley, who was prone on her back on the floor.

"I—I can't breath right," she gushed. Blood soaked the carpet from her wound, and the shoulder poked against the skin, probably broken.

Chainey couldn't muster up any sympathy for the woman who had brokered the murders. She could understand pleading for her life, willing to give up somebody with a gun at your head. But Salley had gotten into this for the dough. Then again, hadn't Chainey? Sirens pierced the distance. But she needed an answer. Chainey bent down.

"Who?"

"I'm hurt, here."

Chainey slapped her lightly with the Beretta. "You're going under the knife, Ginger. When you come out of your anesthetic haze, is it my face, my hand on the intravenous drip you want to see?"

Salley gave her the name, the person who paid her to find a gun hand. Chainey saw there was no other trail of blood on the rug as she left behind Salley moaning from her wound and self-pity. Holt must have been wearing Kevlar, she thought.

Down the stairs and into the day, Chainey saw a man lying on the sidewalk. He was a wizened customer, dressed in a suit that had been old twenty years earlier. He had a hand to his head, and from his voice she knew he was the heretofore unseen client.

"You, you." He pointed accusingly at Chainey.

She was too nonplused to swear. This clown was going to blame her for everything short of an anthrax outbreak. Pick 'em up and put 'em down, she admonished herself as she ran away from the scene of the crime as fast as she could.

CHAPTER FIFTEEN

The race was on to get to Tosches. Holt, she reasoned, might have an advantage in that department. But regrets were for the ones who went bust, and Chainey wasn't through yet. She hailed a cab parked on the west side of the Golden Nugget. Then she made another call.

"Victoria," she blurted when the woman picked up on her private line. "I'm coming after your beau."

"What are you going on about?" the voice thick with the residual effect of booze said.

"He's behind all this shit."

"You're trippin', as they say, Chainey."

"We'll see." She hung up and touched one of her horseshoe earrings. "Let's see if I've got any left," she muttered.

The cab driver smiled knowingly.

She was dropped off at the El Morocco about ten minutes later. The traffic was still restricted due to the martial law edict, though there were more individual cars on the street. She paid the driver and took up position outside the place. It was one thing to enter the casino's main floor; any sucker could do that. But getting up top, getting into the innards, where the monitors, counting rooms, and, most importantly, the admin offices were, was a whole other matter.

But she guessed Tosches would have heard about Salley by now, and that would put the fire under him.

Less than a half hour later, an unmarked side door, partially hidden by a canopy of vines and other crawling plants, opened. Out stepped Tosches with two men built like flesh-and-blood Land Rovers. The Rovers sandwiched the casino owner as his Lincoln town car was brought around.

"Loose the rhinos," Chainey advised. "We need to talk." She made sure her hands were up and in plain sight.

One of them was reaching for his piece, but Tosches stopped him. A LVMPD car went by.

Tosches stuck his tongue in one corner of his mouth, as if probing for food particles. "Yeah, you're right, Chainey. Let's take a ride, shall we?"

"Sure." She walked with him to his car and he opened the door for her. She got in and slid across the backseat. He also got in. The other Rover, this one with a bull neck, made a move, but Tosches held up a hand. "Follow us," he ordered.

Bull Neck hunched a shoulder and closed the door. "Okay, Marty," Tosches told his driver. "Wait for Hope and Crosby to come around and then let's go on out to the ranch."

Chainey looked at him quizzically.

"You want to know, you got to go there or it's nothing. That fuckin' Holt isn't what you'd call stable. And I want to be somewhere I can fortify."

Live dangerously, baby. "Let's roll."

The car took off when the two bodyguards had pulled around in their Navajo SUV. Tosches raised the soundproof window between the back and the front seats of the car.

"How come you haven't been to the cops?"

"With what?"

"Oh, yeah," he said. He dipped a hand inside his coat, and Chainey got nervous. "You can calm down, Ma Barker." He withdrew a rectangular silver case and from it a thin, crooked cigar. It was the kind Clint Eastwood lit up in those Sixties Man With No Name movies Wilson McAndrews used to go see at revival houses. He sucked in some smoke. "You want money?"

"I got that. Now I want satisfaction."

"Don't we all?"

"Why'd you do it?"

He settled back on the seat, enjoying the ride and his smoke. Blue-white vapor drifted around them, as if they were traveling through stygian depths. As the smoke thickened, it was sucked up into a small vent in the ceiling. Behind a grill, a small motor could be heard whirring.

"I'm telling you this for two reasons, Chainey. The first is, I didn't want a scene outside my casino. What with the law looking for you, plus I don't know who you been talking to. I know that crafty Cuban Jew you work for still has uncollected markers around town, and . . ." He let his words taper off.

She let him go on wondering just what kind of relationship she and Maltizar had. "That was a lot more than two reasons."

"I'm making a point here, all right. This isn't debate class." He smoked some more. "The second thing is, that bastard's got me worried."

"Why did you have him kill Moya?"

"That's just it, Chainey, I didn't. But it's like once he's set in motion, the fuckin' guy is a robot who only understands one kind of programming." Behind them, the Navajo swerved, then righted itself. The Lincoln was queued up for a checkpoint.

"Get in here," Tosches said. He let down part of the backseat revealing a compartment.

"Like hell," she said.

"They must have your picture up there, Chainey. And if I wanted to kill you, I'd have done it. We're just heading out to my place near Echo Bay."

She took out her piece. "Any blasting, and I blast back."

"I wouldn't expect any less."

Not having much choice, she got into the compartment, and the cover was sealed again. She rode in the dark. Chainey could hear muffled voices when the car stopped. She expected any second to have the seat ripped away and nightsticks raining down on her. Then came silence, the humming of the engine causing a vibration beneath her. Any second she might feel the first horrible sting of a bullet impaling her. Involuntarily, her finger began squeezing the trigger of the Beretta, her lethal security blanket.

"Okay, we're through," Tosches said, taking the seat back away.

Chainey got out, glad to be in the light again. The SUV carrying the other two was close behind them. She noted absently that only one of the Rovers was up front. Her gun was holstered.

"It wasn't supposed to be murder." Tosches watched the scenery go by. They were heading toward the ramp for the 15 Freeway north.

"Really?" she said, unconvinced. "You wanted to nick the champ, huh?"

Tosches expelled a nervous burst of air, smoke jetting out in a gust. "I need to have a title bout at the El Morocco. That's the only thing I can see that will buoy me. Jeffries was never gonna do it there; he was locked into Victoria and Kuwada."

She condemned him with her glare.

"You can get off your high horse, Ms. Chainey. This was about survival, not greed. Getting a title bout would just about keep me afloat. I wasn't going to see a dime from it."

"What about this idea of yours to build an amusement park up in the mountains?"

"Fuckin' Kuwada." He shook his head. "What could I do? I told you, I need to get some cash flow happening, and I need it quick."

"Or he buys you out?"

He fixed her with a look. "That's right. The land is worth more to him undeveloped, rather than something I've sweated to build up for all these years. I'm so goddamn overextended, it feels like my guts are made of rubber bands. You gotta understand, Chainey, I'm the last of the old-timers. When the Desert Inn closed, I was crying, baby. 'Cause I knew I was looking at my future."

"You wouldn't be poor if you got bought out." Chainey could see Reese lying still in that room and got a chill.

He clucked his tongue. "You're not following what I said."

Below, they passed one of the ubiquitous golf courses in and about town. It was so green, it looked like the lawn had been spray painted using a template. "I'm from the past, Chainey. I don't have an MBA and have my investment banker's number on speed dial." He stubbed out his cigar. "My undeclared partners are certain gentlemen who to this day maintain a social club on Flatbush Avenue in Brooklyn. They may not be spring chickens, and certainly not what they used to be, but those gumbahs have long memories—very fuckin' long memories."

"So you have to produce—"

"Or get scarce real quick. And I'm too old and slow to be lookin' over my shoulder in my golden years."

"Who is Holt?"

"Hitters don't fill out applications, you know that, Chainey."

"Where did Ginger dig him up?" She didn't go into the fact that she knew he'd already asked Degault, and probably a few others too, for leads.

"Seems Ginger tells the fortunes of a few working girls past and present. Anyway, the way I understand it, one of 'em, who gets around, was once flown into this air force base to do some hotshot covert jocks all pent up, waiting for some kind of operation to go down. Some of that disruption shit in Nicaragua or Guatemala, one of those spic countries we're always fuckin' with. Holt is one of these hitters."

"Uh-huh."

"Okay, excuse me for not being politically correct. Anyway, we meet, he's given the assignment. And I explained myself clearly, Chainey. I didn't make a mistake. I told him to wound the champ. Just so it would take him out for a while, and that way I could set up a match between Muhammad and the next guy coming up, probably Sugar Shack. But that kill-happy bastard sonofbitch takes out Jeffries, cold."

The Lincoln had taken an exit and they were now traveling near yet another golf course. This one was the public facility, and it too was of a green beyond compare. Chainey wondered if Las Vegas residents were willing to have beautiful golf courses over enough water for drinking.

"And now he's running around taking care of any and all loose ends."

"Yeah, and I figure I'm last on his list, behind you. And that's why I intend to hole up till that maniac is caught and brought down like the wild animal he is."

"And you expect me to do your dirty work?"

"You got incentive, don't you?" They were now on an access road leading to a gated entrance and a sign marking it private property. Marty, the driver, came to a halt before it and got out to open the gate. The Navajo idled a car length behind them.

"How'd you sneak him into the arena?" Marty got back in and the two cars drove inside.

"I asked Victoria for a set of tags, then had a guy I know who does that kind of work alter them to make it seem Holt was a workman." Before them stretched a modest two-story ranch house. Off to one side was a corral, with several horses grazing in their pen.

Soon the vehicles were sloping down a circular drive of cobblestones, and the Town Car pulled to a stop at the double-door entrance. In a "Beverly Hillbillies" touch, there was a larger-than-life statue of Rodin's Thinker in the middle of the driveway on a stone pedestal. It was made of a patinaed bronze, and several spots of bird droppings splattered its surface. Marty got out and opened the car's back door. Then he went to the house to unlock the door.

The Navajo pulled in behind. The Rover remained in the driver's seat, his hands gripping the steering wheel. His partner's shadow was outlined in the rear seat.

"Maybe I'll let him come for you, then pick him off like that, Tosches." Chainey gladly stepped into the open.

"Or he comes for you and I wait." Tosches was looking back at the Navajo. "Let's go, you two," he yelled at his men.

The driver's door of the Navajo opened and the bodyguard put one foot on the ground. "Mr. Tosches," he hollered, and suddenly he went down on the pavement, crimson spurting from one of the arteries in his neck.

"Oh, God," Tosches yelled. He pushed Chainey aside in

panic, and she fell back against the Lincoln. He ran for the open doorway of the house, Marty having already retreated inside. Holt jumped out of the SUV, gun clacking. He cut down Tosches, who collapsed on the clean steps of his ranch house.

Chainey was crawling across the Lincoln's front seat. The rear window imploded from the gunman's rounds. Chainey returned fire and got the driver's door open. Marty had the keys, and she didn't know jack about hot wiring a car. One other skill she'd have to brush up on, if she made it out of this alive.

She heard the door to the house slam shut. Chainey peeked over the seat again, and a round singed close to her head as she ducked out of the way. If she guessed right, Marty was at least calling the cops from inside the house. She would try the same on her cell but couldn't afford to divert her attention. She snaked to the driver's side and clipped off two just as Holt was trying to sneak up on her. This drove him back to hide behind the SUV. The bodyguard, whose throat he'd cut, lay on his back on the ground. The other one was no doubt a corpse inside the vehicle. Holt must have been waiting inside the car when they left the El Morocco. Devious fuck.

Chainey released the emergency brake as several more rounds came in through the missing back window. Holt was aiming toward the car's ceilng, trying for a ricocheted shot. One round pinged off the metal frame, separating the windows, and the bullet entered a section of the cushion near Chainey's head. She had to put her gun on the seat. Using both hands, she forced the shift selector into neutral, and the heavy car started to roll back, as she'd intended.

Holt fired more rounds and Chaney returned the favor. Before the Lincoln's rear bumper made contact with the grill of the higher Navajo, Chainey was already leaning out the passenger's side. Looking beneath the cars' undercarriages, she saw Holt's shins where he was crouched. He'd tensed for the impact as she'd hoped, and that gave her the time to squeeze off shots at his lower legs.

One bullet struck sparks as it caroomed off the cobblestones. But the other shot went true and sank into his calf. He barely grunted, and then his legs were out of sight as he positioned himself behind the right rear tire. Chainey climbed into the backseat and got herself situated to shoot back, chancing to peep over the rise of the upper rear seat cushion. The angle from the Lincoln to the higher-sitting Navajo only permitted her to see part of the SUV to her left. That meant Holt would try from her right—her blind side.

She unhooked her cell phone, but she'd been using it too much in the last few hours; the battery was dead. Contemptuously, she tossed the useless device into the front of the car. Suddenly realizing she didn't have to be totally in the dark, she climbed back in the front and closed the doors but didn't click them completely shut. The Lincoln's rearview mirrors, mounted on either side of the front doors, afforded her partial views of each side of the Navajo.

He would wait until he heard sirens and then make his move. He probably had the keys to the truck on him and would use them to climb through the back of the vehicle to get to the driver's seat. If Chainey popped her head up, he'd blaze at her as he got the truck running and backing away. But he'd have a chance at him, and that was why he wasn't going to force his play unless he had to.

Chainey looked back and forth at each of the mirrors. Holt, pressed against the left side of the Navajo, tried to shoot out one of the mirrors. Chainey was fast. She kicked the driver's door open, sprawled across the seat, stuck her gun out and popped off two rounds of her own.

She didn't get him, and cursed herself for being too slow. The mirror on the Lincoln's driver's side had been shot out. Things got quiet again. Could be, she reasoned, Holt was going to come at her from the driver's side. Then again, he was sneaky and might try for the passenger side of the Lincoln, even though the mirror on that side was intact.

A minute stretched by with her alternately glaring at the mirror and back at the other side of the car, where the door hung open. It occurred to her that the goddamn bastard could be climbing over the roof of the Navajo, trying to line up his shot that way. *Pick a side, Chainey; which one to dive through?*

Another minute came and went, and the tension was eating her up. She was in a semicrouched position, her back against part of the dash. She had to be careful not to let herself slip beneath the steering wheel, but it was hard for a woman with long legs to tuck them away. She could see over the top of the front seats but would have to turn to look at the mirror. This was getting to be too vulnerable a position for her. She had to do something. She was going to have to roll out the side where he'd shot out the mirror, on the theory he would attack from the other side, to catch her by surprise.

She was scooting that way when a shotgun boomed, and the Lincoln rocked from the impact of a 12-gauge spread. Marty had come around the side of the house, leveling the scattergun at both vehicles. His idea, it seemed, was to knock down anything that moved and let Jehovah deal with the body parts.

"Moron," Chainey yelled as the driver let loose again. "Shoot the man," she stressed. This time Marty at least aimed for the rear of the Navajo. Fuck it, now or never. Chainey unlatched the door and went out the passenger's side, then ran for the Thinker statue on a beeline away from the Lincoln.

Holt raised up to shoot at her, but another discharge from the shotgun sent him to cover again. Chainey slid like going in to home plate, banging her knee as she put the statue between herself and the hired killer. "Call the fuckin' cops, Marty," she hollered.

"No. Mr. Tosches wouldn't want me to do that." He ducked down beside the house as Holt took a shot at him.

"What difference does it make?" Chainey asked. "He's not going to be doing much complaining."

"I have to talk to someone in charge first," the driver responded.

"You are; you got the biggest gun," she screamed. A hinge creaked, and the shotgun went off again. On her belly, Chainey looked around the base of the statue. She couldn't see or hear

Holt, but she did notice the Navajo swaying some on its shocks. The fucker had gotten inside and was now climbing toward the driver's seat. No doubt Marty the driver had seen the rear hatch door open and taken a shot.

"Shoot out the front side window," Chainey ordered.

"What?"

Amateurs. "He's trying to get away."

Marty peppered the truck with more pellets but didn't do much damage. Holt had the engine going and the vehicle in gear. He backed up, disengaging from the Lincoln, which listed but remained where it was. He righted the vehicle, and for a moment it looked as if he was considering ramming the statue.

Marty had become emboldened and stepped out from the side of the house. He shot once more with his semiauto shotgun as Holt got the SUV going along the loop of the driveway.

Chainey crouched and shot at the tires, not hitting them. Holt had the driver's window down and shot back. Bullets zinged off the Thinker's arms and back. The Navajo was getting away.

"The keys," she demanded, running for the Lincoln.

Marty was at last getting hip. He tossed them to her and she was in and gone. There was a bad wobble in the frame, but she'd get over it. Chainey gunned the engine and the car gobbled road as the Navajo ripped through the gateway, which had been left open. The vehicles raced along the access road, Chainey keeping steadily on the man trying to get away.

The Navajo reached Craig Road and bore left, making a pickup truck brake harshly. Chainey kept up the pace, and the two vehicles zoomed along the thoroughfare as other drivers braked and honked at them and bystanders gawked. The Navajo's rear tires screeched, and Holt made a sharp left across the raised median. A Camry slammed into a Mazda van, and Chainey had to veer around the accident riding the brake pedal. She too rode over the median. But the Lincoln wasn't as high off the ground, and she could hear part of the car's underbelly rend and tear. Astonishingly, Vic Damone's voice suddenly filled the interior of the car. Briefly, Chainey considered whether she'd taken flight into another dimension where only crooners existed. But then it was clear to her that all this jarring of the car had triggered the CD player in the dash. As he sang "Impossible You," she closed in on Holt.

It was apparent he was heading back to the ranch house. That made sense; the more the two were out on the streets playing *Gone in 60 Seconds,* the more likely they were to get busted by the law. For Chainey it would be an inconvenience; for Holt, it would probably be a shoot it out till death rather than be captured. He seemed just that resolute and unsteady.

The Navajo was running a red light when Holt's luck gave out. A FedEx truck had been barreling along the cross street and hadn't slowed down even though the driver must have seen him. The truck broadsided the Navajo, knocking it on its side as its front end crumpled and the radiator exploded, releasing steam into the late-afternoon air. The Navajo skidded to a stop, after knocking a light pole over.

Electric cables flailed about, and sparks like fireworks jumped from their naked entrails. Holt climbed out of the driver's door, which was facing up. Chainey was already out of the Lincoln and aiming her piece. A security guard was rushing out of a jewelry shop nearby. He had a clear line of sight at Chainey.

"Put that fuckin' gun down," he bellowed. He was grasping for his own holstered weapon.

"I don't fuckin' believe this."

The security guard, a young man with the side of his head shaved and a stand of twisted hair atop it, had his gun out, "Don't make me bleed you, lady."

Holt, of course, was running away. He was limping from the leg wound, but he was making tracks.

"Drop that fucking' piece." The would-be cop had bent to an effective-looking shooting stance.

Chainey did as ordered. Getting capped for all the wrong reasons was really going to ruin her day.

"Now suck some asphalt."

"Look here, Shaft—"

The muzzle of his gun jerked upwards.

"It's your world," Chainey mumbled. She went prone on the ground. Holt was already a ghost. A small crowd had gathered, and several people clapped, happy that justice had been served. Liquid quietly dripped from the oil pan of the Lincoln, through the hole she'd inadvertently punched in it.

CHAPTER SIXTEEN

Chainey had gone numb from the questioning and prodding she'd undergone for the last five and a half hours. Because of the state of emergency still in effect when she was arrested, at first she was formally taken into custody by some MPs from Nellis Air Force Base. She was tossed into the cooler there. Then someone went out to see Marty the driver at Tosches's place, and an LVMPD plainclothesman named Mann showed up to take custody of her and do the initial interrogation.

Subsequently, she was transported by Mann to the Las Vegas Metropolitan Police Department's main headquarters on Stewart. From there Sheriff Lambert took over. He pressed hard, saying he had an eyewitness who put her at Moya Reese's room at or about the time of her death. Chainey assumed her pudgy pal had given her up.

But she was too tired and too stubborn to tumble. Cops routinely bullshitted prisoners in an effort to elicit what they wanted to hear. If he had her cold, so be it—'fessin' up in the sweatbox wasn't going to get her any goddamn star points when she was arraigned.

Chainey stuck to her story about the search for missing sports merchandise belonging to the Riverhead. That in the course of that assignment, she'd run across Holt and his connection to Tosches. The trail led her to Ginger Salley and the shoot outs that occurred on her premises and at Tosches's place. The casino owner was alive and in surgery. Salley too was recovering. Yes, she acknowledged contritely, she should have stayed at the scene, but she was afraid that Holt would take flight from the state.

Yes, she responded, she understood that her permit to carry did not entitle her to act as if she was a law enforcement officer in pursuit of a suspected felon. But Chainey countered that as a licensed, bonded, and insured courier, she was expected to go the extra mile for her clients. That was why Truxon, Limited, had the reputation it had.

Lambert looked at the two-way mirror as if inspiration from the cops and the D.A. on the other side was forthcoming.

At one point in the interrogation, Lambert had been called out of the room. She assumed the ballistics report had been done and must have shown that the gun that killed Reese matched the one that had taken Tosches down. Add Marty the driver's account of Holt—which matched what Chainey had said about the man—and the sheriff had no choice but to admit the existence of the hired gun.

After three more rounds of questioning, shouting, and berating from Lambert, she concluded that he didn't have much on her. Maybe he had the guy from the room next to Reese's, and maybe he did see her from a distance when she left. Or maybe he was a singer and had a perfect ear for sound and pitch. Maybe he was Superman and had X-ray eyes, only the walls were lined in lead. But it was clear her little fat man had split before the law had arrived. He no doubt had his own reasons for that.

"I'm lawyering up, now, Chief," she finally announced calmly. Chainey had calculated that giving Lambert much of what he wanted had been smarter than clamming up in the first place. But now she was restless and had places to go.

"That's the refuge of the guilty," he announced haughtily.

"I want to talk to my lawyer, now."

Lambert put in twenty more minutes of hammering at her

but finally relented because he knew she knew the deal. "Make your fuckin' call, Chainey."

She buzzed Rena Solomon. Through her, she got Hiss to arrange for his lawyer, Juleyka Saldago, to come over to the station house.

"Great, just fuckin' great," Lambert commented upon hearing that Saldago was soon to arrive. Apparently, he'd had previous experience with the counselor. Chainey had never met her but smiled inwardly; her streak was still hot. She just hoped she didn't cool off yet; no, not just yet.

And so it was night again, a little past nine, when she next got out on the streets. The bail had been set and Maltizar had put up the bond. The main charges were obstructing justice and fleeing the scene of a crime. The sheriff had threatened an endangerment charge, but since she hadn't discharged her gun on the city streets the assistant D.A. had nixed that one. Lambert had confiscated her Beretta as evidence—"yet another gun," he commented forlornly—and she was facing a suit from the city for tearing up city property. But Saldago wasn't too worried on that score.

Saldago touched Chainey's elbow as they walked out of police headquarters. "We're going to countersue Tosches for putting you in harm's way. And of course we'll get those charges knocked down."

Walking down the main steps, Chainey looked all around. She wouldn't put it past that gunner Holt to try something even with all the cops around. Solomon was waiting.

"I'm damn sure getting the exclusive."

"You are, I promise, Rena. But right now I need to borrow your car."

"I'll drive you," she said.

"Uh-uh. Where I'm going your innocent eyes can't see. Juleyka can drop you off."

"Very funny."

"I'm serious." She stuck out her hand.

Eventually Solomon said, "Damn" and handed over the keys. "You're not going to do anything foolish, are you?"

"Do I need to be out of hearing range?" the lawyer asked.

"Just a private matter, Counselor. Pesky loose ends."

"We're not talking about hair, are we?" Saldago asked.

Chainey was already walking toward her friend's car when Lambert came out onto the top step. "Y'all be careful out there, Ms. Chainey." He adjusted his cowboy hat so he looked like Randolph Scott in one of his oaters. "We got an all-points out for this Holt character. But you'd be advised to keep your head low."

"I plan to be so low as to be invisible, Sheriff."

"Right," he said, unconvinced.

Four blocks from headquarters, Chainey lost the tail Lambert had put on her. Now, where the hell would Holt be waiting to ambush her?

CHAPTER SEVENTEEN

Some part of him told him that he wasn't doing this right. Some part of him tickled below the gray fuzziness encamped in part of his brain, reminding him that he needed to be professional about this. He'd gotten away pretty much untouched, and he should be goddamn grateful for that. He should have been on his way to Spain, where he'd hidden out before, after the business in Burkina Fasso went rancid. But the gray fuzziness was consuming more of the space in his head, and he now found it comforting, not threatening, as he had before.

But that big bitch Chainey had to be taught she couldn't go around walking the walk in a man's world. He lightly touched the dressing on his leg wound. The lesson had to be handed down that she was no hairy-armpit role model for those testesterone-chawing broads wrestling with bulging muscles and boxing like they had the same coordination and strength as men. Like they were as smart or as tough as men. Bullshit. The natural order of things was man, then woman, who came from man. It sure as hell wasn't the other way around. Ball busters like Chainey had to be taught that if they pranced and preened as if they were superior, they had to be slapped down quick to provide an example to the others.

That's why he knew she couldn't resist the little note he'd left for her at the concierge's desk at the Riverhead. She couldn't turn down a challenge from a mere man—no, not her; she was going to prove to her sistahs that she could take any man. Shit. As he hunkered down, waiting for his target, he absently rubbed his thumb over the emerald eyepiece of the rifle. Oh, she would come all right, come right to slaughter.

Chainey made another stop at Sly's on West Bonanza Road for another gun.

"Day-um, what you doin', girl, giving these gats away?" he'd quipped. But he handed over a piece after he could see she wasn't in the mood.

She'd already alerted Maltizar, and he'd make sure that his employees were covered. The courier also told Degault what had gone down, and left a message for Solomon, explicitly telling her to keep scarce until she called her because Reese's killer was on the loose. She didn't think Holt would go after anybody but her, but there was no sense being careless.

Headlights out, she slowly drove her new millennium T-Bird down the road to Tosches's house. Martial law had been lifted while she was being held. Driving out to the place, numerous National Guard vehicles had passed her on the way out of town. And when she'd been getting her belongings from the property sergeant, Chainey had overheard two cops talking. It seemed that Ms. Ashford, née Sub-Commandante Khali, had been formally charged with robbery, and she was singing like Toni Braxton. McDaniels was going to get nabbed. He'd want to make a deal and would talk about the money she retrieved from him. That would just have to be Victoria Degault's concern.

The first shot spider-webbed a section of windshield as it bore through the glass and into the head of the driver. The glass then collapsed in on itself. Simultaneously, the passenger's door was opened, and Chainey threw herself out into the roadway. The second shot chewed a chunk of earth at her heel as she went over the low retaining wall. Chainey landed in moist dirt amid transplanted palm trees and got to her feet.

The pilotless T-bird continued along in neutral, finally quietly crashing against the Thinker statue. The dummy torso Chainey had put in the driver's seat after she'd come through the entrance gate, slumped forward on the wheel. A big, nasty hole was dead center in its plastic forehead below the cap and wig.

She looked around, the night vision goggles she wore giving everything a green, shimmering pall. She saw Holt stand up on the roof of the ranch house, but she didn't shoot. It was too far for her handgun to be accurate. And there was an advantage in having him think she was literally in the dark. He loped down the rear of the roof and she went forward. The problem was, there too much open ground once she cleared the trees toward the house.

Conversely, she reminded herself, as she inched forward, Holt wanted her bad. Chainey got to the edge of the small grove. She crouched behind a date palm, alert for any signs of the killer. He had the advantage with the rifle and was probably wearing his own pair of night vision goggles. She scanned the area ahead of her.

Small numbered papers were all about, marking the locations of the ejected shell casings from the previous shoot-out. The milky outline indicating where the bodyguard had fallen on the cobblestones looked like some fourth dimension being who'd expired on her plane. And no one had bothered to scrape up his segmented body. The Lincoln and the Navajo had been towed away, so that only left her car and the Thinker as possible shelter.

Behind the house to the west was more brush and hillside. To the east, on the righthand side, was open ground that circled into more palm trees. If Holt was moving, he'd come at her that way. And if she stayed outside, the high-powered weapon was too much of an advantage. Close quarters were called for.

She took several deep breaths, like an athlete preparing for a match. As fast as she could, she flashed into the open and toward the left side of her vehicle. A shot came from the far trees as she gained the side of the car. It went wide and ricocheted off the cobblestones with a thunk. So Holt was in fact heading her way.

Squatting, Chainey reached a hand into the fashionable black Union messenger bag slung rebel-style around her upper body. She withdrew a couple of the items she'd bought off Sly.

Again, gathering her nerve, she waited, then tossed two squat canister-shaped grenades ahead and to her right, spacing the throws. White-hot mini-suns went off, and she was enveloped by them as she dashed toward the front door of the house. Holt knew what she was doing and shot where he anticipated she'd be. But Chainey managed to get to the house. She didn't attempt to go through the front door, where Holt had been aiming, and where she theorized he would continue to shoot. She'd run to the west side, away from his line of sight once the flash grenade's phosphorous powder subsided.

She could barely see; the dark lenses she'd fastened to her goggles were nearly opaque. They were ideal for the intensity of an incandescent flash but useless otherwise. She clawed at them, even as she had to keep going. Holt would hang back out of caution, but not for long. She got one lens off, and it slipped from her greasy palm. Like a high-tech cyclops, her one green eye glared out at the world. She found a side door and blasted at its lock with her gun. Then she rammed through and fell inside.

She got the other lens off and quickly assessed her surroundings in the gloom. Chainey was in the washroom. Putting her shoulder to it, she shoved the dryer in front of the broken door. Then she went into the main part of the house. The interior was well appointed, but Chainey wasn't on a *House and Gardens* scouting expedition. What she wanted was a bottle from the wet bar. She retrieved some Cutty and got herself ready.

Goddamn, that bitch was cunning; he had to give her that. Holt worked his way toward the house, crouching and alert for any movement or sound. She must have night goggles too, he reasoned, just like he did. He went across the arc of the driveway and came down beside the Thinker. She'd reduced the odds by going to ground. He had to get in, and he couldn't be sure that broad hadn't rigged an explosive on the front door or a window.

She'd had a bag around her, but there were a finite number of devices she could be carrying.

Still, pick the wrong entrance and it was moot as to her limited number of tricks. But this had gone on too long, and he was going to see an end to it. When you put them in the crosshairs, you pulled the trigger; he'd tried to get that weak-livered Tosches to understand that. He'd been given the job and by God that was what he'd done. Wound him, nick him, the slick bastard had whined. You know, gimp him up some so he can't box for awhile, he'd said. What kind of directive was that? When you put the trigger on them, you popped them. Clear. Simple.

When they'd blackballed him they'd manufactured all kinds of double and triple talk about psychic break and misaligned values and other headshrinker terms to mask the truth. It was all political. They'd selected him and trained him and set him loose and then were aghast when he carried out his work too well. They said neutralize and he neutralized. You couldn't penetrate an area unless you had intelligence, and the stumblebums at Ops didn't know dick. So he improvised, and if it meant extracting information from a townsperson, some old woman pretending to be ignorant, well, that didn't stop Holt. That didn't stop him from juicing her with the car battery and wire alligatored to her clit. He knew the hag was lying.

And certainly no long-legged twist was going to get the better of him. Not in this godforsaken world. Recharged, Holt got up and zigzagged to the front of the house, his back slamming against the wood frame, going as flat as humanly possible.

"Did you hear me, you fancy whore?" he yelled. "I'm coming for you, honey. But don't wet yourself, it'll be over soon." He peeled away and went around the east end of the house. Oh, he was going to enjoy killing her.

The trick, Chainey was discovering, was to have confidence in your decisions. It was one thing to formulate the plan and go over and over the strategy in your head until it was second nature to you, like your own name. The wait was what got you off-balance. You didn't know when exactly to execute your plan. The unknown factors got to you. But it was when you relaxed that a bullet would unerringly take your life.

How long had it been since she'd heard Holt yell out? A minute? Two? Or an hour? She didn't dare look at her watch for fear that would be the moment he'd strike. And then it happened fast, because that was how it had to happen.

The window in the dining room was busted out, and instinctively Chainey aimed her weapon that way. But Holt didn't come in there, but right in the front door. It was so fast, he couldn't have run around to that position. He must have found something in that little house off to the side to use. His rifle was blazing and he laid down a carpet of fire, decorating the furniture and walls with air holes.

Chainey was crouched down and to his left in a small study bordered by French doors. She tossed her last flash grenade, but he was already in motion. It went off, and Chainey realized her mistake in using the thing in tight quarters. Especially without her dark lenses in place, she was as handicapped as Holt.

She was blinking, her eyes watery and the green haze of images before her bleary. The rifle was lying upright against the couch, as if it was an ordinary part of home decor. From a far corner of the room she sensed more than detected movement and went flat just as the sound of his handgun racked the air.

"Now what, girlfriend?" he taunted. More rounds, and Chainey rolled behind the washer she'd ruined the hardwood floor shoving into the living room. She needed something heavy to slow down his fire, or at least to obscure her figure.

He blew off some more rounds, and a couple went through the hollow upper part of the machine. A slug dug its way into her upper back, and she had to grab the washing machine to keep from falling out. *Not now, keep going, Chainey, keep going,* she told herself.

More shots, but she had the rag lit and dove out, her arm chucking the Molotov at his advancing figure. She cried out when her body hit the hardwood floor. The bottle and the ignited alcohol exploded at his feet, and some of the contents leapt at him.

"You fuckin' stupid bitch," he screamed. He didn't panic. Holt did what any soldier trained to protect himself would do, and dropped and rolled to extinguish the flames. He also kept his gun hand extended, firing blindly to keep her back.

"You're the one on fire, asshole." Chainey threw a bottle of Glenn Fiddich and it exploded in flames on Holt's rolling body. He screamed in agony and beat at his body with his hands. Holt bumped into an end table, upsetting a lamp that crashed into myriad pieces.

Holt was standing, his arms losing strength as the second- and third-degree burns assailed his body. Blackened skin and cloth hung from him, neither distinguishable from the other. He staggered and, like a blind drunk, collided with the couch. He went over, smoke exhaled from his fried lungs.

Chainey was over him, her own blood soaking the back of her shirt. His green eyes looked up at her from where he lay upside-down on the couch, his face gray. He tried to talk, the words coming out as whispered stammering. She pumped two bullets into his skull.

All her reserves left her and she sank to the floor. She crawled to the phone and dialed 911, gave her location, then passed out. The killer's body smoldered on the couch.

CHAPTER EIGHTEEN

"I killed your friend, Chainey."

She could only stare at him as she leaned on the cane. "Why?" she croaked.

"Panic; I just fuckin' panicked," Tosches replied, lying in his hospital bed. As these things went, they'd both wound up at the Desert Springs Hospital, the same facility where King Diamond was. The rapper's prognosis was still iffy, and there was uncertainty as to whether he'd regain the use of his legs.

"I'd paid off a gofer in Jeffries's training camp so I knew who came and went, who was seeing him, all that. I was still trying to work an angle then, find some way to get him to fight for me."

A nurse went past Chainey, in robe and pajamas, standing in the doorway of Tosches's private room. She frowned. "And you knew then that Moya had been up to see him a few times."

"See him, bang him," he continued. "When that maniac Holt tagged him I was beside myself. Then she runs out, saying what she said, and I had to talk to her, had to know if she suspected I was behind all this shit."

Chainey sagged against the door frame. "She probably assumed the Nymnatists had done it. That they'd found out she'd convinced him to leave them and had killed him for it. That's why she went on the run."

Tosches nodded slowly. "I still got juice in this town, Chainey.

I spread cash quick and found out where she was holed up." He spoke in a monotone, glaring at nothing as he lay propped up in his bed, hooked to monitors and IVs. "I went to see her, pretending like you and Victoria had sent me to see about her.

Hate set Chainey's wan features, making an ugly visage.

"Yeah, I'm a real scum fuck," he said. "But I was scared, Chainey. I couldn't be caught."

"You might have had to own up to your deeds," she snarled.

He went on, pressing to finish his narrative. "I got in her room and I must have lost it. I'm babbling, explaining how she's got to be cool, and I guess I let it slip that I knew more about what's going on than I should. She comes for me and hits me a good one."

Chainey frowned. There was a bruise on his jaw, but she'd assumed it happened when he was felled by Holt's bullet.

"I had on makeup when we were in the car," he answered her unspoken query. "She was gonna wail on me, she was so worked up. Reese was on me, crowding me back and punching me in the gut, and I pressed the muzzle right against that muscle of hers. I—I shot her before I knew what I'd done." All the life went out of his voice. It was as if he was telling her about an incident that had occurred a hundred years before.

"You shot her twice."

"Yes, I did."

"Why tell me now?" she asked finally. "Holt would carry that killing with him too. You'd be home free."

Tosches grinned thinly. "I'm not free, Chainey."

"Should you be up?" Simon Kuwada asked. He was walking along the hallway toward them, a bouquet of roses and African violets in his hand.

Chainey couldn't find appropriate words. How did she tell him that the bastard recuperating three doors from her had killed her friend? How could she put into words that she was thinking of coming back later and putting a pillow over his face?

"Come on, you two can catch up on your misadventures later." Kuwada put an arm around Chainey's waist and started her back toward her room. "Glad to see you're all right too, Dean."

"Yeah."

That night Tosches made a call on the cell phone that had been smuggled in to him. Marty, loyal Marty, brought him three items he'd requested in a plain brown paper sack. Items, Tosches's joked, he said he needed for protection and re-creation. The driver had wanted to stay but was loyal-as-they-come and departed. In the morning he would get the Lincoln out of impound and shine it up just the way his boss liked it. And when the hospital said Tosches could go home, he'd come get him in that fine chariot of steel and iron.

A little past three in the morning, Code Blue was called as the monitors in Tosches's room had suddenly flat-lined. The night nurse led a troop of interns and other nurses as they rushed into the room with their electro-stat cart and whatnot to try to revive the patient.

All their jaws went slack at the sight of the owner of the El Morocco casino sitting up in bed, a section of his skull off to one side, hanging on by his hair. The gun he'd inserted in his mouth was clamped in one of his tanned hands. The body's reflexive action had jerked it back, and the hand and gun lay listless across his belly. His other hand lay palm up and open. In its center was a pair of dice showing three. Somebody mumbled, "He must not have made shooter's point."

Late at night, three days later, Chainey got a call on the phone by her bedside.

"Hello?"

"Rested up?"

"Who is this?"

Silence.

"You're the one who planted the bomb."

She stayed cool; she didn't want him to know he'd shaken her. "Why are you after me?"

"Soon."

The line clicked off.